FROM THE DELTA TO THE DMZ

FROM THE DELTA TO THE DMZ

SEAN KELLY, WAR CORRESPONDENT

PAUL SINOR

To the men and women who served in Viet Nam, especially those who never came home.

And as always to Jewell who waited.

You have never lived till you have almost died.
For those who have had to fight for it,
Freedom has a flavor the protected will never know.
—Anonymous saying from Viet Nam

Contents

Chapter One

Life in a war zone, no matter the country or the conflict, is the ultimate dichotomy. Men are in combat someplace fighting for their lives while others are in rear areas having the time of theirs. Viet Nam was no different.

I had a friend whose father made the landing at Normandy on D-Day. He reached the sea wall unscathed and made his way through France and into Germany with an infantry unit. He spent almost two months in the snow at Bastogne during the Battle of the Bulge and finally was given a four-day pass to go to Paris when the Germans surrendered. He and a friend found a hotel room, several bottles of liberated wine, and, although he didn't tell his son, I imagine some ladies of negotiable affections to accompany them to the room. Once in the room, he took off his shirt and twisted his arm too far back, cracking his collarbone. True or not, that was his story. He came home with scars from the surgery to repair the bone and no purple heart for combat wounds.

In Viet Nam, men were wounded or killed in combat a few miles outside some of the larger cities in the country, while others were getting injured or killed by accidents at the military bases, run over by civilian taxis and busses, or killed by jealous boyfriends who claimed the same Vietnamese girlfriend.

No one wanted to die in country, but for many, there was a certain amount of honor if they were killed in combat.

As a war correspondent, I was not assigned to any particular unit. I had the luxury, if that is the proper word, to roam the entire country and report what I saw and heard. In most cases, all I had to do was show my press credentials, and I could catch a ride to almost any place I thought there was a story worth reporting. Many times, I had no real idea or unit I wanted to see. Sometimes, Wess Price, the photographer who worked for many of the correspondents like me, and I would hit a dry hole when we landed, and other times, we found something that we had not anticipated. I kept a board in the office where I always came back when I was in Saigon. On the board, was a list of places and things I heard about that I wanted to check out or see for myself. As I checked one off, I usually added two more. With any luck, the war would not last long enough for me to complete the board.

My only obligation was to the Nielsen News Network, the syndicate that sent me to Viet Nam and paid my salary. I was contracted to write a mostly weekly column for a group of newspapers back in "the world," as the United States was known by the military over here. When I first arrived, I immersed myself in doing my job. I went all over the country chasing down stories, watching people get shot at, and unfortunately, seeing a few get shot and once or twice see them take their last breath. When I was not out with a unit, I was in Saigon. It was here that I met the other reason for my being here and not wanting to go home.

Her name was Carmen, and she worked for the US State Department as a civilian.

I had spent the previous evening with Carmen, the woman I was now irretrievable in love with. We met and after several dinners together and a few days of leisure seeing the limited sights of Saigon, we found that we were in love. There was no such thing as "dating," as we knew it back home. No Friday nights in the back row of the local movie theater followed by a stop at either the soda shop or a restaurant, depending on the age of the couple. Here, it was dinner at a military officer's club or a local restaurant. Look out the window at either place, and there was no question that you were in a war zone.

Every officer's club in the city had armed guards at the entrance, and the best Vietnamese restaurant in the city was across from the Presidential Palace. It was surrounded by rolls of concertina wire and had several sandbagged machine gun emplacements at the entrances. Fortunately, the food there was well worth the effort of making one's way past the gun emplacements.

Carmen worked for the State Department and never fully explained to me what she did, and I never dug too deep with my questioning her. She knew what I did, and we both knew we saw and did some things that would follow and probably haunt us forever, but they were not dinner table conversations.

I had a room at one of the hotels that had been contracted out by the US government to house military officers and civilians working with the military. A few rooms were available for civilian contractors and others who were either attempting to make a difference or a profit. Even though I was getting paid to be here, I felt that I was at least attempting to make a difference.

I had a contract to write a weekly column that had started out being for a small syndicate out of my home state of Florida, but as I got deeper into the war, it was picked up by several other syndicates and now reached newspapers all over the US. It was more than I ever expected, but it was something I relished as a journalist.

All I had to do was find an interesting topic to write about each week and do it in a way that the reader got a feel for what was happening to their sons, husbands, neighbors, or, in most cases, people they had never heard of. I never got deep into the blood and guts of the stories. The people back home saw that on the news every evening at dinnertime. I tried to give the background on what they were seeing and why they were seeing it.

After checking my board and deciding what I wanted to do next, Wess and I caught a C-7 Caribou. It was a plane developed by the Canadians and used extensively in Viet Nam. It could land and take off on relatively short runways and had sufficient cargo space to carry supplies or personnel to isolated locations. With a rear ramp that let down, it was sometimes used for training paratroopers. For me, it was the perfect transport to get to the remote firebases and towns where I found the stories I looked for.

We sat sideways against the walls of the plane as we lifted off from Tan Son Nhut, the massive airbase in Saigon. It was where flights bringing most of the replacement or returning personnel landed. It was where I looked up one day and saw the largest plane I had ever seen making its final approach. It looked like it had a bubble on top. I learned later it was the Boeing 747.

Every time I got into any type of aircraft in Viet Nam, I thought of those men and women who had fought in World War Two and Korea. Unlike them, we did not have to worry a great deal about being shot down by anti-aircraft fire. In the south of the country, a few fixed-wing planes were brought down by heavy machine gun fire or RPGs or Rocket Propelled Grenades. It was the Air Force and Navy jets bombing across the border in North Viet Nam, Cambodia, and Laos, two countries that we denied being in, that had to worry about the heavy stuff.

Once I had been in a Huey helicopter that made a stop at a firebase and picked up an empty tank that had held propane gas. The tank was sling-loaded beneath the helicopter, and as we were approaching the landing strip at the Can Tho airfield, we began to take ground fire. I'm sure some well-informed local Viet Cong recognized the tank and was shooting at it. Although it was empty, it probably had enough gas left in it to create a bomb big enough to bring down the helicopter. Fortunately for us, the person shooting at us was a bad shot or couldn't hit a moving target, so we landed safely.

Once we were on the ground, the crew chief checked the Huey and was not happy to find several bullet holes. Better the Huey than the tank, I thought.

Shortly after Wess and I lifted off, I noticed one of the men, who was obviously an FNG, or Fucking New Guy, as first-timers were called, with his duffle bag on the floor in front of him. He had a gold bar on his right collar, indicating he was a Second Lieutenant. This was, no doubt, his first assignment after graduating from a college ROTC program or OCS. The bag was filled with things he would probably never use, depending on his assignment. If he were going to a field unit, he'd throw them away to save on weight. If he stayed in a rear area, he'd trade them on the black market for money, girls, or anything else he could get.

I felt Wess nudge me with his elbow and nod his head toward the man. FNG had pulled a dark green towel from his duffle bag and was holding it in his lap ready to catch anything he had eaten in the last few days. His face was not quite as green as the towel, but it was getting there. Two minutes later, the towel was full, and he was patting his feet on the floor of the aircraft to keep from filling up another towel. As a new lieutenant, or Butter Bar as he would be known until he either proved himself or got promoted to First Lieutenant and got to wear a silver bar, he did not need the added embarrassment of throwing up in front of a group of enlisted men, especially if one or more of them would be under his command.

We felt the plane slow, and the landing gear drop, so our attention was diverted from the FNG to what we were going to do or look for once we were on the ground.

The plane landed on a runway made of what was known as Perforated Steel Planking or PSP. The long strips of metal with holes in them had been in use since WWII and were effective when building bridges or runways. Placed on the ground as level as the engineers could get it, there was no need for pavement or cement. Planes could land on the PSP, do their business, and then depart.

The metal rattled beneath the plane as we touched down and rolled to a short taxi strip that ran off to one side and ended near a small wood shack that served as the terminal and operations center for the airfield. After easing to a stop in front of the building, the pilot cut power to one engine to allow those onboard to deplane and the ground crew to load cargo and outbound passengers. The entire operation took less than five minutes. That gave them time to do what they needed to do and not enough time for someone outside the airfield to set up a mortar or RPG and take the plane out.

Wess and I unbuckled our seat belts and joined the others who had caught a ride as we made our way off the plane. The day was a typical one for that time of year. Hot. High humidity. The smell of diesel and aviation fuel. The whine of the one engine still running was not sufficient to drown out the sounds of the airfield. Heavy trucks ran across a dirt track beside the runway on the way to or from places unknown to us. A jeep pulled up to the end of the building, the driver hitting the brakes and causing the jeep to slide to a stop. The sounds of a country and western song were mixed with that of a soul song coming from two different cassette players inside the terminal. The music choices of the men in Viet Nam was as diverse as the men themselves.

The Armed Forces Viet Nam Radio network programmed enough variety to please everyone at least once a day. The one that surprised me was the Saturday morning Polka Music hour. I often wondered how many people in the country even knew what a polka was and if they did, could they do it.

Once inside the terminal, we saw a large sheet of plywood that had been painted black and nailed to the wall. *All incoming personnel check here for messages or assignment* was written across the top. A small group of the men who had been on the plane with us, crowded around the board to see if their name was on it, and, if so, where were they going.

I watched the lieutenant as he searched for his name. He found it and traced it across to the unit designation. I saw his face regain some of its color as he saw he was being assigned to the 196 LIB.

"Let's follow him and see what happens," Wess suggested.

With no other immediate ideas, I agreed and approached the officer. "Excuse me, I'm Sean Kelly, and this is Wess Price. We'd like to follow you and do a story about what happens and how you feel on your first day in country." I hesitated since I didn't really know if it was his first day or not. "This is your first tour of duty, isn't it?"

"That obvious?" he asked as he turned from the assignment board to face us.

"We kinda got that impression back on the plane."

"Yeah. That was kinda embarrassing. I've never had air sickness before, and I hope I never have it again. I'm not real big on flying, but I guess I'll have to get used to it....although..." He looked back at the board. "I may have lucked out on assignments."

"How's that?" I asked as the other men who had gathered around the board were moving toward the door, looking for rides to their units or to the counter to ask for more information.

"I'm a Signal Corps officer. As I understand it, they tend to keep us back in the rear areas, if there are any in Viet Nam, and it looks like my assignment is to the 196th Library...whatever or wherever that is."

Before either of us could say anything more, we heard a loud voice telling everyone who was going to several different units or locations to load on a bus outside. The 196th was one of the units he called out.

"Sounds like I need to get on that bus." The lieutenant shouldered his duffle bag.

I looked at Wess. "Let's tag along. We can see what happens when a new man arrives and how he is processed into his unit."

"Sounds like a plan. I'll shoot it beginning here in the terminal." He had his camera hanging from a leather strap around his neck. He pulled it to his eye and took some shots of the terminal to capture what was inside. He pointed it to the check-in counter where the men who had been waiting for their normal twelve-month tour to finally get a chance to leave were lined up. Two counters had signs indicating they represented two of the largest banks in the United States. This was where those departing could exchange their Military Payment Certificates, or MPC, the currency used by the military for greenback dollars. For many, especially those who were in the rear area, they represented the bank they used while in country.

Along with the US military personnel, there was a large number of Vietnamese military in uniform and a smaller number in civilian clothes, many of whom were women who were girlfriends, and a few who had married US servicemen but were unable to travel back home with them.

After watching Wess take his photos, I caught up with the lieutenant. "I'm a correspondent for a newspaper syndicate back in the States. I'd like to follow you and do a column on what happens when a new person arrives in country. You game?"

"Yeah, I guess so. Will I be able to tell my folks about it or where to find it?" We boarded the bus and took a seat. At first, he attempted to hold his duffle bag and the suitcase he had brought with him in his lap, but I pointed to the seat in front of us, which was unoccupied, and he placed both pieces there.

"Yes, I'll let you know when and where it will be published." I pulled out my notebook. "The first thing I need is your name and hometown."

"My name is Charles Heite, but everyone calls me Chuck. I'm from a little town outside Lexington, KY."

Before I could ask anything else, the driver closed the door and pulled away from the terminal. A second enlisted man, an Air Force Sergeant, stood beside the driver and faced us. He held up his hand to get our attention. "On behalf of Uncle Sugar, I want to welcome you to Sunny Southeast Asia. We hope your stay in Viet Nam will be at least as long as what's on your orders. There are a few simple rules you need to follow. Starting with the ride on my bus. Number One. The mesh wire on the windows is there for a reason. It's to keep some of the locals who are less than appreciative of your presence from returning a grenade that someone lost. Number Two. The most beautiful woman you will meet here wants to marry you and have your baby. If that's not possible, she'll let you buy her a Honda or an air conditioner or anything else she can get from you. In exchange, she'll give you a condition that can't be cured with a nuclear strike, and if you value your dick, you'll keep it in your pants. Number Three. If you want to keep from shitting away at least twenty pounds, don't drink the water. Put the drink in the ice and not the ice in the drink."

By this time, we had driven out of the airfield compound and were on the streets of Saigon. A few of the men on the bus were on subsequent tours and had seen what Saigon traffic looked like. For others, seeing a mass of motor scooters, many with up to six passengers on them, on the wide boulevards was a new sight. The motor scooters, along with US jeeps and other military vehicles, three-wheel motorcycle taxis, and a variety of US and foreign autos, took up every inch of each street and parts of the sidewalk.

The announcements continued. "And Number Four, for those of you going to units in the field, remember: If it moves, shoot it. If it doesn't, salute it, and if you can't take it with you, burn it." He looked around to see if anyone was paying attention to him. "And finally, the best place to get a hot bath is the local steam and cream. If you don't know what that is, you'll find out."

Wess was standing beside the man in the doorway of the bus, taking photos of the men. He came closer to us and took one of Chuck.

"I don't mention people by name or unit, but there is a Hometown News

Release Service that I can give your information to that will send it to your local paper.

During the remainder of the ride, I found out he had gone through the Reserve Officer's Training Corps program at a small college in Kentucky. He had no great desire to be in the Army, but ROTC was a way for him to get a free education and a job for at least a few years after graduation. He had a "girl" back home but was not sure she was as serious about him as he was about her. His father had been in an artillery unit in WWII, was not a fan of the military, and tried to get him to drop out of ROTC. We continued with small talk and watched about half the busload of men depart at the two stops we made prior to arriving at the transfer point for his unit.

By the time we arrived, it was getting late in the day, and the roads would be off-limits after dark, so we were taken to a large building that served as a reception station and theater.

A sergeant stood at the front of the seats. Each person coming in was loaded down with what they had been issued and what they brought with them. The ones who were on second or more tours were evident by the small number of personal items they brought.

Wess and I went to the front and introduced ourselves to the sergeant and told him what we were doing. We had to promise to mention his name in any hometown release we did in order for him to let us continue. After getting settled into seats, the sergeant began to call out names and specific assignments.

Finally, he called out Heite, Charles M. Second Lieutenant. Goes to Bravo Company, 2nd Battalion of the 1st Regiment, 196 Light Infantry Brigade.

As soon as he did, I watched the color drain from the lieutenant's face. "Light Infantry? I thought it was the 196th lib…" He stopped, knowing he was about to make an un-recoverable mistake in front of a room full of mostly enlisted men. He was not going to a library assignment. He was going to an Infantry Company, most likely to be a Platoon Leader.

We watched him as he joined a small group of others who were also assigned to the 196th. "So much for working in the library," Wess said.

"Yeah. I knew it was the Light Infantry Brigade but I didn't want to break his heart his first hour in country."

* * *

We spent two days with the Brigade and found out that Lieutenant Heite had been assigned to a line company as a Platoon Leader. Even though he was not an infantry officer, he was in what was called a "branch immaterial" position, meaning any officer could fill it.

Wess got the photos he wanted, and I got enough information to do a column on the Brigade's actions in the field. We caught a flight back to Saigon and spent three days catching up.

On the third day, Wess came up to me, holding two cups. He handed me one. "Here, you may need this." Those were words nobody wants to hear in a war zone.

"I'm afraid to ask, but why?"

"The lieutenant that thought he was going to be assigned to a library…"

"Yeah." I knew what he was about to say without asking.

"Killed on his second day on patrol. They were on patrol and got caught in an ambush. One of his men got hit, and he ran out to pull him back to safety. Report said he was wounded but kept going. He got the man back safely, but the lieutenant died on the medevac before they could get him to an aide station."

Wess took his time as he sipped his coffee. "My contact said they're putting him in for a Silver Star."

"Damn," was all I could say.

"Yeah. Me too," Wess said as he returned to his desk and his workload for the day.

DATELINE: SAIGON, SOUTH VIET NAM

I remember once going to a cemetery where a friend of mine had recently been buried. We both were in the second grade. He was playing alone in his basement, where we had played many times, when he lit a match near a container of gasoline. The fire quickly consumed his clothes, and at our age, we had never heard the command to drop and roll. He ran out of the basement, the fire on his clothing following him. He made it to the hospital but died three days later. My parents kept his death from me until several weeks after the funeral. He and I went to different schools, so there was no talk of his tragic death in the classroom.

The day my dad took me to the cemetery and I saw the headstone with his name and the date of his birth and death carved on it, I remember asking him how old you had to be to die. My dad, who was not a man to show his emotion, pulled me to him and told me when it's your time to go, you're gonna go no matter how old or young you are.

Several days after arriving at his assignment at the 196th Light Infantry Brigade Headquarters, a young Second Lieutenant's time was up. He was on his second patrol and it's doubtful that any of the men who were with him even knew his name. Unlike World War Two and Korea, few units deployed together. Replacements were constantly coming and going through the pipeline.

I met him on his flight to the Brigade's Headquarters. He was a recent graduate of the ROTC program at his college in Kentucky. He was probably twenty-three or four, single, had a "girl" back home he probably planned to marry after he returned, had both parents still living, and had his entire life ahead of him, and like my childhood friend, it didn't work out for him.

He will get a military funeral back in Kentucky, complete with an honor guard, a bugler playing Taps, a flag folded, and a Silver Star, the third highest award for gallantry, handed to his mother.

One day in the future, some father may take his son to the cemetery. When his son sees the dates on his stone, he will do the math and ask, "How old do you have to be to die?"

There was no answer then and there's not one now.

Chapter Two

Even though I got a regular paycheck from the owner of the syndicate I worked for, I was my own boss in Viet Nam. He occasionally sent me a message by telex or on the phone when we got a good connection and asked me to do a story about something specific that he had heard about or seen on the news or wire that he felt the readers of my column would find of interest. Most of the time, I agreed and did what he asked. Occasionally, he asked for something that I could not or did not want to cover. After I explained my reason, he and I disagreed only once, and I had to defer to him…hence the regular paycheck.

Since I was my own boss in reality, if not in fact, I worked the days and hours I wanted to, or the ones the story I was following dictated. I never quite knew what to call my relationship with Carmen. To say I was her boyfriend made it sound like we were in high school. We were more than just friends, but even though in the back of my mind I could see us having a life together after leaving Viet Nam, I had not broached the subject with her enough to be called her fiancé.

Her job with the State Department kept her out of Saigon about as much as mine did. The difference was that I usually found myself slugging through the jungle with an Army or Marine platoon while walking along a rice paddy dike with an Advisor team. She, on the other hand, was usually at some Corps Headquarters or attending a meeting with generals or admirals.

The downside of all of this was that she had been shot down in a helicopter once and captured by the Viet Cong. A quick reaction force made up of US Navy SEALS was able to find and rescue her before she could be further harmed or moved to a remote jungle camp in Viet Nam, Cambodia, or Laos. Her helicopter was shot down south of Saigon, so she was probably too far from the border to have been moved to a POW compound near Hanoi like the Air Force and Navy pilots who were shot down. I'm sure a female POW would have been something the NVA would have used in every way for propaganda.

Once I got too close to the action, and I was wounded. When I got released from the hospital in Saigon, she cared for me at her home. Unlike what we think of as a home in the States, hers was more like a villa, complete with a maid and an armed guard provided by the State Department.

We tried to coordinate our schedules so we could spend time together. She had been at a meeting on a Navy ship in the South China Sea and had just gotten back to Saigon when I got a message at the office that she was in town. I immediately canceled the trip I had planned to go to a camp north of Saigon to see how the engineers were clearing the forests. Given a choice between three days with tractors and bulldozers and three days with Carmen, the boys playing in the dirt would have to wait.

At a time in the not-too-distant past, Saigon and much of the rest of what is now South Viet Nam was a magnificent city. The French influence in the architecture is evident in almost every building in the city. Traffic is as cluttered on wide boulevards like those in Paris as it is in the French city itself. Theaters have signs on them announcing that they are *Cinemas* and not movies. Street vendors sell hot loaves of *ban mi,* which is nothing more than the baguettes that the French taught them to make.

Without the presence of tens of thousands of men and women in uniform, military vehicles, jets, and helicopters flying overhead, and the distant sound of artillery, it would be a pleasant place to vacation.

If only.

I took a taxi from my building to Carmen's house. It was late in the afternoon, and I wanted to get there prior to the time when the civilians and many of the military personnel who worked in the city left work. Even in a war zone, many people kept office hours. By the time they left work, the streets would double in traffic.

Carmen's maid knew me and welcomed me into the house in both English and Vietnamese. Out of necessity, rather than desire at first, I made a conscious effort to learn the basics of communicating in Vietnamese. I found that when I was in the field, especially with the Advisors, being able to speak a few sentences with the locals was invaluable.

After Mai welcomed me with a greeting, Carmen welcomed me with a much-needed kiss and a drink. "Do you want to stay here tonight or go to a club or restaurant for dinner?"

There were enough excellent restaurants in the city that one had a choice of cuisine, much like any other large city. The problem was that once you finished dinner, there was no leisurely stroll down the street to window shop or buy an ice cream or have a cup of coffee at an outdoor café.

If we chose to dine out, we would catch a taxi, have dinner, and catch a taxi home. After dark, the streets belonged to the military of both sides. Cyclos, which were three-wheel bicycles with seats in the back and a man peddling up front, were the vehicle of choice to ferry the military to strip clubs, bars, or massage parlors. Saigon was the most crime-free city in the world. If someone was robbed, mugged, or even killed, it was reported to have been done by Viet Cong and not one of the many "cowboys" or young Vietnamese hoodlums who roamed the streets and preyed on the military.

We chose to stay in and let Mai prepare dinner for us. While we waited, Carmen fixed another drink for both of us, and we went to her bedroom. Her bedroom was a large room with white painted walls, a fan slowly turning overhead in the middle of room, near the foot of the bed. The bed was wrapped in a sheer covering that was a mosquito net. It looked more like something out of a movie about Arabian nights, than a protective covering to ward off the little pests that would drive you crazy if it was not in place.

She pulled it back, exposing an opening that was a safe place to enter the inner sanctums of the bed during the day when the mosquitos were not out and looking for blood. The sun was setting on the opposite side of her house, so we were in partial darkness. She was backlit by the limited light coming in through the one large window in the room.

"Stand in front of me. I want to look at you," I said as I took her hands in mine and gently guided her to where I wanted her.

"Like this," she whispered.

"I want to watch you undress. Take your time."

She hesitated for a moment, then unbuttoned her blouse, starting at the button just above where her bra peeked out when she moved in certain directions. I watched as, first, her dark blue blouse was slipped off and dropped to the floor. Next, she slid off her light-blue slacks. Finally, she stood in front of me in only bra and panties.

"Turn around."

She turned to face the window, and I reached up and unfastened her bra, and she let it fall into the growing pile of clothing on the floor. I slid my hands down her sides and stopped at the top of her panties. Using only a finger on each side, I hooked them into the silk that remained between us and slipped them off.

"Turn to face me and put your hands over your breasts."

She did as I asked. "Now you," she commanded.

She didn't have to ask twice, and in seconds, I was as nude as she. I reached out and took her hands in mine, and removed them from her breasts.

Nothing more needed to be said as we joined together in the bed.

We were both covered in a sheen of sweat when Mai called from outside the bedroom door and informed us that dinner was ready.

"Please place it on the table, and then you may leave," Carmen instructed.

Carmen slipped from the bed and pulled a deep purple silk dressing gown from the large cabinet that served as her closet. "You need to see a tailor and get a robe made for yourself," she said as I followed her and put on my pants.

We had dinner, and then we both knew the night was over. She was leaving again the next morning for a meeting with the IV Corps commander in Can Tho, in the Mekong Delta region of the country. I had checked off my desire to visit an infantry unit headquarters in Ah Sah Valley from my "to-do" board.

After sharing another drink, I went outside and found a cyclo driver who spoke a little English. I gave him the address of my hotel and as I climbed into the passenger seat, I turned to see Carmen standing at her bedroom window.

Without saying it aloud, we both knew that any time we parted, it could be for the last time.

DATELINE: SAIGON, SOUTH VIET NAM

Unlike World War Two and maybe even Korea, the men who served in Viet Nam did not form lifelong relationships. They generally came by themselves to a new unit or assignment. They had to get to know anyone who would be their friends, and if they were lucky, in twelve months, they were gone. Few of the men in uniform came as a part of a larger unit where they had already made friends and knew the person in the bunk next to them in the barracks, beside them in the foxhole.

It was the same with the civilians who were here. Most were US or allied government employees or contractors. A few foreigners came here and opened businesses. Tailor shops were run by Indians or Pakistanis. French and Russians ran restaurants. Chinese merchants sold everything including counterfeit US watches, to anyone who would purchase them. The Chinese shops were also the place to exchange your MPCs for the best rate.

Your social life was what you made of it. If you were in the field, it was a day or two back from an operation where you could do the thing you missed most. Not drink. Not eat. Not have sex. Sleep. Just sleep.

For those who were in the rear areas, there were USO entertainers at almost every base. Some were named entertainers whom the audience had heard of, others were acts that had, for some reason, been selected to come to Viet Nam. One night at a Navy base I listened to a female barber shop quartet. I'm sure most of the men in the audience had never heard a barber shop quartet in the past, but they were female and "round eyes" as any non-Asian female was called, and that's all that mattered.

Local clubs in the large cities had Vietnamese, Korean, or

Philippine bands who did terrible renditions of American popular songs in heavily accented English.

Many of the military personnel had girlfriends whom they paid by the month. The girl kept a house where she and her boyfriend could spend time when he was not working. It was usually furnished with goods he purchased at the Post Exchange or on the black market. If he did not extend when his tour of duty was finished, she pledged her undying love for him, and as soon as his plane was wheels up, she was available for the next GI. A fact of life under the circumstances.

For the very few, me included, there was a chance to meet someone special. I did, and I have no idea how our relationship will work out, but I'm more than willing to give it a try. Romance has reared its head in every war since the beginning of time.

Why should this one be any different?

Chapter Three

Go to almost any large city in the world, and certainly in the United States, and if you want to go from point A to point B, there will be a bus or a taxi that will come by in a few minutes, and it will take you where you want to go.

That's almost the way it is in Viet Nam. Only a few cities had anything even closely resembling a regular bus service, but there were taxis of all descriptions in every city and village in the country. The taxi may be an actual automobile, or it may be some type of motorcycle rigged with a passenger compartment in the front or back. Another method was a cyclo with a driver up front on a bicycle peddling his ass off to take you where you wanted to go. I have used all of these at some time or another as I traveled throughout the country, but it seems I travel most by helicopter.

The system for flying on helicopters is that there is no system for flying on helicopters. Unless the helicopter is engaged in an actual combat mission, if it's headed in the direction you want to go, and there's room on it for you, in most cases, all it takes is asking a member of the crew for a ride. Several times, I saw a grunt from the field who needed a ride to a hospital or medical appointment or to a location where he could make a phone call, either through the Red Cross or the Military Affiliate Radio Stations network, pull the Crew Chief aside and give him a VC flag or some other piece of military gear as the price of admission.

For me, once they saw I was a civilian and I told them what I did, all I had to do was promise to try to get a hometown news release story about them. Most of the time, all I had was a name and a unit, but that was enough for the folks back home to know their family member or friend was alive, at least at the time I saw them.

I had been in Three Corps snooping around and didn't find anything that I could cover in the next day or two. Usually when I went to a large base, I asked to tag along with a unit going on some type of operation. It may be a combat patrol or a supply run. It didn't matter. Those were the typical things the men and women in Viet Nam were doing, and reporting back to the readers was what I was sent over here for.

The dust was stifling when the large Marine CH-46 made its approach to the red earth landing strip. This firebase had not yet been in operation long enough for the engineers or Navy Construction Battalions or CBs to put down the PSP to make a better landing area. The massive helicopter had two blades spinning atop its curved body. The earlier versions of helicopters in Viet Nam were called Flying Bananas, and for good reason. That's exactly what they looked like.

There were two versions of the massive one in front of me. The Marines called theirs the CH-46, and the Army called theirs the CH-47 or Chinook. Both were used for transporting equipment and personnel. It was not unusual to see one overhead with a 105 Howitzer artillery piece slung beneath it. That one was sometimes followed by a second one with a cargo net beneath it loaded with artillery shells.

As soon as it landed and idled down, the rear ramp dropped, and a group of men in mixed uniforms ducked and ran to the make-shift operations shack on the side of the landing zone. The passengers were a mixed bag of Navy, Army, and Marine uniforms, a few in civilian clothes and at least two in Vietnamese uniforms.

I was inside and watched as they filtered into the building. Most were loaded down with a rucksack and a weapon of some sort. One of the civilians had a Model 1911 Colt .45 automatic pistol in a brown leather shoulder holster. It was not hard to recognize him as a CIA Field Officer of some sort. He walked straight through the building and got into a waiting Jeep parked outside.

I turned from him and to a young Army Sergeant standing behind a desk that had been made from three-point five rocket launcher boxes that has been broken down into usable wood. "Excuse me, Sergeant. Where is that chopper that just landed headed when it leaves here?"

He looked up at me, expecting to see someone in uniform. "Depends."

"On what?"

"On who you are and why you want to know." He had a clipboard in his hands, which he placed on the top of the desk. A clipboard is the universal sign that the person holding it is either in charge, thinks he is, or wants you to believe he is.

"I'm a correspondent. I work for a civilian syndicate, and I have blanket travel authorization." I pulled out my identification card and the small credit card size laminated card that was from MACV Headquarters. It said I had permission to fly on any military aircraft in country at the discretion of the aircraft commander.

He looked at it and shook his head like he really understood that I was not bullshitting him. "Okay. Bird's going to Nam Can. Probably RON there and then tomorrow…who knows. I the pilot says it's okay with him, you can load with everyone else." He picked up his clipboard and walked away.

The pilot and his co-pilot, a Marine Captain and a First Lieutenant, were standing by a cooler that held several bottles of soda. At some point it probably had been filled with ice, but there was no trace of it now. They were drinking the warm soda and obviously enjoying it.

"Captain…" I looked at the nametag on his flight suit. "Miles, I'm Sean Kelly." I extended my hand. "I'm a correspondent, and I'd like to catch a ride with you when you pull out if you have room."

He finished his drink and extended his hand. "You know where we're going?"

"The Sergeant over there at the counter said Nam Can. That's down in the Delta, right?"

"Yeah, 'bout as far south as you can go and still be in Viet Nam. Nothing down there but half a SEAL team and some Army Advisors that got stuck working with Ruff Puffs."

Like most things in Viet Nam, there was an American name for them.

There were two types of local forces used for protection and operations. Regional Forces and Popular Forces or Ruff Puffs. I had been on operations with Advisors and their local troops in the past, but I had not worked with a SEAL team, so that immediately interested me, and I wanted to see what they did and how they did it.

"Sounds like a place I'd like to go. When do we lift off?" I asked before he could tell me I couldn't go.

I watched from the open doorway as several large crates were loaded into the vast open space in the middle of the helicopter. Passengers were seated along the sides in seats that folded down when not in use or if there was too much cargo. The seats were functional and that's about it. Nylon straps held a long metal pole that provided a place to sit. The straps were attached to the bulkhead and held the seat and passenger in place.

After about thirty minutes, the two pilots walked out and did a walk-around inspection. It was a routine requirement, but in most safe areas, it was done more to make sure if the unit's commanding officer was looking, he saw the crew following directives. I knew if they had set the big machine down on an outpost or a firebase in an active combat area, the ramp would be lowered, the cargo and passengers would be hustled off, and they would take off as soon as possible, having never shut the engines down.

When they were satisfied, the crew chief motioned toward the building, indicating any passengers were safe to board. I had seen the two American officers, one a Captain and the other a First Lieutenant, standing by a group of Vietnamese for the last ten minutes. The Americans were dressed in tiger stripe fatigues, indicating they were either Special Forces or Rangers. Like the Vietnamese with them, they were all armed. Some had standard-issue M-16 rifles, some had old M-1 carbines, and a few had shotguns. From the uniforms and the weapons, I knew this was not a standard issue US Army unit and I wanted to find out who they were, and where they were going and to do what.

I fell in beside the Captain as he watched the Lieutenant lead the Vietnamese soldiers to the helicopter. "Excuse me, Captain, I'm Sean Kelly, and I'm a correspondent for a newspaper back in the States. This looks like an interesting unit you have. Care to tell me about it?"

"No, not really," he said without breaking stride as we walked.

"Just an overview. Nothing classified."

"Sorry." He ducked by force of habit, as he approached the helicopter and its twin blades gaining speed as they rotated over our heads.

"Okay, I guess I'll just have to figure it out based on your uniforms and the strange variety of weapons you're carrying." I nodded at the weapon he had slung over his shoulder.

"Sit beside me on the lift, and I'll tell you what I can." He walked up the ramp and disappeared inside.

I felt the heavy bird lift off and head out toward the base at Nam Can. It was a small base in the Nam Can Forest, somewhat of a misnomer since the area was more of a swamp than a forest. It was on the southern tip of the country and was near to where the Mekong River finally emptied into the South China Sea. I had seen it from the air several times, and each time, I felt fortunate that I was over it and not in it.

From the air, you could see the multitude of small waterways that crisscrossed the massive delta region. At my home in Florida, we would call them creeks and give each a name, but here, they were so numerous that only those who traversed them on a regular basis knew where each one went or came from. The land between the ribbons of dark brown water occasionally was the home of a couple of the small houses that made up the hamlets or villages in the region. There were no roads. The only way for the locals to navigate the forest was by foot or boat.

Massive trees took up most of the space on the dots of land. Areas between the trees were covered in tangles of smaller trees, vines, and undergrowth that spent each day trying to reach the limited sunlight that was available.

There were stories of saltwater crocodiles, boa constrictors, and other creatures that made for scary bedtime stories if such a thing existed in Viet Nam. All things considered, I did not want to spend any time on the ground or in the water there.

When we lifted off, the Captain got up and went to speak to the Lieutenant. He had to yell but with the other sounds inside, his words probably could not be heard by the soldier seated next to the man.

Finally, he returned and turned to yell at me. "Okay, we're Advisors to some Vietnamese Rangers. We're going on a body snatch operation. It's a high-level VC officer. That's all I can tell you."

In the real world, one not at war, a *body snatch operation* would be considered kidnapping. The mission was not to kill the person, but to capture him alive. He would then be taken to a safe area and interrogated. If he gave any usable information, subsequent operations would be launched before his information grew cold. He didn't give me much information, but it was a start.

I was thinking about what else I could ask when the first hole appeared in the floor in front of me. There was no need asking what it was. I had seen similar holes in the past. They came from a large caliber machine gun that someone was firing at us. I watched as several more punctured the thin metal between us and the shooter. One round caught a young Vietnamese soldier in the thigh as it came through the floor.

The heavy machine gun was a .51 caliber and was designed to use captured .50 caliber ammunition. Very smart. Their gun could fire the smaller .50 caliber, but the larger .51 caliber round would not fit inside the US-made .50. The size of the round did not matter to the man who was now looking at a completely destroyed left leg. From across the aisle, I could see bone protruding from the wound.

We couldn't see it, but the smell was a dead giveaway. One of the two engines at the rear of the helicopter had been hit and was trailing burning oil. I had no idea if we could stay in the air with only one engine, and I hoped and prayed that I did not have to find out.

I knew the pilot was taking evasive action as we were shifted in our seats as he turned sharply from the left to the right and then I could tell we were trying to gain altitude as the holes kept appearing.

I turned at one point and looked out my side of the helicopter's small porthole window and saw the massive swamp of the Nam Can Forest below us. I remembered all the stories I had heard about it, and it was not a place one wanted to be if an emergency landing was needed.

The crew chief was up and walking down the aisle, examining the holes. A medic with the rangers was attempting to treat the soldier, who was clearly going into shock and was near death from the massive loss of blood from the wound. It was clear that the round had cut a major artery, and there was no way a bandage and a tourniquet were going to save his life.

The crew chief stopped by the Captain and yelled something that I could not hear, but from the look on the Captain's face, it was not good news. After checking more damage by looking out the porthole, the crew chief pulled his microphone down from the side of his headset and spoke into it.

After the conversation, he went to the front and stood just behind the bulkhead, separating the flight crew from the rest of us. He opened a door and pulled out several bundles. It took a moment for me to realize they were life jackets. Passengers in aircraft that are in the air do not need life jackets. Only those passengers in aircraft that may be about to leave the air and go into water need them.

That, I found out, was us.

The crew chief removed the M-60 machine gun from its mount in the open door on the side of the helicopter and then motioned for me and the Lieutenant to come to him.

By the time we got to him, he was holding life jackets and handed one to both of us as we got closer. We watched as he put his own and repeated the process for ours. Once we had the jackets on, he lifted his microphone and pulled us closer to him.

He yelled so we could hear above the sounds of the crippled helicopter and the dying noises made by the engine. "We're probably going into the water. There is a Navy ship not far from where we'll ditch, and we're going to try to get as close as we can."

The look on our faces said this was not something we were prepared for. "I'm going to open the side door so you can jump. If I lower the ramp, we'll never get out of here. As soon as we get to an elevation over the water, I'll give the word, and you have about thirty seconds to un-ass this thing, or the blades will cut you in half when we hit the water." He looked at us. "You got no choice. Give out as many life jackets as we have and the rest can get a head start to seeing Buddha."

The Captain nodded and looked at his next in command. "None of our people know how to swim, so get as many in jackets as you can. They won't jump unless one of us goes first. That'll be you." He then turned to me. "You go second. They need to see us, or they won't even try to get out."

I knew he was probably right, but still, I did not relish the thought of jumping from a crippled helicopter into the South China Sea, even if a ship was en route to rescue us. I also knew if I had any chance of living, it was going to be in the water.

A Vietnamese Sergeant recognized the situation and came forward, took the life jackets, and handed them out. The men were bunched together and fought over the jackets until he pulled a pistol and shot into the floorboard of the already wounded aircraft. One more hole was not going to make any difference, and he knew it.

The Vietnamese who had jackets put them on after discarding all their field gear and weapons. I saw several pull a companion to them as if they were going to jump together.

Up front, the crew chief was waving for the Captain to move his men to the door. The Lieutenant was standing, one hand on each side of the opening, ready to jump, when the crew chief rushed forward and grabbed him by the back of his shirt and frantically waved him away from the opening.

As soon as the Lieutenant stepped back, I felt the unmistakable, bone-shattering slam of a massive twin-rotary blade helicopter filled with American and Vietnamese military and one civilian make a hard landing. The Lieutenant immediately disappeared out the open doorway despite the Crew Chief's attempt to hold him. Everyone who had been standing was knocked to the floor by the bird or slammed against the side.

I was in my life jacket, so I felt if I could get through the open door on the side, I'd at least have a chance of survival. I had a small snub-nosed pistol I won in a poker game that I carried in a holster secured to my belt in the back. It was always covered by a shirt that was never tucked into my pants, so I didn't have to worry about someone having a problem with an armed civilian. Were there sharks in the South China Sea? I had no idea, but I had six .38 rounds to shoot if there were.

Before I got to the door, I saw the Lieutenant. He was not wet and appeared to be standing. Unless he was the Second Coming, I didn't think he was walking on water. Before I could get a grasp on his situation, I saw half a dozen men piling into the open door.

They were sailors and the pilot had managed to make it to the Navy ship before we crashed.

After we got everyone out of the crippled helicopter and safely onboard the ship, we were greeted by the ship's commanding officer. The pilot walked over to him, pulled off his flight helmet, and saluted. "Permission to come aboard, sir."

DATELINE: SAIGON, SOUTH VIET NAM

My home state of Florida has the Everglades.

Our neighboring state of Georgia has the Okefenokee Swamps.

Louisiana has the Mississippi Delta.

South Viet Nam has the Uh Minh and the Nam Can Forest.

All these vast expanses of land, mud, water, and creatures that swim, crawl or walk have one thing in common. People only go into them for specific reasons. In the first three it's generally to hunt or fish or to see the wildlife.

It's the last two that are of concern to me. The Uh Minh and the Nam Can are two of the most desolate places I have ever seen. Fortunately, "seen" is the only reference to them that I have, although I thought that was about to change recently.

When you put your life in the hands of someone else, you never know if they will value it as much as you do. The men and women in Viet Nam do that on a daily basis. No matter if the person is in the field facing a regiment of North Vietnamese Army regulars or in a village that is controlled by the Viet Cong. Up to and including the commander of all the military in Viet Nam, everyone has someone who is in charge of them. You can only hope that the person in charge is as interested in saving your life as he is in saving his.

Fortunately, I had just such a person in charge recently. I was on a helicopter that was in the process of being shot down by enemy fire. We were flying over a vast area of swamps, rivers, and mangroves called the Nam Can Forest. With several holes in the helicopter and an engine fire, we had no place to land, so we headed out to sea. The flight crew had to make a life-or-death decision. Land in the South China Sea or try to make it to a nearby Navy ship.

The pilot made the decision to try for the ship and made a landing that the crew of the ship and the helicopter thought impossible. Instead of ditching at sea, he brought the massive helicopter down on the deck of the ship.

Making life or death decisions daily in Viet Nam is as routine as saying, "Pass the salt" at dinner at home.

Routine, not easy, but necessary.

That's the things you don't see on the nightly news.

Chapter Four

Sometimes, I get more than I bargained for when I find what I think will be an interesting unit or mission. Once I wanted to accompany a recon team that was working the border near Laos. It was a four-day mission and I knew once I decided to go, I was going to be there as long as the rest of the team was. Little did I know that what was supposed to be a dangerous, but routine mission for these men would turn out to be something that none of them would ever talk about.

They were supposed to sit by the trail, watch for the enemy, not engage and report back what they saw. Instead, several nights into the mission, we were attacked. Several of the men on the team were "wounded," and many of the enemy were killed.

At daylight, when an extraction was called for, it was determined that the enemy force that had attacked us and had suffered numerous casualties, was not a regiment of NVA or a platoon of VC, but a troop of hairy monkeys on their nightly feeding frenzy. Like all the men on the patrol, I was sworn to secrecy and only reported the incident later in a column. I learned that night that sometimes I would get more than I bargained for.

I wasn't military, so I had to ask permission, or sometimes forgiveness, when I accompanied a unit on an operation. Most of the time, I went alone, but on occasion, I was accompanied by Wess Price, a freelance photographer who accompanied many of the correspondents when we went to where the stories originated. Sometimes, if I wanted to find out what a particular Army or Marine combat unit was doing, I had to remain in a rear area and monitor the action by way of radio communications with the unit in the field or in contact. Very few of us actually found ourselves with a unit in contact with the enemy. For that reason, I liked to visit one of the many advisory units throughout the country.

The Army and Marine Corps had a unique method of putting advisors in the field. The Army called them Mobile Advisory Teams or MATs and the equivalent for the Marines was the Combined Action Program teams. They usually consisted of five or six Americans and a Vietnamese interpreter. They lived in the villages they supported and, in most cases, lived no better than the locals, which meant, by American standards, they lived like animals.

Some teams had prefabricated team houses airlifted to the village or outpost where they were assigned, but in most cases, they lived in whatever they could build from local, stolen, or scrounged building material. They lived a twenty-four-hour-a-day existence that was no better than the unit they advised.

Viet Nam is divided into forty-four provinces, which in the US, would be roughly the same as a state. The provinces were further divided into districts or counties. The country had three different types of Army or ground forces. The Army of Viet Nam was like the US Army and was designed to fight throughout the country. Each province had Regional Forces operating within the province, and lower on the pecking order were the Popular Forces, which were given the mission of village defense. The Army of Viet Nam were called the ARVN, and the latter two were Ruff Puffs. All three had American Advisors, but only the last two were readily available for me to visit. I knew that when I went to either a Ruff or Puff location, I was probably going to see, and become involved, in combat actions.

I had hitched a ride on a C130 heading north from Saigon. The crew said the plane was scheduled to end the mission for the day and land at the airstrip in Phu Bai, in I Corps or the northernmost section of the country. The region was mostly mountains, and since it was the closest to the border between the two countries, combat there was mostly between North Vietnamese Army or NVA forces and conventional US forces. I had not been with an advisor unit that far north, so I wanted to see what it was like for one to be faced with NVA and must defend their positions with either Ruff's or Puff's.

I was curious, but also cautious, and even though I wanted a story, I did not have a death wish, so I planned to leave the city and find a unit in a smaller village. There were NVA units in the area, but the advisor teams generally faced only Viet Cong, a much less formidable, in most cases, force.

I caught a flight heading out from Phu Bai to one of the district capitals or headquarters. We landed at the airstrip and were met by both Army and Marine representatives who unloaded the cargo the plane brought to them. Most of the resupply came by trucks, but there had been a rash of ambushes along QL 69, one of the main roads in the country that ran from the DMZ to the Delta. Both sides of the conflict used it to move troops and equipment, so it was the biggest ambush alley in the country.

Trucks backed up to the loading ramp at the rear of the plane after I and the other passengers got off. I watched as the loadmaster orchestrated the offloading of large containers of ammunition, rations, medical supplies, and unmarked boxes. Several men stood by the ramp and watched as their fellow soldiers and marines loaded their designated cargo into waiting trucks. When the last large container was moved down the ramp, I found out why the other men were standing around. The loadmaster signaled to the other crew members still working inside the plane to bring another pallet forward.

As soon as it was pushed from the dark of the cargo area to the daylight shining on the ramp, I knew why everyone was still standing there. The pallet was a double load. It was half filled with cases of beer and half filled with soda. The loadmaster had the crew hand a case of soda and then a case of beer to a representative from each of the services. There was no one there from the Air Force, so I assumed they took their share prior to loading.

The pallet was empty except for one case of beer. By that time, everything on the pallet had been equally divided. The loadmaster called one man from each group to him. He reached into his pocket and pulled out a coin, which he flipped in the air and then caught. He turned it over and slapped it onto the back of his hand.

I watched as he pointed to the Marine. It was his job to call either heads or tails, and if he was right, the extra case was Marine property. The call was made, and I saw the man dressed in Army fatigues pump his hand in the air. He won, and the beer was his.

I didn't notice the sounds of the active airstrip as I watched the action at the rear of the plane I had just arrived on. When I left the plane and headed to the airfield operations shack, I heard the not-too-distant sound of artillery as it exploded. I knew from experience and the reaction, or lack thereof, of the men on the airfield that it was friendly outgoing, and not something to worry about. Just as I entered the doorway of the building, I heard several rounds of small arms fire coming from the end of the runway.

An Army Master Sergeant was standing by the doorway, with the always present clipboard in hand. "Hey," he called out to me. "Hang on a minute, and I'll be with you." He watched as the loaded trucks left the runway and two more pulled up to the rear of the plane, ready for whatever they were carrying to be offloaded into the plane. The first thing I saw was the large containers that were used to ship bodies. I didn't want to count them as they were carried from the truck to the plane. It would be the first of several times they would be carried until they were finally given military honors.

When the last one was carried aboard, and the truck departed, the Master Sergeant put his pen in the pocket of this jacket and walked to me. "Who are you, and what can I do to help you stay alive?"

"I'm looking for a way to meet the commander of one of the Marine CAP Teams."

"What the hell you want to do that for? You look like a man with good sense to me."

"I hope I am, but I'm also a correspondent. I want to do a story on the men who work the closest with the locals. That's the mission of the CAP Teams, isn't it?"

I knew that initially, General Westmorland was not a fan of the teams or the concept of working at the lowest level. His battle plan was to defeat the NVA and the VC on the battlefield. That was a plan that would have worked in a conventional war, but what the American and its allies in Viet Nam were involved in was anything but.

"Yeah, they work with the locals, all right. There's a district headquarters about half a mile down the road. Somebody there can tell you where to find a team." He stood in silence and just shook his head as he went back to work.

A young Marine Lance Corporal had overheard our conversation and eased up to me. "I'm headed that way. I can give you a lift unless you want to walk."

"No, I think a ride would be much better." I picked up my small bag and followed him out the door. When we got in his Jeep, I asked him if he could fill me in on the area.

"It's pretty much a free-fire zone. They shoot at us, and we shoot at them. I don't know who's keeping score, but I imagine it's about even. Our guys mostly run into hard-core NVA units, but the guys you want to visit usually have contact with the local VC, although some of them are pretty hard asses themselves."

We stopped in front of a building that had once been a very nice example of the French influence in the area. That was prior to it being, once again, in the middle of a war zone. The right front corner of the structure had taken a direct hit from either a mortar or an RPG. It had not done enough damage to destroy the building, but it was definitely wounded.

"Go inside and to the right. That's the operations room. Somebody there'll fix you up." He waited until I got my bag and then sped away.

Inside the building, it was like a duplication of a city hall in a small town in the US. Several offices had women seated at typewriters, and a few doors were closed and had signs on them. I assumed these were where the men responsible for the operation of the district were located. I heard a burst of English on the radio, so I knew I was close to the operations center. I followed the sound and found a room with a row of radios sitting on what appeared to be wood doors supported on stacks of empty crates that once held artillery shells. I was met at the door by a Major.

"This place is off limits unless you got business here." He was serious but not hostile when he spoke. I imagined any explanation of why I was here and what I wanted would be sufficient. I explained who I was, why I was there, and what I wanted. After listening, he invited me into the inner workings of the operations center.

After a fifteen-minute conversation explaining how nuts I was to want to spend any time with a CAP Team, he got on the radio and made arrangements for a sergeant from a team to come and pick me up.

An hour after arriving at the District Headquarters, I was introduced to most of the men on the team. A CAP Team consists of a Marine thirteen-man rifle squad and a Navy Corpsman as their medic. Their mission was to train the local Regional Force in tactics, fire control, defensive tactics, and combat patrolling. The commander of the CAP team was an advisor to his Vietnamese counterpart. As long as they were not on patrol but outside the confines of their village or outpost, the American was in charge.

It was explained to me that half the team, headed by a lieutenant, was on a recon patrol and was due back by seventeen hundred. Any night operation was generally conducted with the captain in charge, and most of the team included.

The team leader, Captain Harold Bankston, took me to a small building not far from the team's house to meet his counterpart, the District Chief and commander of the Regional Force company assigned to the district.

By the time introductions were made, the team's executive officer, Lieutenant J. R. Dalton, had returned from his recon patrol. "Good news, Dai Uy," he referred to the captain using the Vietnamese rank. "We tried to avoid contact, but we got our nuts in a wringer and had a small firefight in a village right here..." He walked to a large map and pointed to a place that looked like it was not too far from where we were.

"KIAs?"

"We got three of theirs and a prisoner. None of us or our little people were hit." His reference to little people was how any Vietnamese military who were with American troops were identified. The lieutenant looked at a large bottle on the District Chief's desk. "If that's good water, I'd like a drink. My mouth feels like it's full of cotton."

He was handed the bottle, and he took a drink directly from it. "The best thing is what we got from the prisoner. Two of the KIAs are brothers and the other one is a cousin. You know what that means."

The captain nodded in understanding, but I had to ask. I wasn't so sure I liked the answer when I got it.

That night the entire team was back, and I was introduced to the rest of them, and we shared stories. I found out that most of them had been in country for less than six months, and only four of them volunteered to be on a team. They were a cross-section of America. Some were from large cities, some were small towns, two were Black, one Hispanic from Texas, and the captain was an Academy graduate. We had a dinner made from "liberated" Viet Cong chickens and some vegetables from the local market, some warm beer, and they gave me a place to sleep and an air mattress that I had to blow up myself.

I was awakened by someone shaking my foot. In my still groggy state, I raised up. "What…what the hell…?"

"It's me, J.R. We're going on a mission. The captain said to wake you up and see if you wanted to go with us."

"Uh, yeah…I…I do," I managed to stammer as my head cleared and I became more awake.

"Good, we leave in zero ten."

That meant I had ten minutes to become fully awake and dressed and ready to go. Hopefully, they, like most units, had a twenty-four-hour-a-day coffee pot, so at least I'd get a cup before we left.

A quick cup while I listened to J.R. brief the entire team on what we were about to do. When I heard the entire mission, it was too late to back out, and I realized I was seeing the war at its lowest and most primeval level.

We fell in with the already assembled team from the Ruff Puffs that would accompany us. All together, there were about twenty-five fully armed men ready to go into combat to protect their home turf.

We went on foot and traveled for at least two hours before Captain Bankston held up his hand for the patrol to stop. He conferred with his counterpart and the lieutenant before having the patrol spread out along the edge of a ridgeline. Below us, barely visible in the dark, was a group of about five small hootches or houses. A trail led from the adjoining ridge to the hamlet of houses. Each one had a small fire burning either outside or just inside the door of the hootch.

Bankston came back to where he had me wait with the medic and his RTO.

"They'll be along at sunrise to pick up the bodies of the three that were killed. The funeral procession will start from here. There may be some mourners from nearby hamlets who knew them that will come as well. Anybody in the procession is either a Viet Cong or a VC sympathizer, so they're all targets."

We were preparing to ambush a funeral procession.

At first light it happened just like the Captain said.

The three men killed the previous day were wrapped in cloth and carried by other men in the funeral procession. Most of the men had weapons slung over their shoulders, and I saw two women who were also armed with rifles. The captain had marked out the kill zone, and once the procession was in it, the area lit up with gunfire. For the first minute, it was only going toward the procession, but three of the men and one woman managed to unsling their weapons and return fire, but by that time, it was a wasted effort.

The procession to honor the dead had become a procession of the dead.

It was over in less than a minute, and two hours later, we were back at the team house.

It was just another day in the war in Viet Nam.

DATELINE: SAIGON, SOUTH VIET NAM

How do you un-see things that will forever be imprinted on your mind?

War is a daily dose of sights, sounds, and smells. It invaded all your senses and leaves an indelible print at times. The first time you smell nuoc mam or the fish sauce the Vietnamese put on almost all their food; you will never forget it. The sound of a B-52 bomb run, shaking the earth beneath you, Spooky, the C-130 gunship firing a mini-gun at so many rounds per minute it sounds like a swarm of gigantic bees, the pleading of a wounded soldier, no matter who's uniform he is wearing, crying out for help or his mother, or that of a child caught up in a war they will never understand even if they survive it, will stay with you forever.

Are these things necessary? Put them in perspective. A crying child in your hometown will immediately draw the attention of a parent or caring adult who will do what is necessary to take away the hurt. But what if there is no parent or caring adult left in town? What then?

Can human emotions and dignity be stripped away for twelve months, put on a shelf, and then re-inserted into our bodies? Will it stay on the shelf intact or can it be removed a small piece at a time?

Nobody who is in this war will ever be the same again. Part of everyone, especially the actual combat soldier, will have a piece that is either left behind or has been destroyed.

I left a piece on a trail overlooking a village that no one has ever heard of or will ever hear of again. It happened one morning as the sun rose to begin a new day for a small group of US Marines living a small part of their lives in Viet Nam.

We attended a funeral.

Chapter Five

There was a briefing every day at the MACV compound in Saigon. The news we got was sterilized, and it was what the command wanted us to report. The bottom line was that the war was being won. Body counts were up. The enemy was getting tired of getting their asses handed to them by the boys in the field. The Vietnamese government was in full support of all that we were doing, the weatherman predicted snow for the Fourth of July and the Brooklyn Bridge was for sale.

News crews from the three networks and some of the weekly news magazines knew unless they had been in the field and had stories of their own, this was what they had to give the boss back home. It got filtered, a voice-over track laid on it, and Mr. and Mrs. Smith watched it on television each evening.

It was up to some of the independent or freelance men to bring the real war home. We never knew if what we reported was censored or not, so I decided not to report the blood and guts but to try to get the stories behind the men and women who were here. Because most of the Public Affairs Officers knew me and how I wrote my column, I was treated a little differently from some of my contemporaries. I had been in country long enough and seen enough to wonder sometimes just what I expected to gain from being here. Was I making a difference, and if so, to whom?

One day, I got a message that the Public Affairs Officer for MACV wanted to see me. I had seen him at most of the briefings, known as the Five O'clock Follies, but he and I had never had a one-on-one conversation.

Someone, much before I arrived, managed to 'acquire' a jeep that anyone in the office could use. We all chipped in a few bucks a month and had a Vietnamese man who acted as our driver, gopher, and cleaning crew. He was happy to have a job that paid much more than he could get working anyplace on the open market and when he was not working, we knew we could always find him asleep on the back seat of the jeep. At some point during his time with us, someone, and for some reason unknown to any of us, he was given the nickname 'Slick.'

I went outside and found Slick asleep in the jeep. He took a great deal of pride in the vehicle, and it was one of the cleanest and best-looking vehicles on the streets of Saigon.

After grabbing his foot and shaking him awake, Slick climbed across the seat and settled into the driver's seat. "Where we go?" he asked in heavily accented English.

The MACV headquarters and anything or anyone associated with it was always referred to a MACV. We did not use the initials. It was an acronym. "Take me to MACV headquarters."

We left the safety and security of our compound and hit the scary streets of Saigon. I sometimes wondered which was more dangerous: an enemy soldier with a weapon or a motor scooter driver on the streets of Saigon.

The streets were always filled during daylight hours with anything that had wheels and could carry passengers, crates of chickens and ducks, building material, or anything that could be tied to the back of a two-wheeled rocket.

We were stopped at the entrance to the compound, and I showed the American MP my identification card, Slick showed his driver's license, and we were waved through. I directed him to the main building and told him to wait. He joined a large group of other Vietnamese drivers, many of whom were either already asleep or rubbing down their jeeps to clean them.

I saw a sign indicating it was the office of the PAO, and since there was no door, I entered. A young woman was seated at a desk. She was reading something handwritten on a page from a long yellow legal pad. She read for a minute, then turned to her typewriter and, I assumed typed what she had just read. Finally, she looked up and saw me.

"How can I assist you, sir?" Her almost flawless English shocked me.

"I'm here to see Lieutenant Colonel Christopher."

"You must be Mister Sean Kelly." It was more of a statement than a question. "I'll see if he can see you now." She got up, and I noticed she was wearing the traditional *ao dai* that most women wore. It was a blouse that hung over a pair of usually white pants. The blouse had a long front and back that covered the woman. A conical hat made of straw was also a part of the outfit. Very few Vietnamese women who worked for the military wore Western-style clothes.

When she came from the office, she was followed by the PAO. "Morning Sean…may I call you Sean?" He extended his hand. LTC Christopher was about my height and had a receding hairline. His starched and ironed fatigues quickly identified him as living the good life in Saigon. I didn't look, but I suspected his jungle boots were either highly shined or were coated with a plastic-like substance that kept a spit-shined look.

"No, I don't mind at all." I took his extended hand and noticed he held it out in such a way that it was hard not to notice the massive USMA ring.

"Come in. I've got something I want to run by you." He stopped and looked at the woman. "Miss Kim, would you get us a couple of cups of coffee and see if there are any donuts left."

I immediately thought of someone a world away from this office, out in the field, eating a cold breakfast of a can of ham and eggs, chopped from a box of C-rations while waiting for the next round to crack over his head.

Keller motioned for me to sit on a standard-issue Army sofa. It had a seating area that was covered in a brown leather looking material. The frame was round chrome-plated pipes. Probably made in a prison workshop someplace.

"I've read some of your dispatches, and I have to say, I'm mildly impressed." He laughed at his half-compliment.

"Well…I'm mildly impressed that you read some of them." We both got a laugh, but it was interrupted by Miss Kim, who brought in a tray with two brown mugs of coffee and a plate of doughnuts. I was halfway expecting the coffee to be served on china cups and saucers.

"I have a project that I think you'd be perfect for." He put cream and sugar in his mug and took a bite from one of the donuts. "I want the people back in the world to know what it's really like over here."

"Really?" I said as I took a sip of my black coffee. I learned to drink it black after so many cups with units in the field who would kill for a donut and some sugar and cream. "I thought knowing what it's really like over here was a secret."

"Oh, bullshit. You know what I mean. I'm not talking about combat operations. I want the folks back home to see the people in the village and hamlets. Not the medevacs in the field and the hookers in Saigon. And I think you're the man who can do that."

Outside the office I could hear the noise of people walking by and the conversation that can be found in any large business operation. Someone called out for a sergeant to get his ass in here…wherever here was, immediately.

"What did you have in mind?

"I want to get out to the bush. Away from Saigon. I've been stuck here since I got in country. You've been with all kinds of units and every corner of the country." He stopped as if he was the one who had given me permission to go to those places. "The people back home deserve to know that there are people in Viet Nam who aren't shooting at us and are happy we are here."

I thought about being a smart ass and telling him to go out to the parking lot and speak to any one of the drivers and then go find a couple of hookers on Tu Do Street. With any luck, he'll pick some who aren't part-time Viet Cong, but I didn't. "When did you want to take this field trip, and where do you want to go?"

"I cleared my calendar for the next three days. Let's leave tomorrow. We can take a Jeep, or I can get us a chopper to drop us off and wait or come back and pick us up." He made it sound like we were in some large city in the US, and he'd just call a taxi for our outing.

"I think you need to do a little more planning than just dropping in on a village. Find a place you want to go and see if it's a secure area, and if it is, there's probably an Advisor Team of some sort that can meet you…us and give a tour of sorts."

"See. That's why I wanted you to do this with me. I didn't think of that."

There was a little boy at Christmas, excitement in his voice. "Tell you what. You pick the area, and if you can't contact the Advisor Team, let me know, and I'll push the message through channels. What say we leave the day after tomorrow?"

I spent the next day making come calls and asking for them to be relayed by radio if necessary. I finally happened to catch a District Senior Advisor at a Province Headquarters and explained what the PIO wanted, and although he thought he was crazy for wanting to leave the comfort and safety of an office in Saigon to slog through a village, he agreed to meet us.

We were going to a village in the Delta near the Cambodian border. I contacted the PIO and told him where we were going. His first question was about sleeping accommodations if we spent the night. I immediately knew this was not going to be a vacation for me.

As promised, he had a helicopter waiting for us at one of the chopper pads at the MACV compound. We lifted off and headed southwest for almost an hour. I had provided the radio frequency for the District Headquarters TOC to the pilot prior to lift-off, so when we got close, he radioed them for clearance to set down. Every District Headquarters had some type of landing zone. It may not be for fixed-wing aircraft, but helicopters were their lifelines to any place outside their district.

We set down, and the chopper was immediately surrounded by a group of kids from the nearby village. This happened almost every time a helicopter set down in, or near a village and it was not landing troops on a combat mission. The kids ran with their hands up. If they had learned any English, they begged for cigarettes or candy. If they hadn't, they just held up their hand, awaiting anything that would be put in it.

I was with a group from an Army company coming back from a patrol when I first arrived. As we passed through a village, the kids ran out and held up their hands as they begged. Some of the men threw cans of C-rations, not to the kids, but at them. I was shocked until I heard about some of the kids being used by the Viet Cong to toss grenades into the back of passing trucks. I had a lot to learn.

When we cleared the kids away from the chopper, we saw a man standing with his arms crossed, watching us. I knew it was our point of contact. He let us get well clear of the blades of the helicopter still rotating overhead before approaching us.

"I'm Major Alan Cochran, the DSA." He shook hands with both of us and turned. "Follow me. I'll take you to the PSA, and he'll blow some smoke up your ass about how secure the Province is."

The Province's Senior Advisor was a civilian and a retired US Army Colonel. His office was in a former French villa. It had a courtyard with a fence surrounding it. The fence had been made of cement blocks and was topped with barbed wire and broken glass bottles embedded in the top. If this was secure, I'd hate to see what he'd do in a combat area.

We spent an hour in his office and listened to him tell us how the Province had recently declared almost all of its villages secure based on the criteria set forth by IV Corps Headquarters. When we had no questions, he turned us over to Major Cochran, who led us out.

"We'll take my jeep out to Ap Ben Koi. I've got a couple of men from one of the local teams to meet us. The village is a good representation of everyday life in this part of the country."

We got in and bounced across, and through, some potholes in the dirt and gravel road that would have knocked any American auto out of alignment. The ride took a little over thirty minutes. We stopped once and he asked the PIO to hand him the handset from the radio mounted in the back of the jeep. He called the men on the ground at the village, and after confirming that it was still safe, we continued. Both the PIO and Major Cochran were armed with a .45 automatic pistol In addition, Cochran had an old .30 caliber M-1 carbine in a holder attached to the dashboard.

When we got to the village, introductions were made, and when neither of the two Sergeants saluted LTC Christopher, I could tell he was about to say something when Cochran intervened. "Nobody salutes in the field unless you've got a death wish. The bad guys always shoot the officers first and then the RTO."

Christopher stood with his hands on his hips and looked around. "About what I expected." I didn't know if that was good or bad.

The part of the village we were in was probably listed as a hamlet. A series of hamlets usually made up a village. It would be something like the houses on one street in America added to several other streets made up of the town.

The houses were made of bamboo or other local wood and had a straw roof. It was usually one room, with sleeping mats made of woven straw rolled up during the day. A crude table and chairs made of wood, possibly from ammo boxes, dominated the main area. A small table would be set up with a Buddha statue and a long incense stick burning. There usually was a piece of fruit or a small amount of rice on the table as a tribute. Most Vietnamese were Buddhist, but the altar was to honor ancestors.

If there were kids, depending on age, they may be naked. Up to two or three years of age, they wore a shirt and nothing else. The old men and women of the village would be sitting outside the house. The women would be chewing Bedel nuts and spitting long streams of juice that were sometimes mistaken for blood by FNGs. Their head would be wrapped in cloth like a turban. The old men would be smoking if they had anything to put into their pipes.

A fire would be burning inside or just outside the door for heating water or food. In addition to the altar inside, many of the houses, or hootches as they were known, had a large stone, multi-colored elephant outside. The elephant had a flat surface on its back.

For the first time, Christopher asked a question. "What's the significance of the elephant?"

"We're not really sure, but the teams call them BUFFIES."

"Why would they call them that."

"It stands for Big Ugly Fucking Elephants. Some of the villages like to hide explosives and weapons in them. Our guys usually smash them when they go through a village."

Any able-bodied villager would be working, usually in a nearby rice paddy. It was back-breaking work, bending over all day in knee-deep mud and water, planting sprouts of rice by hand. The women who had small children would come back several times a day to nurse.

There were no young men in the village. They would have been "drafted" by the ARVN if they were found during the day or by the Viet Cong if found at night. Draft was universal in Viet Nam.

Major Cochran took us through the village pointing out the life of the average resident of the war zone. I knew after about an hour that LTC Christopher did not have to worry about sleeping accommodations, and he was ready to go.

In a matter of hours, Lieutenant Colonel Christopher, the Public Affairs Officer for MACV had learned all he needed to know about the everyday life of the people the mightiest military force in the world was here to save.

The last thing I heard him say on the helicopter ride back to the LZ at MACV headquarters before I shut him down was, "I think I may write a book about my experiences in Viet Nam."

DATELINE: SAIGON, SOUTH VIET NAM

I recently came to realize that we, the men and women who are over here, and you who may be reading this column, know very little about this place we call South Viet Nam. The thirty-second snippets you see on your television every evening show men at war. You see the men slogging through the mud of the rice paddies in the Delta, or cutting their way through the triple canopy jungle that is so thick the sun hasn't touched the ground since before most of the men were even born. Twenty seconds of a helicopter landing to pick up wounded is old news.

What you don't see is the people we're supposedly doing all of this for.

Most of the population lives like their ancestors have for centuries. They live in small groups of houses in what is referred to as a hamlet. Several hamlets make up a village. The village is the center of their lives. They have all they need. A one-room house made from bamboo with a straw roof, a table, chairs, sleeping mats for everyone, and a rice paddy close by that may be communal property or one they work in for a small wage and rice for themselves and their family. If they're rich, they have a water buffalo to help in the rice fields.

The children sometimes are naked until they're three or four years old. The old women sit outside their homes and chew bedel nut, the old men smoke.

Overhead, you may see the con trails of a B-52 bomber, one of the most expensive pieces of American war equipment, while below, the oldest man in the village may have never traveled more than ten miles from where he is standing. Ask him to point to the direction of Saigon and he has to take three or four attempts. He has no idea and no need to know. What happens, or what will happen, there will make no difference in his life.

Sometimes I wonder….

Chapter Six

"**M**edic."

"Medic!"

The first time I heard that call was on what was supposed to be a routine patrol with a platoon from the 9th Infantry Division near the Cambodian Border in IV Corps. I had gone to the Corps Headquarters several days prior to the patrol to speak to some of the men who lived in the largest city in the Delta.

I knew many of the men and the women who were assigned to the units in and around Saigon, and some of the larger cities in the country had a fairly easy tour of duty. They got the same monthly amount of hazardous duty or "combat" pay as the men who got shot at on a daily basis. The difference was that if they got shot at, it was usually by accident by someone who did not know how to handle a loaded weapon.

Can Tho was the IV Corps Headquarters city. It had as much of a big city feel as found in South Viet Nam. Off-duty military men strolled hand-in-hand with their Vietnamese girlfriends to movies that were featured every night in theaters on the bases. Many lived off the bases in houses maintained by their girlfriends and had maids, and other household help paid what would be a pittance in the United States.

The offices were filled with the men who wrote the operation orders and made the war plans that the men in the field were expected to carry out. I wanted to follow an order from its inception to its completion.

I went to the office of the G-3, or the Colonel, who was the Operations Officer for the command. The first person I saw was a Sergeant Major who wore a combat patch on his right sleeve, indicating he had been with a combat unit in the past. The one he wore was from a unit that had not been in combat since World War Two.

"Morning, Sergeant Major. I'm Sean Kelly." I handed him my press card. I found it easier to identify myself and give some idea of what I was doing in fatigues with no unit patch in a combat area as soon as I met someone in authority. Few people in the military service have more authority than the senior enlisted man sitting outside their door.

"You a correspondent." It was more of a statement than a question.

"Correct. I do a syndicated column, and I want to follow an operations order from its inception to the unit that carries it out."

He pursed his lips like he was giving it serious thought. "I suppose you got at least a SECRET security clearance."

"Correct. I'm cleared for rumors as high as ridiculous." I had heard someone in Da Lat say that, and I thought it summed up the security chain of command.

He must have liked it because he smiled. "Yeah, we get that a lot around here. Hang on, I'll see if the Colonel can see you." He kept my press card, left his desk, and went to an open door down the hallway.

The building had been some kind of government compound prior to the American takeover of the facility. It was a faded pink stucco color on the outside and was the second structure when a person entered the gated compound. It was guarded by armed guards from both American and Vietnamese military police units.

"The Colonel said give him a few minutes, and he'll see you." The Sergeant Major handed me my press card. "Got some coffee brewing over there," he pointed, "if you want a cup."

I went to the pot and was pouring a dark black mug with an even darker black brew when a tall, man who was starting to go grey came out of an office with a cup in his hand. "You Kelly?" he asked as he sidled up to the pot beside me.

"Yes sir, and I assume you're the colonel." I finished pouring my cup and held the pot so I could fill his.

When I finished, he nodded toward his office. "Thanks. Come on back and tell me what I can do for you."

Two hours later, I was waiting for a helicopter at the helipad that would take me to the location of a battalion about to send an infantry company on a recon mission of a suspected area where the Viet Cong had been actively recruiting, or more accurately kidnapping, men and forcing them to join their ranks.

The ride was uneventful as we flew over the green squares of rice paddies that make up all the usable land in the Mekong Delta. From the air, the ground looked like a souvenir postcard.

"Having a great time. The weather is clear, the rice paddies are a dazzling shade of green. We can see the quaint houses of the natives and see them working in the fields, doing back-breaking work to plant and harvest the rice. Wish you were here."

We managed to cross over this postcard landscape without getting fired on, so I considered it a successful flight. When we landed, I was met by a sergeant who pointed to a jeep.

"If you're Kelly, I got your ride." He reached for my small AWOL bag that contained a change of clothes and my shaving gear, along with a tape recorder and extra batteries I bought at the main Post Exchange in Saigon.

"I'm Kelly, and I'll take care of my bag," I said as I followed him to the jeep. We were passed by three Soldiers, one with his arm in a bloody sling, who boarded the helicopter. "Wounded?" I asked.

"Yeah. He was on guard duty last night, and he said a sniper shot him, but I think he probably sat down and went to sleep, and a cowboy tried to rob him." The local thugs who preyed on the military were called cowboys.

We got in the jeep, and he drove the short distance to the battalion headquarters. When we got to the building, I was directed to the battalion commander's office. At a desk outside the door, a Captain sat at a desk and cranked the handle of a TA-312 field telephone. "TOC, this is Captain Nelson, the old man wants to set up a briefing for a correspondent of some kind…" he stopped talking and looked at me, "that wants to see what real Soldiers do." As he grasped the handset, he smiled, letting me know he was joking. Maybe. "Roger, he wants it ASAP. All he needs is the location of the Bravo Company jumping-off place for today's operation." He looked up. "What's your name?"

"Kelly, Sean Kelly."

"His name is Sean Kelly. He's a civilian, so tell them to try not to get him killed or wounded. I don't need to do the paperwork." He placed the handset back into the green canvas container for the field phone. "I'm Captain Nelson, the S-1. The colonel is expecting you. We got a call from our higher saying you were coming and we were to support you." He stood. "Come with me, and I'll introduce you."

I followed him into the next office and saw a young lieutenant colonel seated behind a desk. He looked up as we came in but did not stand. "Colonel Rogers, this is Sean Kelly, the correspondent we were told to support." Nelson quickly left.

Rogers looked up from his desk. I immediately did not like him. He gave me a quick look that said he was not happy to see me. He leaned back in the old, wood chair he was seated in. It was one of millions the Army had for offices all over the world. Made of oak with wheels with strong springs in the back so you could lean back while seated.

"I don't know where you've been in country, but we're in an active war zone down here. My battalion has one of the best body counts in the entire IV Corps area. I'm going to let you go out with one of our patrols that's on a recon. There shouldn't be any action, but if there is, keep your head and your ass down and your mouth shut. My officer is in charge. Understand?"

"Trust me, I know what to do in a firefight. Matter of fact, I've even been wounded since I got here. I don't get medals. I'm just here to let the folks back home know what's going on with their husbands and sons."

He just nodded his head as if he understands, then called for Captain Nelson to take me to the TOC.

After a briefing on the mission at the Tactical Operations Center, or TOC, I was told to meet another captain at the LZ who would be leading the mission. Thirty minutes I was seated beside Brad Morrow a captain from Georgia, in the first of two Huey Helicopters headed for a landing zone in the Uh Minh Forest.

Once we were on the ground, Captain Morrow directed his men to head out in a line formation. "I've got one of the best point men in the division. I swear the guy can smell the VC from half a mile." We watched as he led the column out from the LZ. I was with Morrow and his RTO about twenty yards behind the point man.

We had only gone about a quarter mile when the man in front of us held up his hand for us to stop. Morrow immediately held his up, and the signal was passed down the line to the last man. "Stay here," he said to me as he and his radio man moved forward. He didn't have to ask twice.

We were in an area that was out the fringe of a small hamlet. A series of rice paddies were to our right, and a canal blocked us on the left. We had some cover afforded by the trees of the forest, but so did whoever the point man had seen. According to the briefing, we were to avoid contact if possible,report on enemy location and strength, and wait for a larger force before engaging. It sounded good at the briefing, but when I heard the distinct sound of a long burst from an AK-47 answered by M-16s, I knew that plan had just turned to shit.

Morrow broke from the trees and shouted for his men to spread out along the nearby rice paddy dike. He went forward with his RTO and one other man. Only he and the RTO were in front of us.

He slid into the muddy bank of the dike and grabbed the handset from the radio. "Firefly, this is Rocket Point Six in contact." He proceeded to give his location and requested a fire mission at a location he read from his map. Rounds were cracking over our heads as we hugged the paddy dike.

I knew not to ask any questions, so I watched as he directed his men to set up an M-60 machine gun and rake the wood line. At first, we were only getting small arms fire, but when the M-60 opened up, the first Rocket Propelled Grenade or RPG exploded not far from us.

"I see him. He's at your ten o'clock," Morrow yelled to the machine gun team, telling them the shooter was to their left front. They immediately shifted their fire in that direction.

The small arms fire from the wood line was increasing, so Morrow got back on the radio and called for helicopter gunship support. I heard him swear as his request was denied because of a much larger firefight in another area with another battalion from the division.

He had the long antenna attached to the radio, and it was like a lightning rod as it marked the location of the officer and the radio that could bring in artillery and helicopter gunships. I watched as his second in command, a young Black sergeant scrambled along the dike and came to him. He barely gave me a glance as he gave his situation report.

"I've got seven men down there with me. I think I can take two of them and come in behind the RPG if the M-60 can keep him occupied."

Scott nodded and pointed to his map. "We're here, and this hamlet is part of a village that's about three hundred meters out front. I think these guys are from the village, and if we put some lead on them, they'll withdraw."

Before the sergeant could answer, I heard a voice call out. "Medic."

There was someone or maybe several someones who were not concerned with the politics of the war, public opinion, upcoming elections, or anything playing at their old neighborhood theater. They were in pain, and the only person who could help them was a medic. I had seen the medic for the patrol earlier in the formation. He carried a large OD-colored bag slung over his shoulder where everyone else had a rifle. The medic was a non-combatant and if both sides agreed to the Geneva Convention, he did not carry a weapon unless it was for self-defense. The medic on this patrol was unarmed.

When the call went out, he usually did not know if it was the wounded man who was able to call himself, or if someone was doing it for him. It didn't matter, he ran to the sound. I watched him slip and slide in the water and mud of the paddy as he ducked and ran to the man. As he ran, he paid no attention to the bullets that dug into the ground in front of, and behind him. I could not see who he was treating, but I did see several other men scramble to his position to help.

Morrow got on his radio again. This time he was loud enough that if any of the enemy troops spoke or understood English, they would get a lesson in profanity as he again called for artillery and now for a medevac to be on standby.

I saw the sergeant and the two men with him as they left the limited protection afforded them by the dike and headed for the woodline to take out the RPG team. Somebody from the other side saw them at the same time.

The second man behind the sergeant took several rounds, and I saw him buckle and crumble to the ground. His two companions stopped and, with the VC still shooting at them, pulled their wounded comrade back to the rice paddy dike.

Again, I heard the call for the medic.

Before he could get to the second man, I heard the sound and felt the concussion as the first 105 Howitzer round found its target. As more rounds hit the tree line, we saw several of the Viet Cong drop their weapon and run. They were easy targets and were quickly picked off by Captain Morrow's men.

I was in the position with Captain Morrow, his RTO, and two other men. Rounds were still digging into the dike where we were hunkered down, and as each one hit, they seemed to get a little closer to finding a live target. One threw dirt in my face, and as I turned my head to clear my eyes, I saw a splash of blood erupt from the chest wound in the man next to me. Someone, I'm not sure who, it may have been me, yelled for the medic.

The RTO immediately shucked off the radio, reached into the cargo pocket of his uniform shirt, and pulled out the clear plastic that was used to wrap the radio batteries.

He low-crawled to where I looked helplessly at the man who was struggling to hang on to what little life the VC had left him.

When the RTO got to him, he immediately pulled his jacket apart and exposed the gaping wound. With hands covered in thick, coppery-smelling blood, he pulled the plastic bag apart and placed it on the wound. "Here, hold this in place. I've got some morphine."

Without waiting to see if I would do as he asked, he reached into the pocket of his jacket over his heart and pulled out a small bottle with a morphine syrette in it.

"Do it." He said to me. "If you don't, he's gonna bleed out."

I held the plastic in place as the blood flow continued, but not as strong as it was before the plastic was placed on it.

After giving him the morphine, the RTO dipped his finger in the man's blood and made a crude M on his forehead, indicating he had been given morphine. I felt another person bump against me as I held the plastic. It was the medic.

"Great job. I've got him now. Just keep the pressure on the wound till I can figure out how bad it is. I've got medevacs on the way.

Twenty minutes after the point man had held up his hand to stop the patrol, the helicopter lifted off with four wounded. Morrow and his second in command, got an update on casualties and ammunition and radioed their situation back to battalion headquarters. From what I could hear of the conversation, it seemed the battalion commander wanted him to follow the retreating VC and see where they went.

"Sir, I can do that, but if they are as strong as I think they are, we need backup." I watched as he continued to talk and even disagree to the point of a small argument, which I knew he would lose, before he tossed the handset back to his RTO.

He was still crouched behind the dike, using it for cover, and motioned for me and his second in command to come to him. "The Colonel is sending Alpha Company out. We're to do a cordon and search of the village to our front. I tried to tell him that if the bad guys lived there, they had already hauled ass and were hiding someplace in the forest, but…shit…you know how he is." The sergeant just nodded. Then Morrow looked at me. "He wants you on the first chopper out of here. No arguments. No excuses. If you don't have what you need for your column by now, you're gonna have to get it someplace else."

I rode the first helicopter back to the LZ at the battalion compound. I didn't go inside to thank the commander before I caught a ride that ultimately took me back to Saigon.

DATELINE: SAIGON, SOUTH VIET NAM

Viet Nam, like any war zone I imagine, although I can't speak from experience, is filled with sounds. Some are quite pleasant, like the sound of a child laughing when they are given a piece of candy by a GI or the sounds of a bunch of mostly drunk military men singing along with a band in a USO show.

On the opposite side of the coin are the sounds you don't want to hear. The sound of incoming artillery. The crack of the first bullet fired by a sniper who you didn't know was around until the round zipped by your head is one you want to avoid.

The worst one for me is someone yelling, "MEDIC." That means someone has been injured and needs medical attention. There have probably been medics along with military units since before written history, and they have saved an untold number of lives. A wounded man in combat in Viet Nam today stands a better chance of recovery than in any war in history, but it all begins with the medic on the ground with him.

Many are conscientious objectors. They feel an obligation to help, but not to fight for religious or other reasons. They go into an active combat zone armed with a medic bag and their personal convictions about what is right and what is wrong. I have seen them in action, and no one can ever question their dedication to their jobs.

When the call for a medic is heard, they respond without hesitation. Many have lost their lives because of this immediate response when bullets fill the air between them and the person needing their healing hands.

They are not doctors or nurses. Most have had no formal training other than what they got prior to coming to Viet Nam, but they work miracles on the battlefield. Before any combat mission is planned, the commander wants to know all he can about the enemy. How many are there? Where are they? What kind of support can I expect? How long will I be out? For many, the most important question they ask is, "What kind of medical support will I have? How many medics and will medevacs helicopters be available?"

It may be the last question he asks during his briefing prior to the mission start.

For the man who will need it, that is, without a doubt, the most important question.

Chapter Seven

At some point, most of the correspondents ran across each other in Saigon. It may be at one of the Five O'clock Folly briefings at MACV Headquarters or a bar at one of the hotels where we stayed. The ones the folks back home saw on the network evening news sometimes were given a place to stay at the MACV compound. It was generally thought that for one of them to be injured or killed while chasing a bunch of grunts in the field would not be good for the image the US was trying to portray back home.

Wess Price, a freelance photographer who shared office space and sometimes accompanied me when I went to the field and I were having a drink at the Continental Hotel bar one evening when we both found ourselves with no place to go and nothing to do when we got there. The bar at the Continental was my favorite place to get a drink, a real meal, and relax. But that was my second reason for liking it. The first was that I met the woman whom I was now seeing on a regular basis, and if I was honest with myself, that I was in love with.

Her name was Carmen, and she worked for the State Department. I never asked her exactly what she did for them, but I knew she was very high in the Saigon pecking order for the SD. She spent almost as much time roaming the country as I did. She had a villa in Saigon, and when we were in town together, we spent our time there.

She was out of the city, so I had to settle for Wess as a dinner companion. We always tried to have a conversation about anything or any place except Viet Nam, but it never worked. We were surrounded by it no matter where we looked. The bar was filled with men and a few women in military uniforms of all the services. The ones in civilian clothes were government employees or contractors, with a few tourists thrown in for good measure.

Occasionally, we ran across a tourist who, for reasons unknown to me, wanted to see Saigon. Most of them were either French or Russian. If they were French, they probably had been in the country back in the early 1950s and may have had a girlfriend they were trying to find again. The Russians were spies.

"What next?" Wess asked as we waited for our second round of drinks to be delivered. The cooks, bartenders, and wait staff were all Vietnamese men who had managed to avoid or pay their way out of military service. Their salary was nothing, but they lived for the tips they got, and they lived better than most of the people in Saigon.

"I think I'm going to find a firebase and see what they do." A firebase was a small contingent of military personnel who were part of a larger unit but were not on the main compound. In most cases, they were where the artillery guns were located. The firebase was constructed by the unit, and in addition to the guns, it had bunkers where the men lived. Up north in the mountains, the bunkers were usually dug in. If the firebase was in one of the first three corps areas that made up the country it was not a problem. There was usually a hillside or a piece of relatively high ground that could be leveled off, and holes dug in and fortified with sandbags or other building materials to make it safe. For those in the Delta in Region IV, dig three feet down, and you have a swimming pool. In the Delta, bunkers were above ground and were easy targets.

"Where you going? Army or Marine?" Wess stopped talking when the waiter reappeared with our drinks. In Saigon everyone was on somebody's payroll for gathering information. "I don't know. I'll probably just go over to Hotel One and see where the next chopper I can get on is going." Hotel One was the main helipad in Saigon and a place where everyone went to catch a ride.

"Want me to go with you? I'm free for the next few days." Wess watched as a Marine colonel came in with a very attractive, and much younger,

Vietnamese woman on his arm. Unlike most women in the city, she wore Western-style clothes. She had a skirt that was as tight and short as I had ever seen. Her high heels caused the muscles in her calves to tighten, making her legs look longer than they were. The couple attracted attention in a bar that was used to seeing military men with their Vietnamese girlfriends.

I tapped on the table to get Wess' attention. "Down, boy. That one's taken, but if you go outside, I'll bet you can find one just like her."

"I'm just window shopping. I'm not buying." It was an unfortunate fact that many of the women in Viet Nam were more than willing to do what was necessary to find an American boyfriend. If it lasted no longer than his tour of duty in country, she would move on to another one. For the lucky ones, it was a real romance, and even though it took a long time and a ton of paperwork, a marriage was possible.

We ate our dinner, had one more round after that, and spent an hour listening to a Korean band make a passable effort to play the most popular songs the military heard on Armed Forces Viet Nam Radio, or AFVN daily. We left together and caught a pedicab from one of the many lined up outside the hotel.

The next morning, I awoke, took a shower before the hot water ran out of the dual tanks the hotel had installed when the Americans took it over as a BOQ, or Bachelor Officer's Quarters. The mess facility on the bottom floor served a decent breakfast if your palate ran to the taste of reconstituted powdered eggs and milk. Mine didn't, so I grabbed a loaf of *ban mi*, the small loaves of bread that was one of the best things the French taught their former colony to make. I had the cook toast it and sprinkle it with cheese, so that, plus a large mug of coffee, was a good meal.

When I went to the field, I always carried an AWOL bag with at least three changes of underwear and sox along with my shaving gear, a bottle containing a combination of medications. I had Tetracycline, or "no sweat pills," so named because they were an all-around antibiotic good for just about anything. I also had a few Imodium. They were needed in case you got a bad case of the shits from eating local food or water. They were so strong that a handful dropped behind Boulder Dam would shut off electricity on the West Coast. Last in the bottle was Compazine for nausea caused by taking the Imodium. Along with the meds, I carried a separate bottle with what looked like a very small tube of toothpaste. The difference was that this one had a needle at the end and was filled with a quarter grain of morphine. All the medics carried similar items, but after being hit once in the field, I knew how valuable morphine was, so I didn't want to be responsible for taking a syrette that was destined for a wounded military man.

I had several small notebooks and a box of pens and pencils I always brought along just in case. When I first began going out to see units in the field, I got in a poker game one night and won a snub-nosed .38 pistol, which I had tucked away in a small leather holster I attached to my belt in the small of my back.

I had only drawn it once, and that was when I was on an ambush with a recon team that was attacked in the middle of the night by a group of monkeys. It sounded like a North Vietnamese Army Regiment, so we were all prepared. It was almost daylight when we sprung the ambush, and at daylight, we discovered we had been attacked and killed a dozen monkeys.

After two hours of waiting and talking to a couple of Army captains, I decided to try to find a unit in the Delta. There was at least one US Army division working in the area, so I knew I could find a firebase or at the least an outpost to check out. If I had to choose, I think the IV Corps or Delta Region is my favorite part of the country. Flying over it, you are mesmerized by the expanses of rice paddies, green when the rice is growing and a completely different color at harvest time. It stretches to the horizon and beyond. No mountains to break it up. No giant craters from B-52 bombing runs. Few structures beyond the huts or hootches in the hamlets and villages along the many waterways that lead off from the mighty Mekong River. On previous trips to the Delta, I've heard farm boys from the United States even comment that they'd like to come back and have "a little place" here.

As a courtesy, I always checked in with the senior command in an area as soon as I got there. As we flew, I knew we were someplace south of Saigon, but without a map and an idea, I did not know exactly where. Since it really didn't matter, I decided to just get off at the first place we landed and take my chances.

I watched as the crew chief on the UH-1 or HUEY helicopter moved from where he had been manning one of the two M-60 machine guns mounted on either side of the helicopter. He was talking to either the pilot or co-pilot through the internal communications system in his flight helmet.

When the conversation was over, he pointed to me and two other men, a sergeant and a lieutenant who, like me, had jumped onboard prior to lift-off. "Make sure you're strapped in," he yelled over the sound of the blades and the air rushing across the seating area. I always wore the seatbelt that was provided, but out of habit, I checked to make sure it was secured as I felt the helicopter twist to the left and dip as we approached the LZ.

As soon as the ship settled to the ground, the crew chief made a motion for us to unbuckle and get out of his helicopter.

I ducked beneath the still-spinning blades and headed for a building at the edge of a large open field. At one end of the field, away from the structure, were three large black rubber fuel tanks. They looked like pregnant inner tubes for an extremely large tire, but they held the fuel needed by helicopters operating out of the field.

Inside the building, I was greeted and checked out, but a Private First Class who looked like he should have retired during the Korean War. I knew immediately that he had a story because I'm certain he had once had more than one stripe on his sleeve. I mentally filed it away for another time. "Excuse me, but exactly where are we, and what's the senior command in the area?"

He had half a cigarette dangling from the corner of his mouth. Somehow, he managed to speak around it. "What the hell do you mean, 'where are we?' If you don't know where you are, what are you doing here?" He stood behind a counter that had been constructed from old ammo boxes. There was no paperwork or anything on top, so I had no idea what his job was.

"I'm a correspondent and I wanted to do a story about some of the men on firebases. You know, those operating away from the flagpole. Not bound by as tight a set of regulations as some of the others."

He nodded in understanding. " You want an interesting story? That's why

I'm out here. This is my world. I'm the king. Nobody fucks with me." He stopped. "Maybe you want to do a story on me, 'cause I'm a walking story."

"I'll bet, but maybe on the way out, but right now I need to see whoever's in charge so I can let them know what I want and see if they can help me."

He pointed outside the open door. "Across the LZ 'bout two klicks is the company headquarters. We're split from the battalion, so the CO has a firebase with two 105 guns that he's responsible for. That may be what you're looking for."

After speaking with the CO, a captain who was the company commander, I was given permission to catch the swing ship out to the firebase later that afternoon. The swing ship was a helicopter that made regular swings through an area, resupplying the men with food, ammo, water, fuel, and, most importantly, mail. A sack of mail tossed from the helicopter was grabbed before a case of C-rations or a case of beer.

The swing ship landed at the same place where I arrived earlier in the day and I hopped aboard. The company commander said he'd radio ahead and let the lieutenant in charge on the firebase know I was coming.

It was only a thirty-minute flight as we passed over the green rice paddies. At one point, I saw the crew chief swing the M-60 into firing position as we swept low over two sampans on one of the many waterways. The pilot circled the two vessels and I saw an old man stand up in one of them and wave in an effort to keep the crew chief from opening up on him. Satisfied that they were not Viet Cong, we continued to the firebase.

The firebase was unlike most I had visited. This one was on level ground. The biggest advantage artillery had was if it controlled the high ground. Here in the Delta, there wasn't any. That was something I wanted to explore. I met the lieutenant and his sergeant who took me to the two guns and introduced me to the crews. In an hour, I had seen everything on the base. It covered about ten acres. The guns looked like they had been placed on a pad constructed to keep them from sinking into the ground when fired. The hootches, or living and working places, were all made from logs, sheets of PSP, and any other building material they could scrounge, trade for or steal. Everything was lined with sandbags. I saw one structure that had obviously taken a direct hit from an incoming mortar round or an RPG fired from close range. I didn't ask if anyone had been in it at the time.

The lieutenant took as much time as he could in an attempt to impress me or to have something to do. A firebase such as this one probably had one or two listening posts outside the wire during the day and at least one at night. Other than that, they had nothing to do except wait for the call for a fire mission.

The lieutenant took me to what he called his headquarters. It, like the other structures on the firebase was above ground and made of a variety of construction materials. It had a double row of sandbags around it and a similar set of sandbags on the roof. It would probably withstand a direct hit from a small mortar or an RPG, but if there was anyone inside at the time, they would be walking around in tight left-hand circles until their ears stopped ringing. The hootch served as their radio room and had a small table where a man sat to monitor the radios. He had a pad of paper on the table. Around his neck was a chain heavier than the ones that held dog tags. It held a small book about the size of an index card. On its pages were the radio frequencies, call signs, passwords, and counter signs for the unit. It was one of the most important items on the firebase. If it was lost or captured, the enemy would have access to all the information they needed to mount a serious attack. It was to be protected at all costs.

The man with it around his neck was dressed in fatigue pants and an olive drab undershirt. He didn't have any visible rank insignia, but I knew he was probably an E-4 at the most. He nodded as an indication he knew I was in his domain.

"This is where most of the activities happen, or at least begin here on the firebase," the lieutenant said as he picked up a handset from one of the radios. "This one is in the battalion net. We can do a fire mission for anyone within the range of our guns. It doesn't always have to be our company, although it usually is."

"How many fire missions do you do a day?" I asked.

"Depends. If we have a unit in the field, we may fire ahead of them to prep the LZ. Once they're on the ground or especially if they're in contact, we keep their location keyed in so we can fire as soon as we get the call."

He turned to the man at the desk. "When is the next patrol scheduled to go out?"

"Ain't got nothin' set up right now, sir, but you know it can change in a second."

"Let's go outside, and I'll show you the guns," the lieutenant said with a tinge of pride in his voice.

Unlike most of the rest of the world, there are only two seasons in Viet Nam. Hot and monsoon. It was fall back home, so we were at the edge of the fall monsoon season. The area was relatively free of rain. As I looked across what I could see of the land around the firebase, I thought some of the rice paddies looked like football fields. The green rice was just the right height to give it the appearance from a distance of a well-manicured football field planted with a heavy stock of grass. Since it was football season in the US, it was an easy transition for me to make as I looked across the landscape.

The entire Delta region was a sanctuary for the Viet Cong. There were few hard-core NVA units in the area as we were too far to logistically support them, but the VC took up the slack and kept the war going. There were a few villages and hamlets close to the firebase and everyone knew that a certain portion of the draft-age population men would side with the VC in a firefight. The fact that they didn't wear uniforms and usually worked their fields during the day made them almost impossible to identify, so everyone was suspect.

When a village got a reputation of having a large population of Viet Cong supporters, it was targeted for one of several programs. It may have a visit by a South Vietnamese unit who tried to convince the resident of their need to convert to good citizens and forget the VC. If that didn't work, a military operation called a Cordon and Search was conducted. An American or a Vietnamese unit would surround the village, usually in the middle of the night, and roust everyone from their homes. Anyone proven or suspected of being a VC or a VC sympathizer was taken away. Finally, if all else failed the village was eliminated. Usually by a bombing mission.

In the Delta those missions were flown by the US Navy using OV-10 aircraft called Black Ponies. To give everyone a chance, a flight would be made over the village, and leaflets dropped warning the residents that it was time to haul ass. Since most of the residents couldn't read, the leaflets had sketches of a village being bombed and dead people on the ground. They got the idea across, and the people fled. The downside of the leaflet drop was that the bad guys also fled, so they just moved to a new location, and nothing much changed.

I wanted to spend enough time on the firebase to see a fire mission. The first night passed with no calls for support. I think I was the only one on the base who was disappointed.

In the late afternoon of the second day, I was standing by one of the 105 Howitzers when the assistant gunner looked up. "Hear that?" he asked.

I turned my head to try to locate the sound. "I think so. Sounds like a plane. Not a chopper with a fixed wing."

"Yeah, we get them down here sometimes. They come from the navy base down on the coast. Most of the air support the units in contact down here comes from the Navy. They've got the Black Ponies and the Seahawks…the helicopters with the .50 caliber machine guns."

"That's a lot of firepower for a helicopter."

"Yeah, I hear that they have to fire from both sides at the same time to keep the chopper stabilized. Probably not true, but it sounds good." He stopped talking and looked for the plane, making the sound he and I both heard.

Finally, it got close enough for us to identify. "It's a Black Pony. Somebody must be in contact." He motioned for the sergeant who was in charge of the gun to look up. "I wonder why they didn't call us first?"

The sergeant stood looking up. "Maybe it's a SEAL team. They'd call the navy first."

By this time, several other men had heard the sound and were looking up in the direction of the plane. The lieutenant came and stood at the back of the massive weapon. He had a pair of binoculars hanging from a strap around his neck.

He raised them and, after twisting the focusing wheel, got a good look at the plane. "It's a Black Pony, all right."

It seemed to be taking a slow, almost circuitous route as it closed the distance. As we watched, it made one pass over the village and then turned and came directly over the firebase.

"Son of a bitch," the lieutenant said. "They've never buzzed us in the past."

"I think it's a warning that they're about to do a bombing run on the village." The sergeant had his hand on his forehead, shielding his eyes so he could get a better look at the plane. "Here it comes again."

As we watched, it dropped low on its pass over the firebase. When it got to the edge of the base, a snowstorm of leaflets was tossed out and were blown in all directions by the wind and the back blast from the plane's engines. Most seemed to be falling outside the concertina wire circling the base.

The men on the firebase went from a moment of idle curiosity to a full-blown panic in less than five seconds. The first to react was the lieutenant. He yelled to one of the sergeants standing outside the doorway of the main hootch. "Get on the horn and find out if they're doing a bombing run. Nobody told us if they are."

He almost pushed one of the men on the gun crew toward the wire. "Go get one of those leaflets. I want to know how much time we have before they start dropping shit."

Several men were already scrambling over the wire and paying the price. The concertina wire was fitted with not only barbs, but with razor-like attachments that grabbed clothing and flesh and shredded both with equal disregard.

I watched one of the senior NCOs from the base grab a leaflet in mid-air. He held it as he ran back to the base. Instead of the panic I had seen earlier, I saw what I thought was a smile. As he made his way back inside the wire, several other men had picked up similar leaflets, and they, too, were smiling.

He was almost back to where I stood with the lieutenant when we saw the Black Pony headed back toward us. If the base was lucky, the plane would not hit the radio antenna that was in the middle of the fire base. As it passed over, it did a wing wiggle, climbed, and flew away.

I couldn't wait to see what was so amusing about an upcoming bombing run on a village that was less than five hundred meters from the entrance to the firebase.

The sergeant was now laughing as he handed the leaflet to his lieutenant. "You know what day this is back in the world?"

I watched over his shoulder as the lieutenant read it.

GO NAVY...BEAT ARMY!

Back home, it was football season.

DATELINE: SAIGON, SOUTH VIET NAM

Rah, Rah, Rah, Sis Boom Bah

Not something you'd expect to hear in a war zone. Even here in Viet Nam, sports play a big part in the lives of the men and women who are here, especially those from the United States, Australia, and New Zealand.

It's not unusual to find a pick-up game of baseball or football at some of the larger bases. MACV even has a tennis team at its headquarters in Saigon. The Australian and New Zealand version of football differs from that played in the United States, but they are just as passionate about it as we are.

Games played in the US are heard later here in Viet Nam. The Armed Forces Radio Network, or AFVN, sometimes will rebroadcast a game or, if possible, send it out live. In the larger base camps and headquarters where they are able to show a movie, most of the films will be preceded with a reel showing clips from football or baseball games that were played for months and sometimes even years in the past. For those watching them, it doesn't really matter. It's a taste of home.

Some of the men followed the games played by a college they attended or otherwise had a special allegiance to. For many, especially the "ring knockers" or military academy graduates, the game they followed was the annual slugfest between the Army and Navy academy teams. It was a rivalry going back to the first game in 1890. Ask any academy graduate and they will tell you how many games their team won and the score. To say it was a rivalry was to call an alligator a lizard.

The graduates were like salmon returning to the stream where they were spawned as they filled the stands each year. For those who couldn't make it, the day was set aside as almost a religious holiday so that nothing took the place of listening to the game on the radio if they couldn't be there.

It was no different here in South Viet Nam.

I was recently on a remote firebase in the Mekong Delta when a navy plane flew over us. That usually indicated they were about to do a bomb run on an area controlled by the Viet Cong. They did a leaflet drop to warn the local citizens what was about to happen and give them time to leave the area.

As the plane flew over the firebase and dropped the leaflets, all the men were shocked since they always were told when a bombing mission was about to take place. The commander of the firebase rushed to contact his higher headquarters to get an update, while several men gathered the leaflets to determine when and where the bombing mission was to take place.

Siss Boom Bah....

It was Saturday back in the world, and the navy was dropping leaflets all over the Delta that simply said:

GO NAVY...BEAT ARMY.

It didn't work.

Chapter Eight

R&R. Rest and recuperation was the time that the military gave those serving in Viet Nam to get out of the war zone. Recharge their batteries. Get some decent food. Get away from the flagpole. Let their hair down. For many of the men, it was a time to visit some of the most interesting and spoken-about places in the Orient. Why were they so interesting and talked about? One word. SEX

Bangkok was one of the favorite R&R destinations. For the men who went there, the R&R didn't stand for Rest and Recuperation; it was for Rape and Rampage, although there was no need for rape. The bars in Bangkok were well known for the quantity and quality of the girls who worked there and serviced the men from Viet Nam.

This was a city where anything goes. The men who chose Bangkok over going to Australia, Taiwan, or even Hawaii went for only one purpose, and that purpose was met in ways they had only read about or heard about from returning GIs.

When I first arrived in country, I asked a sergeant in the 101st Airborne Division how he viewed his twelve-month tour.

"This is my second time, and I've got it figured out."

We were in the back of a truck taking us to a rally point where the men would leave the truck and begin an operation in a nearby village. I was curious as to how he had it broken down.

"See, the way I figure it. Sometime within the first three months, I'll probably either get wounded or sick. If it's not too bad, I'll spend a week or so in a hospital and then back to my unit." He stopped to light a cigarette.

"Then at the midpoint, say six months or so, I get a week for R&R. I go to Bangkok, get my ashes hauled, spend all my money, and if I'm lucky, not come back with a case of the clap. I spend three more months and if I didn't get wounded or sick the first three, it'll happen the last three. Another stint in the hospital or if I'm close enough to my DEROS…" He stopped and looked at me. "That's the date to rotate out of station or service or something like that, but it means when I get to go home. If I'm close enough, they cut my tour short, and I unass the area."

The way he said it made sense, at least to him.

We got to the rally point and unloaded the truck. Wess was with me, and he had been shooting photos of the men and the area we passed through all the way from the base camp. He and I jumped down from the truck and went to where a young captain stood with three men with the insignia of a sergeant first class on their sleeves. He was the officer in charge of the operation, and the three sergeants were there to make sure he did it right.

He saw us coming and stopped talking to the sergeants about the operation. "Gentlemen, these two men are correspondents. They're gonna be tagging along with us." He looked at me. "It was the battalion commander's idea, not mine. He's the one who approved it."

"I appreciate you letting us join you, and I assure you we've done this before, so we know where we stand at all times. We are not here to cause any trouble or get in the way." I wanted to defuse the hostile feelings as soon as I could.

He turned back to the sergeants. "They are our guests, so to speak, so we have a certain obligation to take care of them, but remember, the mission comes first."

He pulled out a map and pointed to a spot. "This is our LZ. The first squad will be in the lead ship. When they hit the ground, I want them to set up from twelve to three. Second squad is in lift three and they will go from three to six, third and fourth will take six to nine and nine to twelve and tie in with first squad. I'll be with second squad."

He was using the clock method to set up the perimeter. Twelve o'clock was always the direction of travel. Twelve to three meant the first squad took a quarter of the perimeter to the right. The rest of the clock was filled in by other squads. It was an effective method and everyone understood just where they were supposed to be.

"Are there any questions?" He waited to see if any of his sergeants spoke up and then they didn't, he folded the map. "Let's go kill some gooks."

The small group broke up, and the sergeants left to brief their men. The captain motioned for me and Wess to follow him. He went to a nearby area that had once been a large growth of bananas. The trees had been either blown down by the back blast from helicopters landing and taking off or cut down to make a landing zone.

"I've got a lift coming in here in ten minutes. I want both of you on the ship with me. From our intelligence, if you care to believe them, the area we're going to is relatively secure. I can't imagine the old man letting you go someplace to get killed on his watch."

I did not find that reassuring, but I let it pass. "Like I said, this is not our first operation. We know you're in charge, and we will respect that.'

"Why do I feel like there is a *however* coming?"

"Because you're a very smart man. So, the however, is that we also have a job to do, and taking photos and writing about what we see and do is a part of that."

We heard the helicopters coming. Hearing the sound of helicopters in Viet Nam had become as routine as the sound of street traffic back home. We hardly looked up when we heard them. It was only when the pitch of the engines changed so they could land that we paid any attention.

There were five UH-1 or Hueys settling to the ground to our rear. "We're in the second ship, so duck and run. Come in from the front or side," the captain pointed to the second bird on the ground. "I'll be there as soon as I know everyone is loaded."

When everyone was loaded, he came back and gave the crew chief a thumbs-up signal. The crew chief spoke in his headset, and I felt the change in the engine as we powered up for lift-off. As always, we flew with the side doors open and men on machine guns pointing out. I looked out to our side and saw two Cobra gunships shadowing the flight. The old man may have thought the area was secure, but the captain was not taking any chances. The Cobras were there to prep the LZ if necessary or to provide firepower if it was a hot LZ and the bad guys were waiting on us. We would not know until we were almost on the ground if they were needed.

This was not the first time I had been on a chopper heading for what may be a hot LZ. In the past I had been on several combat assaults with both the Army and the Marines. It's not fun, and it's a great way to get killed. The VC and the NVA have the habit of letting the first helicopter land without taking it or the men on it under fire. Even though the Americans know this is a favorite tactic of the bad guys, they sometimes fall for it. The first chopper lands, everyone gets off and hauls ass to the nearest cover. The other choppers make their approach and land, and the LZ lights up like Times Square on New Year's Eve.

The idea is to cripple several helicopters so they either crash on take-off or they're unable to leave the LZ. This makes the area smaller and hopefully, for the VC and NVA at least, no more helicopters filled with combat troops can land. If they can't land to let the men off, they probably can't land to pick up the wounded. It's a win/win for the bad guys.

As we approached the LZ, the two crew members manning the M-60 machine guns opened up. They, along with their counterparts in the other choppers, sprayed the area around the LZ with enough lead to deter anyone from raising their head to fire back. Since we didn't receive any ground fire, the pilots told the crew chief to let our lieutenant know we were going to land. He pointed to me and Wess and motioned for us to follow him. We did not have to be told twice.

With the chopper a few feet off the ground, we slid from our seats to the edge of the opening. We hung our feet out until we could touch the skids. Huey's did not have wheels but landed on heavy metal pieces that looked like those on Santa's sleigh. Unlike Santa, this sleigh was not loaded with toys, but with men who were ready to do whatever was necessary to catch a return flight, not only from this LZ, but from the entire country.

The chopper hovered a foot off the ground and we jumped the rest of the way. The first chopper had already landed, and the men had set up the beginning of a perimeter. We ducked beneath the rotating blades, and I heard the increasing pitch and whine of the engine as the pilot gave it power to lift off. The empty choppers would stay on station, or in the area until the lieutenant was certain the area was secure. If it wasn't, he'd use them for additional firepower or possible medevacs if needed.

The LZ was bordered on two sides by thick, dark jungle. One side was a small river and the other was the rice paddies belonging to the village we could see across the paddies. I knew from previous missions, that once we left the edge of the tree line, we would be facing some of the harshest, most inhospitable jungles in the world. It was not called triple canopy for nothing. There were trees and plants growing fifty meters inside the jungle that had never felt the warmth of a ray of sunshine.

The point man who would eventually lead the patrol into the tangle of trees and undergrowth relied on his machete as much, and maybe more than his rifle. When the lieutenant ordered the man to move out, if there was a path already cut in the jungle, the point man would stay as far away from it as possible.

The order was given. The men who had been smoking put their cigarettes out. I noticed most of the men carried their cigarettes in the plastic bags that radio batteries came in. The bags were carefully folded and tucked into a shirt pocket. Once the lieutenant was satisfied that everything was in order, we began to move. I watched as Wess took photos of the men. Most had an OD towel draped around their neck to keep as much sweat as possible from soaking into their jackets. Some had the sleeves cut out of their jungle fatigues. It was not regulation, but it was done out of necessity.

Each man had extra ammo, several cans of C-rations, and as many canteens of water as he could carry. Their packs or rucksacks were filled with everything they would need and then some. All wore heavy steel helmets with a cloth cover in a green camouflage pattern. In addition to the pattern, most were adorned with *Peace Signs*, or some personal slogan or saying. Wess tried to get as many close-ups as he could of the helmet covers. I'd talk to the men later to see what the signage meant to them. Each cover was held on by a thick, heavy rubber band. Almost everyone had a small plastic bottle of insect repellent stuck in the band. The bug juice was a lifesaver at night when the mosquitos came out or when crossing a paddy filled with leaches.

The two most popular ways of getting rid of the leaches were to drown them in bug juice or torch them with a cigarette or a lighter. If one latched onto you and you didn't find it in time, it would grow to the size of a small cucumber.

I listened to the sound of the point man as he chopped a path for the men behind him. Even though we tried to keep noise to a minimum, the chopping was a necessity.

We didn't know how long the patrol would take, so I looked at my watch. It was a stainless-steel model I bought at the military exchange in Saigon. Even though I, and most of the other civilians were not military, we were authorized to use the military exchanges. Like the military, we had ration cards that allowed us to purchase a limited amount of alcohol and cigarettes each month. The men who didn't smoke or drink usually sold, or traded, their cards to those who did. It was a black market within a black market.

After getting everyone safely off the LZ, the lieutenant released the choppers. We were now on our own. Thirty minutes later and no more than a hundred meters inside the jungle, I head the first shot.

It came from our front, and the first thing the lieutenant did was to signal a halt to the patrol and call for his assistant patrol leader to come to him. By that time, we heard the distinct sound of an AK-47 and several M-16s firing in response. Using hand and arm signals, the men were ordered to spread out and take up positions protecting the patrol on all sides.

I watched as one man came scrambling back from the point element and ran to the lieutenant. "We've got contact in front. It don't seem like too many, but who the hell knows."

Before the lieutenant could say anything, we heard the steady chatter of a machine gun. It was answered by one of ours. The sound came from our rear. There was the distinct possibility that we were surrounded.

One of the squad leaders, the young sergeant I had been talking to on the truck earlier, rushed to our position. "We got what looks like a squad to our rear. I think it was a hasty move on their part since we ain't getting no fire from the left side. It sounds like a rouse to get us to panic, but that ain't gonna happen in my squad." He didn't notice Wess taking a picture of two combat leader discussing a situation that meant life and death for one side or the other.

"Shit," the lieutenant looked at Wess and me. "I can't leave you here and I don't want to take you with me, but I gotta go back with Sergeant Dillard." He hesitated for a second until he heard another blast of the two machine guns. "Follow me. Keep low and try not to get killed."

We did not have to be told twice. I had been shot at in the past, and Wess had mentioned that he had been caught in a massive firefight when he first got to Viet Nam. I was one up on him, since I had actually been hit in a firefight several months previously. I spent a couple of days in the military hospital in Saigon, and then Carmen took me to her house for a week to recuperate. That was probably the best week of my life, certainly the best one since I got to Viet Nam.

We ran in a crouch and trailed behind the lieutenant and Sergeant Dillard, who led us back to his squad's area of responsibility. Two men were positioned behind a large tree, using the trunk for cover, and Dillard headed for them. The tree had at one time been two different ones, but they were so close together as saplings that as they grew, the trunks almost became one, and the mature trees only branched out about four feet above the ground. That gave us a solid wall of protection.

"What are we facing?" the lieutenant asked one of the men who had remained in place when Sergeant Dillard reported the situation to him.

"We got a single machine gun and a couple of guys with AK-47s. The MG keeps firing intermittently, so I don't think he's got enough ammo to maintain a steady rate of fire."

"Have you heard anything from either of the squads on your flanks?"

"No sir. Just some small arms fire at first and now that's died down."

The lieutenant turned to Dillard. "It's getting late. If we can't find out what we're up against, I'm going to call in some artillery and we'll hold tight until morning and see what damage it did."

"I don't think that's a good idea. We need to put an end to this right now and get a lift to take us back to base before dark. Ain't no telling what they can bring in here during the hours of darkness."

Before he could get an answer, the machine gun fired a shot burst at us. The rounds dug into the tree, throwing splinters of wood and bark onto the forest floor. After a second, it was followed by a longer burst.

"See what I mean. He ain't wasting ammo," the other man said.

"I still think we should wait and see…" Before the lieutenant could finish his thought, Sergeant Dillard stood up.

"This is bullshit. I ain't gonna let him keep us here overnight." He pulled a grenade from the shoulder harness on his web gear, and with his M-16 held waist high with his right hand, he left the shelter and safety of the tree where the rest of us hugged the ground and hunkered down.

"Sergeant…"

He either did not hear or completely ignored his commanding officer as he ran in a zig-zag pattern toward the machine gun that was firing a short blast back toward the tree. Behind me, Wess raised up as far as he could to take a photo of the sergeant as he ran.

There were several large trees between us and the position where the machine gun was located. Sergeant Dillard ignored the first one and continued to run, but evidently, the machine gunner saw him and decided that shooting at a man coming toward him was more important than trying to destroy a tree.

The bullets found Dillard and began to kick up the heavy, musty leaves that had been covering the ground for more years than any of us had been alive. They were hitting on both sides of Dillard when he took refuge behind the second tree.

I watched as he pulled the pin from the grenade. He had carried it in his left hand as he ran, but switched hands, and after pulling the pin, he held the spoon down long enough to take a quick peek from behind the tree. Evidently, he liked what he saw as he let the handle fly off, waited a second, and then tossed it.

"Fantastic shot," I heard Wess exclaim from behind me. He was still taking photos of Sergeant Dillard.

The grenade flew true and landed just in front of where we could see the machine gun fire coming from. All we had seen was the muzzle flash and some movement as the gunner and whoever was with him moved around in their position.

As soon as the grenade exploded, Dillard left the protection of his tree and rushed the machine gun position, firing all the way.

"Covering fire. Give him some covering fire, but don't hit him," the lieutenant yelled. Evidently he was heard by men on both sides of where we were as small arms fire erupted along a line of about thirty meters. Foliage on both sides of the machine gun position was chewed up as Dillard continued to run.

Finally, we saw Sergeant Dillard stop his run, and seconds later, with his back to us, he held up his hand, indicating that there was no longer any need to fire.

"You two, go check it out," the lieutenant said to the two men who had remained with us at the tree.

They cautiously left the cover of the tree and went to Sergeant Dillard, who was standing still and looking down. After a quick conversation with him, one of the men came back to our location.

"Sergeant Dillard wiped out the whole thing. There's nobody alive over there. He said it's safe to come to him."

"Let's go, but stay close. We don't know what else may be out there."

The lieutenant, Wess, and I followed the men back to the location where Sergeant Dillard was poking around. There were three dead bodies on the ground. All three were dressed in the dark green uniforms worn by the NVA or North Vietnamese Army. Two pith helmets lay on the ground. A third one looked like it had been placed in a meat grinder. It must have been worn by the man behind the machine gun. From the neck down, he looked fine, but from there up, it looked like his head had been in the meat grinder with his helmet. The full effect from the fragmentation grenade that Sergeant Dillard had tossed in his position must have caught him and took his head off. The other two men had multiple wounds from M-16 rounds.

When we got there and stood over the site, the lieutenant searched the bloody pockets of the dead men, looking for any documents or other intelligence information they may have on them. He pulled a small plastic book from one of them. "It's their party membership book," he said to Wess, who was still taking photos. He held it up so Wess could get a good photo. "Spell my name right if you use the photo."

Satisfied that he had gotten all he was going to get from the dead men, he turned to Sergeant Dillard. "Stupid and uncalled for, but damned gutsy. I'll put you in for the hero button when we get back."

"All the same to you, just call for an extraction and get us back to base camp. I'm due to leave for R&R in Bangkok in two days. I knew if we had to RON or remain overnight, out here, I'd miss my flight. Ain't no medal worth that."

The lieutenant laughed and reached for the handset on his radio. He called in the choppers for an extraction. Before they landed, his men did a sweep of the area and found five bodies from where the first contact was made. Sergeant Dillard went back to the machine gun position and made certain that the other two men who had been with the gunner were dead.

By the time all the bodies were counted, and any pertinent intelligence information had been collected, the first chopper landed.

"Get on the first ship out of here," the lieutenant pointed as he spoke to Sergeant Dillard. "And take these two with you."

I didn't have to ask to know he was talking about Wess and me. We watched as two men who had been wounded were helped aboard. They were followed by Sergeant Dillard and then us.

I can't say I was disappointed to see the landing zone grow smaller as we gained altitude and headed back to the base camp.

Sergeant Dillard's smile lit up the entire interior as we departed.

DATELINE: SAIGON, SOUTH VIET NAM

Everyone in South Viet Nam has a priority. For most, it's simply leaving and returning to the life they had prior to arriving in country. Once here, the priorities change, sometimes daily.

Get a good assignment.

Be assigned someplace safe.

Don't get sick, wounded, or killed usually tops the list.

Once you are here and find out a little more about what you have gotten yourself into, you begin to make plans. Most are based on the reality of the situation, but some are based on speculation, rumors, hopes, and fears. Making long-range plans is a dangerous thing because it tends to take your mind off the present, and that's where you must live. If you are to live.

The military has a lot of incentives for the men and women serving over here. Your pay is increased each month by sixty-five dollars. The military calls it Hazardous Duty Pay, but it's called Combat Pay by those who earn it. Jump out of airplanes, disarm bombs, be a doctor or other medical professional, and your pay increases even more. All the money you make here is tax-free.

Want to mail a letter home? Write the letter, put it in an envelope, and put the word FREE where the stamp normally went, and away it goes.

Extend for another tour when your first one is over, and the Army will give you thirty days' leave and a round-trip ticket to almost any place in the world.

The one thing most of the military personnel here look forward to, and plan on is the mid-tour week off, known as R&R or Rest and Recreation to the military and as Rape and Rampage to many of the men. It's five days that's not charged as leave. You can get a ticket to any R&R site on a military charter flight, and all you have to pay for is your hotel, food, and anything else you want. The anything else usually falls into two categories. Alcohol and sex.

That's not to say that both are not available in abundance in country, but for most who go on R&R, they have spent at least six months in South Viet Nam, probably most of it in places where neither were available. The average age here in the war zone is about nineteen years of age. Most of the men who arrive here do so with very little or no experience with the temptations that come in a bottle or wear a short skirt, calf-high boots, and will do anything asked if the price is right. Every day during their R&R is like Christmas morning. Something new and exciting every day.

I recently met a young sergeant who was on his second tour of duty. He explained how he had this tour figured out. Based on his last tour and on that of others he knew, he broke it down into quarters, each having three months. He explained that during the first or maybe the third quarter, he'd get sick or wounded (again) and spend a week in a hospital or confined to quarters. During the second quarter he'd go on R&R. This time to Bangkok. He took a long time to explain why, but since I don't know who's reading this, I won't go into details. The third quarter would be another chance to get sick or wounded. Finally, at the end of the fourth quarter, he'd leave and return home. It seemed so simple when he explained it.

He had been in country almost six months when we had the conversation. He'd made his first quarter expectations by having a relapse of malaria, which he picked up in his first tour. We were seated in the back of a truck en route to a landing zone where we would board helicopters that would take us into the jungle and into enemy territory. It was supposed to be a safe operation, but…

There were very few safe areas in country and this turned out not to be one, either. We made contact, and the platoon was pinned down by machine gun fire. The patrol leader said he was going to call in for artillery or an air strike, and we'd spend the night and continue the mission at daybreak.

It was not something the sergeant was willing to do. He left the cover of his position and, with a grenade in one hand and his rifle in the other, assaulted and destroyed the machine gun emplacement and the men in it.

When he returned to the patrol leader position, he was told he would be put in for a medal for his brave actions.

His response was to tell his commanding officer that he wasn't interested in a medal. He didn't want to spend the night in the field. His R&R was scheduled for the next day, and that was more important than any medal the Army had to offer.

The man had his priorities in order.

Chapter Nine

When I was in Saigon, I tried to get to what everyone called the Five O'clock Follies at MACV headquarters. This was when the various services had their information officers give a briefing on what was going on, what they wanted the correspondents to report, and what the people watching television or reading newspapers were being told about the war. Unlike WWI and WWII, this war was primarily confined to one country. Even though the Ho Chi Minh Trail ran through Laos and Cambodia on its way to South Viet Nam, we were not actively conducting operations in those countries, although there were some strong indications that cross-border operations were quietly being done. For the most part, the shooting war was confined to North and South Viet Nam. There were demonstrations for and against the war throughout the United States and the other allies who had military personnel on the ground in country.

The briefing was held either in a large room or in a theater. If it was in the theater, it usually was accompanied by a slide show on the screen behind the briefer. Occasionally, we were shown a news story that had been put together and shown on one of the network's evening news programs. It was critiqued and all the points were made which indicated it was doing harm and not helping the war and the men fighting it.

After all the representatives from the services information offices finished giving us the daily dose of propaganda, we watched as he turned to a brigadier general who had been sitting in the front row. This time, we were in the briefing room and not the theater, so he walked up to the podium and adjusted the microphone. If you were making a movie and wanted an actor who anyone watching the movie would believe was a real general, this was the man central casting sent you. He was a little over six feet tall. His jungle fatigues had been tailored and were pressed. He had a crew cut and his hair was steel grey. After trying to pull the mike higher so he could speak into it, he cleared his throat.

"I wanted to speak to you today to relate something that I think you will find of interest. The information I am about to share with you is not classified, but I ask that you respect the privacy of the individual involved." He stopped and looked across the group of approximately thirty men seated in front of him. All of us were civilians or government employees. The civilians worked for a variety of news outlets in the United States, Australia, and New Zealand, and a few were from other countries who found the war of interest for a variety of reasons. I knew there was at least one Russian correspondent and two from France.

"I want to illustrate how the effort is not contained by the borders of the countries around us. The war, if you will, can follow you home." He looked down at a notepad he had placed on the podium.

When he began to read, we all paid attention. By the time he got to the second page, we were mesmerized. Like everyone else in the briefing, I knew that was a story that needed to be told for a variety of reasons. As I continued to listen, it was evident that this would take more than a weekly column to do it justice. I decided to break it into two installments when I got back to my office and sat at my typewriter.

DATELINE: SAIGON, SOUTH VIET NAM
Part 1.

This is the story of Major Andrew Douglas as reported to a group of correspondents at the Military Assistance Command, Viet Nam by an Army General.

Major Andrew Douglas was known by Andy to his friends at MACV Headquarters. He was a graduate of the ROTC program at Texas A&M. From his enrollment at the college and attaining the role of an Aggie; he wanted nothing more than a career in the military. As a distinguished graduate, he was allowed to select his basic branch and selected Military Intelligence. After several assignments as a Battalion S-2, or the officer responsible for intelligence as a junior officer, he finally made captain. As a captain, he moved up the food chain and was assigned to Third Army Headquarters at Fort McPherson, Georgia. As the war in Asia grew and the need for more men grew with it, time in grade for promotions was shortened, and he was on orders for Viet Nam when he made major.

He was home on leave in Miami when he was able to pin on the gold oak leaves of his new rank. Normally, he would have pitched a party at the Officer's Club where he was stationed. It was traditional that the amount of your first month's raise in salary was spent on alcohol. At Officer's Club prices, that bought an incredible amount of liquor. He held his promotion party at the Officer's Club at Homestead Air Force Base not far from his home in Miami. It was the only Officer's Club in the area and was frequented by the military for all the services in the area. His party was a success, and only one person was stopped for a DUI after leaving the party.

After arriving in Viet Nam, he was assigned to the J-2, intelligence office. Unlike the work he did at the levels he had been accustomed to, at MACV, he worked on a joint staff with officers from all the allies who had military personnel in country.

Like most of the men assigned to any of the offices in Saigon, he lived a much better life than the men in the field. He had a nice room at one of the hotels the military had taken over when they moved into town. As a field grade officer, he did not have a roommate. His room was as nice as he could make it. He purchased a small refrigerator, two fans, a television, and a stereo set at the PX at the MACV Annex. Under the circumstances, it was like living in a penthouse. The hotel had a dining room run by the Navy. They served breakfast and dinner and there was a small bar on the roof of the hotel.

Andy was not above having a good time when he was off duty, and he frequented some of the better restaurants and clubs that were approved by the military and considered safe. Like most of the men, he occasionally yielded to temptation and went to one of the massage parlors that offered what was known as a 'steam and cream.'

Ten months after arriving in Viet Nam, he put in for an extension for a second year. It was approved. Andy was a devout Catholic and attended Mass as often as his work schedule allowed. The two dominant religions in South Viet Nam are Buddhist and Catholic, so many of the local civilians who worked on the MACV compound attended Sunday Mass at the chapel on base. It was there that Andy met Kim.

Her full name was Cai Linh Kim, but since in Viet Nam the person's last name came first, it was not uncommon for a Vietnamese to be called by the name that was listed last. Kim was a secretary and had worked for the Americans for three years. She went to a school operated by the Army to learn how to type and familiarize herself with the paperwork that she would be required to do. She had learned the basics of English in their equivalent to high school. After three years, her English language and her secretarial skills had improved to the point where she was the secretary for the Assistant J-2 and worked in the same office as Andy Douglas. She was five years younger than Andy.

Five months after meeting her at Mass, Andy asked her to accompany him to a movie at the MACV compound one night. Kim still lived a very traditional life at home with her parents. Her father had lost his leg in a motorcycle accident years earlier and was not eligible for military service, so he worked as a barber on the compound. Her mother did the daily shopping and maintained the household. After gaining her father's permission, she accompanied Andy to the theater.

One night at the theater turned into more nights together, and a friendship that began in the office, blossomed in the midst of war to a full-fledged romance. Six months after their first real date, they made an appointment with their Priest to explore the possibilities of getting married.

It was not uncommon for US military personnel to marry a Vietnamese national. It was a difficult and time-consuming process, but for them, it was worth it. Eleven months after that night at the theater, they were married. The first ceremony took place at the chapel on the MACV compound. A second ceremony was conducted for Kim's family and friends who were not allowed on the compound.

Andy made enough to rent a house for them in a neighborhood near the Phuoto Racetrack in Saigon. Like many of the men assigned in Saigon, it was not unusual for them to live on the economy.

Their first child was born ten months after they were married. It was a girl, and they named her after both their mothers. While waiting for the baby to be born, Andy extended his tour for another year.

At the end of his third year in Viet Nam, Kim was pregnant for the third time, and his request for another extension was denied. For an officer to advance in the military, they must have the proper holes punched in their IBM cards, and Andy needed some that he could not get in Viet Nam.

Since Andy had been privileged to some extremely sensitive information and intelligence about the war, and had a SCI, or Special Compartmental Intelligence level clearance, he was precluded from traveling to any Communist country or associating with any known members of the Communist Party, among other things. His next assignment would be at the Pentagon, where his knowledge of the day-to-day operations of the war would be used.

Kim was seven and a half months pregnant when the doctors told her that if she did not leave within the next two weeks, she would not be allowed to accompany Andy back to the United States.

Their situation was explained to the personnel office, and Andy had orders allowing him, his very pregnant wife, and their young daughters to catch a military flight to Travis Air Force Base near Sacramento, California. From there, the plan was to take a commercial flight across the US to his home in Miami. It would be the first time any of his family met his new wife and children.

The flight to Travis was long, and Kim was terribly uncomfortable even though they were on a chartered flight using commercial aircraft. The little girls were fitful and by the time they got to Travis, all were ready for the next leg of their journey.

Or so they thought…

Chapter Ten

I almost felt like I had a week off. This would be my in-country or, more specifically, my in-city R&R. I had the remainder of the Andy Douglas story already written, so I didn't have to do much work to have a column ready. I liked to keep at least one column written and stashed in my desk in case I was in the field and not able to get back to Saigon to file it. Wess and Nguyen both knew where I kept it and how to file it if I was not there.

Unless you looked at a calendar, it was difficult to keep up with what day it was. There were very few five-day work weeks of eight hours a day. Some of the larger headquarters allowed their men to have half a day off on either Saturday or Sunday. Most picked the afternoon off since they were already used to getting up early, and by taking the afternoon off, they could drink more and have time for it to wear off before their Monday morning duty day. When she was working at the State Department headquarters in Saigon, Carmen usually took the Sunday afternoon shift off.

As my own boss, I could take any part of any day I wanted as long as I got my job completed. I awoke early on Sunday morning. I had a small coffee maker in my room, so I fired it up and made a pot while I walked down the hallway to the large shower room that serviced the floor at the BOQ. A few of the rooms had their own bathroom and shower, but those were reserved for senior officers and civilians. Since I didn't qualify on either count, I padded down the hallway in shower shoes with a towel wrapped around my middle.

After a shower and a cup of coffee, I decided to visit the Post Exchange at the MACV headquarters compound. I didn't need anything, but I sometimes found something I could send home to my parents. After looking around and finding nothing, I went outside and saw a man selling hand-painted landscapes on pieces of what appeared to be mattress covers. One in particular caught my attention. It was a nighttime scene of the moon resting in safety over the city of Saigon. When I first met Carmen, it was on a moonlit night, and I referred to her as my "Moonlight Lady." It was an immediate sale.

I had been to her office several times in the past, so I decided to pay her a visit and give her the painting. It was a fifteen-minute Jeep ride to the American Embassy compound, where she had an office.

The driver knew the way and also knew he was not allowed on the Embassy grounds, so he stopped well away from the Marine Corps guards at the entrance. I walked to them and before they could ask, I showed them my correspondent's identification card and was allowed to enter. Once inside, I was stopped by another guard and had to sign a book with my name and destination.

When I got to Carmen's office, there were several other men and a few Vietnamese secretaries working in the mostly open area that was filled with desks. Carmen's desk was in a corner and had partitions around it, closing her off from the rest of the activities in the room.

Only one man looked up and challenged me when I entered. "Help you?" he asked.

"I'm here to see Carmen." I held up my identification card, which he hardly glanced at as he motioned to her desk area. "Got it," I said as I nodded.

Carmen had heard her name so she stood and came around her partition to meet me. "What a nice surprise, Mister Kelly. Working on a story?" She asked. I don't know how much the others knew of her personal life, but it was not up to me to divulge anything.

"As a matter of fact, I am, and I was told you may be able to assist me.

"If I can, I'd be happy to." She stepped back and motioned for me to follow her behind her partitions.

I felt like a teenager when Carmen took a quick look around to make sure we could not be seen and pulled me close for a lingering kiss.

"I think I just completed my research," I said as we broke away. "But as nice as that was, I did come here for a reason." I handed her the rolled painting.

"The moonlight," was all she said as she looked at it and placed it on her desk. "Give me a few minutes to finish up here. I have the afternoon off, and we can leave."

I watched as she pulled a large book on Viet Nam printed by the State Department and thumbed through it until she came to a chart and stopped. After making a few notes and comparing numbers to those on the chart, she stopped and looked at me.

"Are we making a difference? I mean, you tell the people back home what the war is really like, and I tell the politicians what they want to hear. Both our messages are filtered sometimes to the point that they are meaningless to the people we're trying to reach."

This was the first time I had heard her speak about her actual job. I still didn't know what it was, but she certainly gave me something to think about.

We left the Embassy, and after having lunch at a nearby hotel that was being used as a transient billet for military personnel coming or leaving Viet Nam she suggested we go to a nearby orphanage sponsored by the Catholic Church. I hoped she had a motive other than looking for a child to take home when she said the children were putting on a show that afternoon.

We had never had a serious conversation about religion, but I knew she was Catholic, but I did not know how deep her faith ran.

We got to the orphanage just as the kids took their places on an outdoor stage. They looked like they ranged in age from about four to ten or twelve. The clothes they wore were probably furnished by churches in the states.

A priest dressed in a black cassock stepped forward and addressed the crowd in passible English. "Today, our children are happy to present to you a program of songs, some in their native language and…hopefully, some in yours." He got the laugh he was after.

The children opened the show with the Vietnamese National Anthem. The kids did a rousing version of the song that everyone stood for. Next they did *God Bless America.* For the next hour we heard a mixture of folk songs and well-rehearsed English version of *The Sloop John B.* ended the show.

A collection basked was placed by the exit and by the time Carmen and I got to it, the attendees had filled it with MPC. I thought it interesting that no Vietnamese were allowed to have the currency used by the military, but I assumed the good priest had contacts on the black market to spend or convert the MPC.

We left the concert and went to Carmen's residence, where we spent the remainder of the afternoon and evening until curfew time together.

The next morning, I went to my office and filed the second half of the Andy Douglas story.

DATELINE: SAIGON, SOUTH VIET NAM
The story of Major Andrew Douglas
Part 2

Major Andy Douglas, his pregnant wife Kim, and their two daughters arrived at Travis Air Force Base in California in the middle of the night. The children had finally gone to sleep, and Andy carried them from the plane to the bus at the end of the steps leading down from the body of the aircraft. They were seated in the second bus and taken to the passenger terminal where Kim found a seat for her and the sleeping children while Andy rounded up their bags. Before leaving Saigon, the Army had sent a crew of Vietnamese workers to pack up their family belongings. For the most part, that only consisted of clothes, his stereo equipment, and a few personal items. Andy had moved his refrigerator and everything else he purchased for their home in Saigon to Kim's parents' house.

With their bags on a cart, they went outside the terminal and caught a bus that would take them to the airport in San Francisco. Andy had booked a flight from San Francisco to Miami with a change of planes in Atlanta. It was the best he could do, and it took the shortest flight time. He knew all of them would be more than ready to get off the plane when it finally landed in Miami. He was facing a nine-hour flight that included almost two hours of layover time in Atlanta. They had crossed so many time zones and date lines that he wasn't sure what day or time it was. All he knew was he wanted to get everyone to Miami and take a deep breath when it was all over.

Kim had to get up and walk around in the waiting area at the San Francisco airport due to the discomfort she felt that lingered from the flight from Saigon. Once on the plane and against her doctor's recommendation she asked the flight attendant for a Bloody Mary. It seemed to relax her, and she slept most of the way to Atlanta. Andy and his daughters occupied themselves with a book of fairy tales he purchased in an airport gift shop.

In Atlanta, they had a meal and found out it was almost noon local time. Again, Kim had to walk around to regain the feeling in her feet and legs. When the flight to Miami was called, they knew they were only a couple of hours away from putting the misery of the flights and the war behind them.

When the gate agent saw Andy, who was in his khaki uniform with a pregnant wife and two small children, she upgraded them to first class. Kim and the daughters took seats on one side of the cabin and Andy took an aisle seat across from them. His seatmate introduced himself as a veteran of WWII. While waiting for the plane to fill with passengers, they spoke about the difference between their two wars. After a few minutes, Andy's eyelids began to droop and his seat companion stopped talking and let Andy slip into the quiet and darkness of sleep.

Andy was awakened by shouting from the back cabin of the aircraft. He turned in his seat and saw two men standing in the middle of the aisle at the front of the tourist cabin waving guns.

The plane was being hijacked.

While one man roamed up and down the aisle demanding the passengers give him their identification or passports, the other hijacker grabbed a female flight attendant and put the pistol to her head, and together, they backed up the aisle to the cockpit door. As they passed Andy, the hijacker was facing the cabin and did not notice him.

The flight attendant knocked, and one of the crewmembers in the cockpit opened the door. The hijacker shoved the flight attendant inside, and Andy could hear him yelling at the crew. In a minute the captain came on the cabin public address system and announced that the plane was now under the control of a man who demanded they fly him to Havana.

A Communist country.

Andy couldn't go there but his options were limited. He thought about rushing the cockpit and trying to overpower the hijacker, but he had no idea if the man would shoot the pilot if he was challenged. Across the aisle from him, his wife's face said she was in pain.

Andy only had one option. Andy Douglas had to become Andy Douglas private citizen on a flight with his wife and children.

The first thing he did was remove all the military insignia and ribbon bars from his uniform shirt. Now, it was just a light tan shirt. He reached into his pocket, pulled out a small Swiss Army knife he carried, and slowly opened it so the scissors were exposed. He stuck the point into his pants just above the knee and slowly cut in a circle, turning his pants into shorts.

His seatmate saw what he was doing and leaned toward him to tell him to change shoes with him since they both appeared to be about the same size. Andy exchanged his plain black Army low quarters for a pair of black wingtips that were half a size too small, but under the circumstances, it didn't matter.

The biggest problem he had was that he was not traveling with a passport. He had his Army Identification Card in his wallet. After he pulled out the green, plastic-covered card, he took his knife and started cutting very small pieces from it. He had an almost full can of soda on his tray so as he cut a small piece, he used the soda to wash it down as he swallowed it. By the time the second hijacker reached the first-class cabin, Andy had completely consumed his Army Identification Card, and there was no indication he was anything but a civilian traveling to Miami.

The Cuban government did not look kindly upon hijackers, no matter their motivation so the plane was escorted by Cuban military jets once it entered their airspace. All it took was a glance out the window as the plane touched down to see the welcoming committee that consisted of numerous military and police vehicles.

When the plane's door was opened, the hijackers were rushed by uniformed military personnel. Another Cuban watched them removed and then announced, in perfect English, that he was a Colonel in the Cuban Army, and he wanted everyone to remain seated and follow his instructions.

It was at that time when Kim let out a muffled scream that immediately got the Colonel's attention. Andy disregarded the instructions to remain seated and crossed the aisle to be with Kim.

The Colonel recognized the problem and gave instructions to one of the junior officers who was with him. Kim was made as comfortable as possible in the seat, and Andy, the Colonel, and the flight attendant, noticed the wet stain on her seat. Her water had broken, and she was about to deliver.

Two people, a man and a woman rushed up the steps leading up to the cabin of the plane. After a hasty conversation in Spanish, Andy noticed a stretcher being brought up the steps.

It was panic time for Andy. Was his wife about to give birth at an airport in Havana?

The Colonel quickly explained that they had landed on a runway at a military base that had a hospital, and the two people who came onboard were a doctor and a nurse. As they were taking Kim out of the plane, another officer rushed up around them and spoke to the Colonel.

The Colonel explained to Andy that a decision had been made to put him, Kim, and their daughters aboard a Cuban aircraft and fly them to Key West, the closest point of US territory, as they did not want to have a child born in Cuba with one parent an American and another a Vietnamese. He said it would take the United Nations to determine the nationality of the child.

The plane was loaded and as the door was being closed, the Colonel handed Andy two boxes of Cuban cigars. One box had a label that said Es Un Nino, and another box was marked Es Un Nina.

The plane was given permission to enter US airspace and land at the Navy base at Key West. The military delegation that met the plane there was just like the one in Havana.

Andy left the plane with his daughters walking beside him and a son wrapped in a blanket in his arms. Kim was helped to a waiting ambulance that took her to the hospital. Andy reluctantly handed the baby to her as she left.

When he entered the flight operations building, a customs inspector was there. The doctor, nurse, and flight crew requested political asylum, and Andy was allowed to keep both boxes of cigars.

Chapter Eleven

nce, at a MACV briefing, I heard that for every "grunt" out in the brush getting shot at, there were at least fifteen people in the rear areas supporting him. That number included the administrative support personnel who were located at fire bases and at compounds that sometimes got hit with rockets and mortars. Most of the remainder were the relatively lucky ones who were assigned to the larger installations at places like Da Nang, Long Binh, Saigon, and a few other choice locations.

Life in the field was rough, to say the least. For the Infantry in both the Army and Marines, a patrol may last from a few days up to a month. Days were spent moving through some of the most inhospitable terrain in the world. A grunt could be chopping his way through a tangle of jungle that was so thick it was nearly impossible to cut with machetes, while at the opposite ends of the country, his counterpart was humping mountains or slogging through rice paddies and mangrove swamps.

Most did not consider or even know about the man they went through boot or basic training with who lived a relative life of luxury in the war zone. The men and the very few women who were assigned to the big cities were referred to as REMFs. That was the recognized acronym for *Rear Echelon Mutherfukkers.*

These lucky ones had the advantage of a workday consisting of ten or twelve hours and usually half a day off each week. Most were assigned a bed in a barracks building someplace on the compound, but if they wanted to, they could usually manage to find a place to live in the city. The room outside the compound, for the most part, came complete with a woman who may be his long-term girlfriend. Others were content to have a different lady friend as needed. They traveled the city on their off-duty time in pedicabs powered by men or motorcycles. Taxis are as abundant in Saigon as they are in New York City. There were USO shows at the enlisted and officer clubs almost nightly. Some were bands from the Philippines or Korea, and other times, it was entertainers from the US.

A good meal was as close as a taxi ride. Drinks at the clubs were so cheap that a two-dollar drunk was not uncommon. Throw a few dollars in a slot machine at the bar and win a month's pay. For a few dollars a month, you could have a *Mama san* who did your laundry, cleaned your room, and occasionally slipped between the covers with you or found someone who would. It was not unusual for that someone to be the daughter of the woman who washed your clothes, shined your boots, and cleaned your room.

The military in the cities got the same hazardous duty or combat pay as the soldiers in the field. Another advantage they had was a ration card and the black market. Buy a fan, a television, a bottle of scotch, or a carton of cigarettes, and you are instantly in business. All could be sold for a tidy profit on the black market.

Many of these REMFs did everything they could to keep from being shipped home. They had it made, and they knew it. To a certain extent, I fell into that category myself.

I had a nice room in one of the Army-operated hotels where officers assigned to units in Saigon lived. We had a rooftop bar with a restaurant and five slot machines. Wess lived in the same building, and once a week, we had Mama San come in and clean our rooms and do our laundry. Even though we were not military, we wore the same uniforms as they did. Instead of a US Army or Marine tape on the jacket, ours said CORRESPONDENT. When we were in the field, we got just as dirty as the troops we were following. The advantage we had was when we came in from the field or were airlifted out before the operation ended, we came back to Saigon and had a few days of rest and safety.

I was having a hamburger at the bar in my building one night when I struck up a conversation with a Military Police officer named Jason Lockridge.

Somehow, the conversation got around to motorcycles, something I knew very little about.

"What do you mean, you never rode one by yourself?" He asked with more than a little attitude.

"It's just something that never interested me. I was more of a hot rod kind of guy. I had a thirty-four Ford when I was in high school."

"You and I need to get together one day and I'll show you around the city and take you to some places you can't get to in anything with four wheels," he said as he ordered another round of drinks for us.

I was having a beer with my hamburger, so I did not object. While we were talking, a band from the Philippines came to the stage and checked their instruments before they played their set. Two very attractive women were with the three guitar players, along with one young man who was plinking on an electric piano. A drummer pulled several stands closer to him. The two women were dressed in very short skirts, long-sleeved tops with strands of fringe that hung just below their breasts, and white calf-high boots.

"And just how are we supposed to get to these places?" I asked.

"Hell, man, I got my own hog. Bought it from a man I know." He winked.

I guess it would not be smart for a Military Police officer to admit to doing business on the black market.

By the time the band was in its third or fourth song and we had determined that the only thing good was the gyrations of the two women, he had convinced me to meet him Sunday afternoon.

He roared up in front of the BOQ five minutes early. I don't know much about motorcycles, but this one was big and loud.

"Hop your ass on the back," he motioned with his right hand.

Once I was on, I leaned forward. "What do I do now? Do I hang on to you or what?"

"Hang on to the seat. Don't do any leaning when we turn. I'll do all of that. Keep your mouth closed to keep the bugs out. Here," he said as he handed me a pair of goggles. "Put these on so you can see. Wouldn't want you to miss anything." I felt the machine launch, and we were on our way.

He drove the streets of Saigon like a native. He paid no attention to other traffic as we weaved between military and civilian cars, jeeps, motorcycles, motor scooters, and pedicabs. I wanted to ask where we were going, but I remembered his warning about keeping bugs out of my mouth, so I kept quiet.

I soon recognized the Cholo District, where the racetrack was located and which was the home of Saigon's Chinese population. We pulled to a stop at a small outdoor stand selling fresh fruit and drinks.

He pulled his goggles up and turned to look at me. "Let's get something to drink, and I'll tell you where we're going." He cut the engine, and we got off.

"How'd you like that?"

"Not bad, but I think I'll stick to having four wheels on the ground." We took a seat at a small table and a young girl who looked to be about ten years old came and stood beside him. The way she looked at us, I knew she did not speak English. I was about to try out my limited vocabulary when he spoke first.

"Hai quả chanh," he said, and she smiled.

"Two lemon aides," I said.

"Not bad. You go to language school before you got here, or is this something you learned on your own or from your steady punch?"

I didn't like him referring to Carmen as my steady punch, but since I wasn't entirely sure where we were or how to get back to my hotel, I let it pass.

We drank our lemon aides, and he placed several large denomination *piaster* notes on the table when he got up.

"That should give them enough time to let everyone know we're in the area." He pulled his goggles down, slung a leg over, and climbed aboard.

"You want to explain what you just said?"

"You want something to write about? I'll bet you dollars to donuts you're gonna see something before we get back. These people aren't friends of the VC, the NVA, or Uncle Sam. They just want to be left alone. By all sides." He drove his foot down on the crank, and the engine came to life. "Climb on and hang on."

We left the roadside stand and headed down a small, narrow alleyway that may have been paved at some time. I immediately knew what he meant by places a four-wheel vehicle could not go, but I still did not understand why we were there. I got my first hint when an old woman tossed a pan of water on us as we passed. Her timing was bad, and the water went behind us. That seemed to excite him as he intentionally revved the engine until the sound bounced off the walls on either side of us.

We made several turns at intersections and scattered a variety of chickens, ducks, dogs, and children as we roared through the Chinese neighborhood.

So far, I had not seen anything I wanted to include in a column.

That was about to change.

DATELINE: SAIGON, SOUTH VIET NAM

I've heard that there are no atheists in foxholes. I can neither confirm nor deny that, but I can assure you there was not one riding on the back of a motorcycle recently.

I met a Military Police officer while having dinner at the hotel where I live. Our conversation covered a number of topics until it got to motorcycles, and I admitted I had never owned one, never wanted one, and didn't even know how to drive one. He immediately offered to take me for, as he put it, something to write about and a ride I'd never forget. He already knew I was a correspondent, so I figured I might see a part of the city I had not seen before.

He met me at my hotel the following day, and we rode through Saigon in a way I had seen others do but never thought I'd be doing. In Saigon, traffic rules are merely suggestions, and nobody pays them any attention. We swerved and weaved our way, passing other assorted vehicles by inches until we got to the Cholon District, which is where most of the ethnic Chinese in the city live.

We stopped at a small outdoor café, and after ordering in Vietnamese and leaving a large tip, he informed me that the locals should know we're coming by now. I was about to learn what he meant.

His comment before we entered the first small alleyway was, "I'm going to take you places you can't go on four wheels." What he forgot to add was that the residents did not like the VC, the NVA, the Saigon Government, the US military, or especially two men on a motorcycle.

He steered us through numerous back alleys where we scattered a variety of chickens, ducks, children, and old men and women as we blew by them. Looking back, I think he was sending a signal that a crazy American was driving a motorcycle through their domain.

After cutting across streets and alleys, some paved and some dirt, he did a maneuver that spun the machine around and slid to a stop. He turned and looked at me. "Here comes the good part." Without explanation, he adjusted the goggles he insisted we both wear, revved the engine, and took off with me hanging on and regretting having what seemed to rapidly be becoming my last supper.

We flew down a side street, then did a hard right turn into an alleyway that was only a foot or so wider than the motorcycle. The sound of the engine bounced off the walls on both sides. Halfway through the alley, we passed an open doorway, and as I glanced in it, I saw an old woman holding something that I soon realized was an American .30 caliber carbine.

She stepped into the alley behind us and fired the first of what I mentally counted to be over a million rounds. I felt like I was in one of the Saturday morning cowboy movies I watched as a kid, as the rounds pinged and bounced off the walls on either side of us as we made our getaway. Either she was the worst shot in Saigon, or God was the third passenger on the motorcycle, as none of the shots found their target…which was me since I was on the back.

We made it out of the Cholon and through Saigon traffic back to my hotel. As soon as we stopped and I got off, I had to decide if I was going to kiss the ground or knock him to it. I decided it was in my best interest to show no fear or anger, so I shook his hand even as mine still trembled and told him how much I enjoyed the ride. I made no mention of the fact that he had almost gotten both of us killed.

He offered to take me again if I wanted to see some of the backcountry. I declined. He left to go wherever crazy motorcycle riders go, and I went to my room to take a shower and change my pants.

Chapter Twelve

When most people think of the war in South Viet Nam, they automatically envision it being combat between US and GVN or South Vietnamese military forces and those of the Viet Cong or the North Vietnamese Army. Most of the combat operations were conducted between those forces but there were other countries involved in the conflict.

Our biggest ally in combat was South Korea. They provided two hard-core units, the White Horse and the Tiger divisions, to the war effort. Australia, New Zealand, the Philippines, Thailand, and Nationalist China also had troops on the ground. President Johnson made a call for other countries to support the United States in fighting the Communists. Almost forty governments responded by providing material support in some fashion.

The other side was supported by Russia, China, and reluctantly by Laos and Cambodia, the latter two allowing their country to be part of the Ho Chi Minh Trail, which was used to resupply insurgents in the south.

The Koreans operated almost independently, relying on the US for logistics and advisors. The two divisions were feared by both the NVA and the VC with good cause. The Koreans had a reputation for being ruthless in combat, taking few prisoners and offering no quarter to those they faced in armed conflict.

The Australian and New Zealand military were more closely aligned with the tactics and philosophy of the United States when it came to fighting a war. They planned and executed their own combat operations and had liaison officers to keep the United States military appraised of what they were doing and the results.

Each country was eligible to attend any training or schools the United States operated for its military. Once, when I was at the Eleventh Armored Cavalry Regiment base camp at Zion, I ran across several Australian and New Zealand students at the American Advisor School there. It was two nights prior to graduation from the school, so the students were having a cookout. Several boxes of steaks were "relocated" from the regiment's mess hall. Cases of Victoria Bitters were iced down, and someone had gone into the local village and obtained several old, grainy, black-and-white skin flicks, which were being shown on a screen made from a white sheet nailed to the side of one of the barracks buildings.

The night was clear and hot. The humidity was a match for the temperature, and I felt like I was back in Florida. Liberal splashes of Army bug juice did not deter the mosquitos from dining with us. A few brave souls sat around, shirts off, beers in hand, watching the movies as they ate.

By the second movie, I'd had enough, so I drifted over to a small group of men where a very large New Zealander was playing a guitar and singing songs that were popular during World War Two. I was amazed that most of the men around him knew the words and sang along. His voice was a pure as any I had heard and I wondered why he was here instead of a recording studio. After a Grammy-quality version of *Bluebirds over the White Cliffs of Dover*, he took a break, and he and a Warrant Officer from Australia came to sit beside me on the long picnic table I occupied.

After introductions, the Australian suggested I might want to investigate a training course they ran down in the Mekong Delta. It was a course teaching night ambush techniques, and the final exam was an actual ambush.

Be successful, return to school the next morning, and graduate.

Nobody wanted to fail the course.

DATELINE: SAIGON, SOUTH VIET NAM

Ba Xuyen is a province in the Mekong Delta region of South Viet Nam. It's generally too far away for there to be many hard core NVA military in the area, however it, like the rest of the Delta is a hotbed of Viet Cong activity. Most VC are part-time soldiers. They operate their farms during the day and conduct raids and operations at night. Thus, there is a need for well-trained friendly military to counter their night operations.

That was my introduction the the Night Operations Ambush Training Academy, or NOAT, run by Australian military personnel.

The students were, for the most part, South Vietnamese Regional and Popular forces along with their American Advisors. The Ruff Puffs, as they were called, were tasked with the protection of their local hamlets and villages. Very few large-scale US military operations were conducted in the Delta, since the enemy was not organized into large units.

I arrived at the NOAT school in the middle of a training cycle. The Warrant Officer in charge of the school, WO Robert Warren, was more than happy to show me the school and explain how it operated.

"It's quite simple, Mate. Our pass/fail rate is one of the best you will ever see. If they come back from the graduation exercise, they get the Owl Badge. If they don't, we save the badges for the next class." He explained as we walked toward an outdoor class being conducted by an Australian and his Vietnamese interpreter.

"The Owl Badge?"

"Right. It's a little badge the South Vietnamese Army designed for us. Looks rather like the American parachute badge. Here." He reached into his jacket pocket and took one out. It had an owl with large eyes and outstretched wings. Simple and to the point. Owls hunt at night and kill their prey. So do graduates of the NOAT.

We listened to the class for a few minutes, then he asked me if I wanted to join in. I thought he meant the class, but he meant the graduation problem.

That night I found myself laying on the ground beside a small canal about half a mile from a hamlet where we were told we could expect some local VC to be collecting taxes. At about three in the morning, the information proved to be accurate, and even though I tried to stay awake, I was shocked awake by the sounds coming from either side of me as the students prepared to graduate.

The graduation problem was not one where you had multiple choices or had to write out the answer. It was real. Live fire. Good guys versus bad guys, and only the participants knew which was which.

I was in the middle of a group of Regional Force men from a district in a province to the north, close to Saigon. Next to me on one side was the American officer who was the senior advisor to the unit, and on the other side was his senior sergeant. Both were on their second tour of duty in country, but this was their first time at the NOAT school. They told me prior to darkness that the only thing I had to do was stay awake, fight the mosquitos, and keep my head and my ass down when the shooting started. Not if, but when. They expected to graduate at daybreak.

I heard the dull whump sound the claymore mine made when one of the men down to my right triggered it with the hand-held firing device. After that, it was a graduation party unlike any I had ever heard of. The bad guys were in our kill zone; the claymore's seven hundred ball bearings, traveling at a rate of almost four thousand feet per second, chewed them up like they were in a meat grinder at the local butcher shop. Two more being fired in rapid succession convinced those who were left that they were in the wrong place at the wrong time. After firing a few rounds from AK-47s and SKS rifles just to make a point, they un-assed the area and headed home.

We waited a reasonable time while the Regional Force men checked for bodies, gathered weapons, and anything else of value, and then we left as well.

Nobody played Pomp and Circumstance, but graduation was over.

I have my NOAT badge and it's one of my prized possessions.

Chapter Thirteen

When I told my dad I was going to South Viet Nam for my job, we had the first real man-to-man talk we ever had. I had listened to him and my uncle talk about their time in World War Two, him being in Europe, and my uncle in the Pacific, but most of their war stories were about funny things that happened to them. Even in their war zones, they found some humor. I'm sure it was to mask the horrors they experienced, but that's what they wanted to talk about.

We were at home in the back yard. Years earlier he built a large barbecue grill out of cinder blocks that was his pride and joy. It had a heavy metal mesh over the firepit and a smokestack that extended over six feet in the air. Over the years, he added a cement pad around it where he put an outdoor furniture set made of rattan. I was in the chair, and he sat next to it on the sofa. Both pieces had begun to unravel and fray from use and weather.

I knew when he asked me to join him and have a beer that it was serious. He knew I drank, but he never really approved of it. He grabbed two bottles from the refrigerator in the kitchen as we passed through the room on our way outside.

The weather was perfect for sitting and having a beer with my father, although I know I would have enjoyed it even if it had been during a hurricane.

He took a long drink and cleared his throat. There was a slight catch in it that the beer did not destroy. "I...I can't offer any advice for you." He stopped speaking, and I leaned toward him to say something, but he held up his hand to stop me. "Don't. Let me finish. From what I've read and seen on the television news, that war over there is completely different from what I experienced. I mean, whoever heard of a person pouring gasoline on themselves and setting it on fire just to make a point?" He shook his head as he took another drink. "I don't know what you're going to see or do when you get over there, but it's still a war zone, and you could get…hurt…or worse. If something happened to you, I don't know what your mother and I would do. All I can say is, be careful and know that we love you more than you can imagine." He stopped talking, placed his half-empty bottle on the small table beside the sofa, and went into the house, leaving me alone to consider what he said and, more importantly, what he meant.

I knew they would keep up with what was happening in the country by watching the evening news and reading newspapers and magazines and the dispatches I wrote. I just hoped they would get a clear picture of what was really happening.

The longer I stayed in South Viet Nam, the more I realized that the news back home was far from the truth about the realities of what was happening. I knew I was as guilty as anyone when I had to sanitize my columns each week. My only hope was that my readers could read between the lines and get some idea of the real situation.

Both sides had their own version of propaganda. The Americans called it Public Relations. I'm sure the North had a name for what they did, but I never heard it. Leaflets were printed by the Americans urging the VC and NVA to give up because they were in the wrong and fighting a losing battle.

The North had propaganda leaflets depicting American servicemen being beheaded for war crimes when they were captured. A popular topic for North Vietnamese propaganda leaflets was showing the wife or girlfriend back home in compromising situations while the man was away. Some were graphic to the point of being pornographic.

The Americans also had the Chieu Hoi, or *open arms* program, which encouraged the other side to come over to the good guys and be welcomed with open arms, all sins forgiven, and we would hold hands and sing happy songs around the campfire. I met a few former fighters who were Hoi Chans, the name given to those who accepted the offer. Many of them were serious and assisted the Americans by being scouts, leading missions to their former colleagues.

The one propaganda program that almost everyone in country was familiar with came over the radio at night.

DATELINE: SAIGON, SOUTH VIET NAM

In World War Two, the soldiers listened to Tokyo Rose, Axis Sally, or Lord Haw Haw. In South Viet Nam, we had our own version, and she was called Hanoi Hannah. The military operated AFVN, which was initially called Armed Forces Viet Nam but later changed to American Forces Viet Nam Radio. Like any major station in the US, it featured a variety of shows. It had everything from news broadcasts and morning wake up shows, to a Saturday Polka Party. Every musical taste was serviced at some time during the day.

There is also a competing radio broadcast coming from Hanoi in North Viet Nam hosted by a woman everyone called Hanoi Hannah. Her show was designed to discourage American military personnel by telling them what an unjust war they were fighting. To make her point, she often had more accurate casualty figures than those reported by Stars and Stripes. She sometimes had accurate data on troop movement, ships coming and going, and other information that either was or should have been classified. She sometimes mentioned someone by name and said their wife or girlfriend was about to divorce them or was pregnant by another man. It was not unusual to hear a radio at a secure location with her on it and then see the radio hit with a can of beer thrown by a GI who disagreed with her.

Her favorite topic is the dissent back home in the streets. She always went out of her way to play up the anger the American people have with the war and the government. Every broadcast includes an offer to give protection to any American who deserts and joins in the fight against the war. I don't know of anyone who ever accepted the offer, but there were rumors of Americans who had defected and were either fighting with the enemy or living deep underground in a city or village in the South.

Three times a day, she made her presence known to the military here in South Viet Nam. The listener had to make up their own mind about the truth of her broadcasts.

Chapter Fourteen

Saigon has been called the Paris of the Orient and if you can get by the fact that everyone in the city is armed and prepared for war, it's true. The architecture is all French-inspired. Large villas surrounded by stone walls topped with barbed wire and broken glass, with armed guards at wrought iron gates, are abundant in the city. French Citrons, one of the strangest-looking cars ever made, are everywhere.

One of the largest French influences and legacies is the second-generation Eurasian women. Daughters born to mothers who either married or became pregnant from French military or civilians during the Viet Minh period are some of the most beautiful women I have ever seen. They are the prized wives and girlfriends of the political and military leaders of the country and have become just as popular with the Americans who are here now.

Carmen was out of town and I had just returned to Saigon from three days in Long Binh. It was a time I used to catch up on sleep, good food, and writing my dispatches. Wess and I went to a cinema where an American Western was showing. Unlike many of the features shown in Saigon, this was not overdubbed. I never got used to seeing a movie star I had grown up with speaking Vietnamese. We left the cinema and went to a bar that had a floor show. This one, unlike many of the places in the city, did not feature an actual sex act being conducted in the middle of the room.

The first time Wess took me to one, he did not tell me what to expect. All he said was, "Let's go get a drink. I know a place."

The place, as he called it, was filled with uniforms. Australian, New Zealand, and US military personnel filled every table, stool, and chair in the place. As we entered, the first thing I saw was a movie being shown on the back wall of the club. It was an old, scratchy black-and-white skin flick. There was music playing so loud that I had to yell to get his attention. "What the hell kind of place is this?"

"Oh, you ain't seen nothing yet," he said as he took my arm and pulled me through the crowd. We reached the edge of the main floor, which was surrounded by men two or three thick. In the middle of the floor, a Vietnamese woman was sitting astride a young man in a US uniform, or at least part of a uniform. His shirt was unbuttoned, his pants were around his boot tops, which appeared to still be laced, and his arms were outstretched. There was no doubt what she was sitting on. Her grinding away was accompanied by yells of encouragement from the crowd.

Almost before she could finish and climb off, another young woman dressed only in a pair of bikini panties pulled another 'lucky' man from the crowd. This one was in an Australian uniform, so I assumed they wanted all the Allied forces to enjoy themselves.

I later learned this was one of many such places in the city.

After we returned from dinner and the movie, I got a good night's sleep and awoke with very little to do. I wanted to attend the five o'clock follies at MACV, but that was hours away. I decided to grab a pedicab and just take a tour of the city. In my limited Vietnamese, I told him to take me down by the Saigon waterfront. After that, we headed back to the center of the city.

When we got near the Presidential Palace, I noticed the traffic had almost come to a standstill.

"What's going on?" My reporter curiosity kicked in.

He replied in Vietnamese, and it took me a minute to unravel what he was trying to tell me. The closest I could get to it was "Buddhist protest."

That sounded interesting, so I paid and tipped him and watched as he quickly peddled away. I always carried a small camera with me. It was something I learned from the men in the field. The one-use cameras fit inside an ammo pouch or, in my case, in the cargo pocket of the fatigue pants I wore. Take all the pictures on the film, turn it into the PX in a mailer, and in a week, you get copies of the photos. I was fortunate in that Wess developed my film in the darkroom he had for his own use.

I made my way through the crowd and saw a group of Buddhist Monks in the center of the square. The monks were a common sight in Saigon and in many of the larger cities throughout the country. They wore saffron-colored robes, had shaved heads, and I don't think I ever heard one speak. It may be that they did not speak around Americans or foreigners, or they did not speak at all.

They parted when an older monk came to them. He took a moment to think, pray, meditate, or something as he stood quietly, and the others around him did the same. With the assistance of two monks who appeared to be much younger than him, he was helped to a sitting position on the ground. As if it was hidden beneath one of the monks robes a large metal can was handed to yet another monk.

My heart sank at this point. I had heard of how the monks were protesting the war and the government, perhaps not in that order in the past. I knew, and yet I was horrified by what I knew was about to happen.

The monk held the can above the head of the seated old man, and a steady flow of liquid poured down on the man, soaking him, his robes, and the ground around him.

After the can was emptied and placed on the ground, the older monk gave a slight nod, and the young monk produced a cigarette lighter. As soon as he did, a scream came from the gathered crowd. Like me, they knew what was about to happen, but none of us did anything to stop it.

I remember as a kid, my dad and I were fishing from a bridge one day. We were enjoying the father-son outing, and I can't recall if we had caught anything or not when we heard a man yell. We turned and saw a woman climbing over the railing and standing on the edge of the bridge. The man pleaded with her, and several people closer to them than my dad and I rushed to his side. My dad pulled me to him and turned my head, but it was too late. I saw her as she leaped into the water below.

We later learned that some men in a fishing boat had seen her and were able to pull her onboard. I never knew her name or what happened to her, but it was a sight I never forgot, and it came to me late at night for a long time.

Flames leaped up from the gasoline-soaked robes as the monk was engulfed. If he made a sound, it was not loud enough to be heard over the screams and moans from the crowd. I had seen men die in combat, both American and the enemy. It was something I hoped I would never get used to, but to see someone deliberately set themselves on fire brought an entirely different meaning to death.

Like the lady on the bridge, I know I will see the monk again late at night for the rest of my life.

DATELINE: SAIGON, SOUTH VIET NAM

Death in a war zone is inevitable. For the men in uniform, no matter the country, they know they have a chance of never going home again. Since coming to Viet Nam, I have seen the dead from both sides. Most were already deceased when I saw them. I was around several when they took their last few breaths. I heard them call for their mothers, for their Gods, and for forgiveness for past transgressions. It's something I hope I never get used to. I have managed to push most of those to the far corners of my mind where I can keep them safely hidden away.

I recently witnessed something that I'm sure will never be locked away. No matter how hard we try, there are some things we cannot unsee.

My intent with these columns is to bring some understanding of what you see on the television news or read in your daily papers. So much of the details are left out for a variety of reasons. I will leave the details of this incident to the television news and the photos you will eventually see. No news footage or still photograph can possibly explain the rationale behind, or the horror, of seeing a man seated on the ground allowing himself to be doused with gasoline and then lit on fire.

What I saw was what I understood to be a holy man of his religion. I have no idea what he expected to get out of this act. To bring attention to a cause? To frighten the leaders of the country? To send a message? If so, what was it? His fellow monks may know and understand. I don't, and I don't expect to ever understand.

Was this a selfless act not unlike a soldier jumping on a grenade and sacrificing his life to save that of a comrade? Did he expect to go to his version of Heaven? How much thought and planning did he do prior to the act? Did he have a family? Did he say his last goodbyes and try to explain what he was about to do? Did they understand? Did they approve?

I will never know.

I will never understand.

I will never forget.

Unlike the men in the field, his was a death of choice.

Chapter Fifteen

When anyone leaves their home country for an extended length of time, they will invariably be confronted with local customs and traditions. I imagine when the first Europeans landed on Asian shores, the customs they found were as foreign to them as those we would find landing on Mars today, assuming Mars was populated. South Viet Nam was my first experience with some very strange, at least to me, customs.

Before I left the United States, I read up on the country as much as I could. I used some National Geographic magazine articles and an old travel guide I found at the library. Neither of which prepared me for the reality of what I would face once I got here.

I was in a Marine regimental headquarters not far from the junction of the borders of South and North Viet Nam and Laos. It was about a close as I could get to the border and still be in South Viet Nam. From previous conversations and briefings, I knew we were running cross-border operations in the north and in the bordering countries of Cambodia and Laos, although the US military and government vehemently denied any such actions were taking place.

As a correspondent, I was treated differently in almost every place I went. In some places, I was wined and dined almost like I was a celebrity. Sometimes, the wine and dine consisted of a box of C-rations and a warm beer, but it was the best the unit could provide. In other places, I was looked on as a pain in the ass and treated as such.

When I arrived at the small headquarters detachment, my treatment was someplace in between the two extremes. The commander, a Naval Academy graduate, wanted to make certain I did a good story on the unit and mentioned his name. He handed me over to First Lieutenant Fletcher, who was acting as the unit's Civil Affairs officer. It was his responsibility to maintain contact and friendly relations with the local civilian population. He and a Master Gunnery Sergeant made regular visits to the Province and District Chiefs in their area of operation. Both knew there was a fifty fifty chance that the men could be batting from both sides of the plate and were hedging their bets that the Americans would be victorious in the war. Just in case, they maintained a loose relationship with the other side as well.

The first day I spent there was much like other first days with new units. I got a standard briefing on what the unit was doing, how many patrols were out, how successful they had been, and the most important statistic: their body count. Unlike previous wars, the United States and most other countries, success was not measured in territory gained, but in enemy dead. Every unit kept a running tally of dead enemy soldiers, and I'm sure the entire male population of North Viet Nam would soon be wiped out if all of the numbers were correct and added together.

That night I went to the mess hall which doubled as a movie theater and watched a comedy that was at least ten years old. The best part was a clip of football games featuring most of the American and National Football League teams. After the movie was over, Fletcher invited me to his hootch.

He shared a small wooden building with another officer who was on R&R in Thailand. Fletcher pulled out a bottle of scotch and two glasses. After filling both about halfway and handed me one. "If you stay here long enough, you get used to drinks at room temperature." He held it up, and we touched glasses. "In the summer, that can be almost boiling."

He downed half of his drink in one gulp. "I asked Gunny Hayes to stop by. I want to set something up for you." Grabbing the bottle, he refilled his glass.

"What did you have in mind?"

"I think meeting some of the local government officials would give you the other side of the story that the commander gave you today. There are more pieces to this puzzle than any of us will ever be able to assemble, but at least you'll have a few more of them."

The hootch was tin-roofed, and halfway up, the sides, screen wire was attached to the studs. Sandbags were stacked two deep up to the screen. Large sheets of plywood were hinged to the roof, ready to be dropped during the monsoon season. The screens were there to keep the bugs out, and the plywood was to keep the rain out. Neither one of which worked as designed.

We could hear the sound of artillery being fired from a nearby firebase. I had heard it so often that it was not a matter of concern any longer. There was a different sound between incoming and outgoing artillery and one had to hear it only once to know the difference. Several men walked by, and I saw their shadows against the screen on the hootch. We had a small Coleman lantern sitting on a wooden ammo box providing our only light. Even though we were in a relatively secure compound, nobody took chances with lights.

There was a soft knock on the edge of the doorframe, and Master Gunnery Sergeant Hayes stepped inside. "Evening, gentlemen," he said in an accent that could have been from any place south of the Mason-Dixon line.

"Evenin' Gunny. Pour yourself a drink and join us." Fletcher had already finished his second scotch and held out his glass for Hayes to pour him another one as well. "I wanted to come up with a plan for tomorrow for taking Sean, here to meet the Province Chief."

"Not a problem. I'll set it up in the morning. I need to go to the village anyway to pay for something."

"Great. Make it happen." He looked at me. "Where you bunking tonight?"

"Good question. I hadn't gotten around to asking earlier."

"Not a problem. You can use the spare bunk in here."

"Okay, I'll leave the two of you alone, and I'll see you in the morning," Gunny Hayes said, and he downed his drink and left.

Fletcher and I spent the next hour talking about his life back in the world and what he was doing here. He was single, a graduate of his college ROTC program and did not plan on making a career of military service. "I thought about it until I got here. I see some of these lifers and what it has done to them, and I don't want to turn out the same way." We never got to the point of his telling me what that 'way' was.

I crawled into the bunk, made sure the mosquito net was tucked in tight all around, and listened to the night sound until I finally went to sleep.

Most of the next day was spent with the Gunny showing me around the compound. I was impressed with how they had managed to build what was almost a permanent base camp in such a remote location. It even had a landing strip that could accommodate the C-130, which came in while we were on our tour of the base.

Late in the afternoon, Lieutenant Fletcher caught up with us and told me that we were to be the guests of the Province Chief that evening. I had only met one other Province Chief since arriving, so I was looking forward to talking to him.

"We'll leave here at sixteen hundred. That'll give us enough time to do a grip and grin and get back before it's dark."

When we arrived at the Province Chiefs office, it was in a white-washed building. I couldn't tell if it was cement over brick or what, but it looked like it had been in place for many years. Several other similar buildings surrounded it, and one had a red cross on it.

We entered and were greeted by several men in uniform, all wearing the Vietnamese rank of either a Colonel or Lieutenant Colonel. Others in the room wore very nice-looking civilian clothing. I noticed that there were no women present. It dawned on me as we entered that unless the Gunny or Fletcher spoke Vietnamese, I would have very little idea of what was going on.

As we shook hands, mine being grasped in both hands by the Vietnamese as a sign of respect, I found that two of the men spoke very good English. After ten minutes of introductions, a large dishpan was placed in the middle of a table. I watched as two junior Vietnamese officers poured two bottles of clear liquid into the pan.

Gunny Hayes slipped up next to me. "You're the guest of honor, so be prepared to share a drink with everyone here." I immediately did not like the sound of that.

The Province Chief picked up a small glass from the table, dipped it into the pan, and filled it. He held it up and said, *"mot, hai, ba, dzo,* and drank half the glass and then handed it to me. I recognized the first three words as counting from one to three. I had never heard the last word, but I was soon to find out what it meant.

As I took it, Hayes whispered, "You're expected to drink the other half. Not to do so would be an insult and he'd lose face with the other men here." I noticed a smile on his face as I downed the other half of what tasted like a mixture of white lightning and root beer.

Another man, this one a Colonel, dipped the same glass, drank half, counted to three, and handed it to me. The countdown Gunny whispered to me was "one, two, three, drink." I quickly realized that if I had to drink half a glass of this concoction with every man in the room, I'd never make it out alive.

After two more toasts, I was beginning to weave, and the room spun around me. About that time, Gunny handed me a cigar. I did not smoke, but I took it anyway. He pulled out a lighter and whispered, "Light it and take a puff, then follow my lead."

I held the empty glass in my other hand, and Gunny took it from me. He dipped it in the bowl, filled it, and held it up. "Gentlemen, in honor of our guest tonight, I propose that when we drink with him, you smoke with us." He downed half the glass and handed the remaining liquid and his cigar to the Province Chief.

The man reluctantly took the glass and, after it was empty, took a long pull from Gunny's cigar. After inhaling, he immediately began to cough and had to grab the table to keep from falling.

The lieutenant followed Gunny's lead, had a drink, and then offered a cigar to the man with whom he shared the glass. Like the Province Chief, the cigar proved to be a challenge.

One of the Colonels carefully took his arm to steady him. That ended our drinking session. The remainder of the time was spent with the leaders, telling me all the good things the two sides were accomplishing and how happy they were to be allies.

As I listened, I occasionally took a puff from the cigar that Hayes had given me.

We left just prior to dark and as soon as we got in the jeep, both Hayes and Fletcher burst out laughing. "You bastards, you knew that was going to happen, didn't you?"

Gunny was driving. "First lesson in Vietnamese culture. Don't ever do anything to embarrass your counterpart or anyone who is important. Your life may depend on it."

"He's right. They lose face, and you may lose your ass. Tell him about the *trung vit lon.*"

"I'm afraid to ask, but what is it?"

We were nearing the perimeter wire surrounding the compound, so he slowed his driving. "You ever heard of Balut?"

The word sounded familiar, but I could not remember it. "Tell me."

"It's a real delicacy. They take a duck egg that's half fertilized or half hatched, boil it, and then pull the embryo out and eat it. Most disgusting damn thing you ever seen."

It turned my stomach just thinking about it.

Fletcher turned to face me. "You're gonna be asked to eat one at some point. The best and only way to get out of it is to say that eating anything that is unborn is against your religion. They'll respect that, and you won't get killed the next day for causing them to lose face."

"And always keep a cigar when you are expected to be the guest of honor."

I left the next day with a bad hangover and a life lesson in Vietnamese customs.

DATELINE: SAIGON, SOUTH VIET NAM

Some lessons are learned the hard way. "Remember to wear clean underwear in case you get in an accident" meant nothing until you were in an accident and forgot to change that morning. Some things we learn with no forewarning.

I had never heard of "losing face" until recently. Like always wearing clean underwear, it's something I'll never forget.

Recently, I had the opportunity, and I thought the pleasure of being the guest of honor at a combination meeting and reception hosted by a Vietnamese Province Chief. Just to clarify, South Viet Nam is divided into forty-four provinces, so I was meeting with the equivalent of an American governor.

In my quest to learn more about the country and the Americans and locals fighting the war, I went to a marine base near the DMZ, the dividing line between North and South Viet Nam. My host, with the Marines, arranged for me to attend the reception that night. He and his assistant, a well-seasoned Master Gunnery Sergeant, drove us to the province headquarters building, where we met the Province Chief and several other local officials and senior military officers.

After introductions were made, it was time to have a drink and toast the guest of honor. The problem was that the drink tasted like a mixture of moonshine and root beer, and as the guest of honor, I was expected to have a healthy drink with each man there as they "honored" me. I had been told earlier that to refuse was considered a serious insult, resulting in the host losing face. After being honored three times, I could see that the night was not going to end well. With half of the men still waiting to toast me, the Gunny Sergeant came to my rescue.

He had done this in the past and knew that the Province Chief did not smoke, so he proposed, after lighting the darkest, most evil-smelling cigar I had ever seen, that if we drank with them, they should smoke with us. He took the first drink, handed the lit cigar to the Chief, and watched as after inhaling, he turned several shades of colors only seen in a box of crayons. A Vietnamese Colonel came to everyone's rescue after recognizing what was transpiring.

No more toast from either side was offered, and we spent an hour talking about things I cannot remember. As we drove back to the marine base, both my companions could not contain their pleasure in my dilemma.

When I got back to Saigon I wrote my dad and asked him to send me two boxes of "el ropeo stinko" cigars. I sent one to Master Gunnery Sergeant Hayes and kept one for use the next time I was a guest of honor.

Chapter Sixteen

Every time I went to the five o'clock follies at MACV Headquarters, the other correspondents who represented television, newspapers, magazines, and syndicates like I did compared notes on where we had been, where we wanted to go, and what we were looking for. Most of us had the credentials to travel to any unit in country and on any type of transportation available to us. Some of the guys like to spend time with only the Marines, the Navy, or had some other unit or location they liked to cover. I knew this was a once-in-a-lifetime experience, so I wanted to see and do as much as possible while making a concentrated attempt to keep my head and my ass down and get home someday.

I had two very important, at least to me, things on the board I had in my office that I had not done yet. I wanted to go out to an aircraft carrier and watch the preparation and launching of a bombing raid over North Viet Nam. I had a contact at the Navy Liaison Office at MACV, so I knew at some point I'd probably be able to do that. The second thing I wanted to do, and was within my own resources, was to go on an operation in a tank.

Tank battles were things that happened in WWII and Korea and not so much in South Viet Nam. The NVA had crossed the DMZ a few times with their PT-76 tanks but were quickly either destroyed or driven back by US Marines in M-48 tanks. I had never heard of serious tank battles, but I knew we had tanks that were a part of the 11th Cavalry Regiment stationed at the Black Horse base camp near Xuan Loc, so I decided to visit them.

I caught a chopper at Hotel One, the helipad everyone tried to use in Saigon. It was a clear and quiet day as we lifted off and flew over the outskirts of the bustling city below us. When I boarded, the crew chief handed me a headset so I could listen to the communications between the crew. We had a young PFC on the left, or port side of the chopper manning the M-60 machine gun. The crew chief was situated behind the one on the right side. The guns, like all M-60 in Huey helicopters, were on mounts that allowed them to be moved in any direction except directly back. No pilot wanted his gunners to get so worked up following targets on the ground that he swiveled so far back that he shot off the tail rotor. I never asked, but I wondered if that was a precaution or a reaction to something that had actually happened.

When I boarded, the crew chief gave me a communications helmet and a way to talk to the crew. The flight was uneventful, and I had a long conversation with the pilot, who was from Oakland, California, and was a die-hard Oakland Raiders fan. We talked about The Snake, Fred Biletnikoff, and George Blanda. He was surprised that I knew who all of them were.

We landed at the Black Hawk airfield and he had called ahead to operations and asked that someone meet us with a jeep since he had a VIP on board. After we landed, we met face-to-face for the first time after talking for almost an hour, and he climbed in the jeep with me.

"Take me to the club," he said to the driver. "And take this gentleman to wherever he wants to go."

After he got out at the Black Horse Saloon, I told the driver to take me to the base commander's office. I had no idea where it was, or who the commander was, but I knew it was a good place to start.

At the headquarters, I was introduced to the Executive Officer, a major who was not thrilled to see me.

"I don't have time for visitors. The old man is on R&R someplace getting his ashes hauled, and we've got troops in the field, so tell me what you want."

"I'll make it quick and dirty," I said after explaining I was a correspondent and the unit would be mentioned in any columns I wrote while I was there. He softened after that and took me to the S-3, the operations officer, and explained what I wanted.

Captain Lee, the S-3, quickly pointed to a large white, plastic-covered board hanging on his wall. It had the designations of the units in the regiment and where they were. "I've got a troop with M-48s about to do a road-clearing operation for a unit headed out for a week. You interested?"

"Only if I'm actually a part of the tank crew or in the tank itself."

"You got a death wish or something?" He looked at me. On the collar of his uniform shirt, he had the insignia of an armored corps officer on one side and his captain bars on the other. On his left shoulder was the patch with the Black Horse in the middle, but the patch on his right shoulder indicated a unit he had served with in combat with. It was the patch of the 187th Regimental Combat Team. The 187th had not been in South Viet Nam, so I knew he had seen combat during the Korean War. "You ever been in a tank?"

"No, and that's one of the reasons I'm here."

"They're hot, noisy, smell like an outhouse, cramped, and if you get hit and survive, just the concussion will make your ears ring, your nose bleed, and you'll walk around in tight left-hand circles for a week. All things considered, they're just a shit load of fun."

An hour after meeting Captain Lee, he and I were standing beside an M-48. It was cranked, and the heat from the massive engine cooked the air behind it. Two men were loading cases of C-rations, extra cans of water, a cooler filled with mostly beer with a few cans of soda, duffle bags, spare parts, and ammo. Everything except the ammo was strapped or tied to the outside of the tank.

Two more men were busy hanging road wheels and track blocks on the sides. Captain Lee pointed to these two. "Those things are to prevent any RPGs or any captured LAWs fired at the tank from penetrating. They'll hit the junk and detonate." He motioned to a man who was situated in the commander's hatch.

When Sergeant Vinson, the tank commander, noticed us, he removed his CVC or communications helmet and climbed down. He was wearing his issue fatigue pants, a dark brown tee shirt, and a pair of leather boots with straps and buckles on them. I had seen them in the past and knew they were called Santa Clause Boots.

Lee explained who I was and what I wanted to the sergeant, who took the information in stride. "Take him out and try not to get him hurt or killed unless it's his fault. He can stay as long as he or you and the crew can stand it. If the gets in the way, send him back, and if that's not possible, just shoot him and dump his ass out." He said it so forcefully that I was not sure if he was kidding or not.

"Good copy, Captain. I can put him to work if that's okay. My assistant gunner is in the hospital and ain't due back for a couple of days."

"Sounds like a plan. Make it happen." They exchanged very loose salutes, and I became a crew member of a tank headed into combat.

"Come on up here, and I'll show you around," Vinson motioned for me to join him atop the tank. He dropped down through the hatch he had been standing in and disappeared inside.

To say the inside of a tank is crowded is like saying it's cold in Siberia. The driver sat in his seat up front, the gunner to the left behind him, his loader beside him and my position as the assistant gunner was behind him. "There's an escape hatch for you, so you can stand up and look around if you want to," Vinson pointed to a metal plate above my seat. "I'd advise only doing it when I'm in my open hatch. Otherwise, you'll be the only target."

He didn't have to warn me twice.

In thirty minutes, I felt the tank lurch. It was fully crewed, loaded with fuel, supplies, and beer, and we were on the move. Our job was to be the lead vehicles in the convoy of trucks and other wheeled vehicles. The theory was that if the road was mined, the tanks would find it first and being bigger and heavier than the trucks, absorb the blast with little or no damage.

Most convoys, if they were lucky, had an engineer mine-clearing team proceed them when they were on the main roads. Either one was not available, or this was not considered dangerous enough to have the engineers work the road ahead.

I was standing in the open hatch making a few notes in a pad I carried when I heard and felt the loud WHUMP as we hit a mine. I didn't wait for Vinson to motion me down. I immediately scrambled down and pulled the hatch shut. I heard and saw the massive 90 MM main gun as it swiveled, and the gunner searched for a target. Vinson was directing him through the CVS helmets that we all wore, so I heard his commands.

"Movement at your three o'clock. Put one in there just in case." The loader was already holding another round, ready to shove it into the breach of the gun as soon as the first round was fired.

Vinson pushed open his hatch, climbed up, swung the .50 caliber machine gun around, and fired into the area he had directed the tank to engage. All the time, the driver kept us moving through what could have been an ambush site.

The remainder of the day passed with no further action, so I was able to ride in the open all the way to the remaining overnight or RON site. During that time, we had left the road and hit the woods. A tree is no match for a tank on a mission. With two tanks running almost side by side we cleared the way for the infantry who followed behind us. With darkness approaching, we stopped, and the crew prepared our position. The first thing they did was pull down a case of C-rations and place several cans on the manifold of the engine. Each can was punctured to allow the steam from cooking to evaporate, otherwise the contents would explode and cook on the manifold for several days and add to the stink already in a tank.

After placing the cans on the engine, they pulled down several rolls of razor wire and encircled the tank and our sleeping positions with it.

"The grunts will put out some patrols and LPs for the night, so we're pretty much left alone. This is when we do maintenance or anything else we need to do, so you can watch or do whatever you want, as long as you let somebody know if you're roaming around inside the wire."

The next day, we were on a road that led through a village when I saw a flash and instantly felt the Rocket Propelled Grenade or RPG as it hit the opposite side of the tank from me. Vinson saw it at the same time and took the hootch where the rocket came from under fire. Fortunately, the road wheels and other pieces the crew had placed on the side of the tank absorbed the blast and it did not penetrate. As soon as Vinson opened up, I heard the steady PING, PING, PING as small arms fire bounced off my side of the tank. By the third PING, I was safely inside. Like the RPG, the small arms only served to identify the location of the shooter and bring the wrath of the tank and the accompanying infantry down on them.

I stayed with the tank for three days, and that was the only real action we saw. The assistant gunner was released from the hospital, and a resupply helicopter brought him out with a load of fresh water, mail, and three replacements for men in the accompanying infantry.

After accompanying the tank crew on an operation, I climbed on the resupply chopper and rode back to the Black Horse Airfield. It was getting late, so I managed to find a place to sleep in a transient barracks that they operated. The building was filled with bunks, about half of which were empty. Those that had men in them or belongings on them indicated there was no separation between officer and enlisted. I saw a shirt hanging from a bunk that had the twin silver bars of a captain on it. A Specialist fourth class was asleep on the bunk next to it.

That night, two senior NCOs set up a table and started a poker game. It was generally accepted that officers did not gamble with enlisted, but like the sleeping arrangements, that rule did not apply here.

I watched the game for an hour and did not play. I wanted to catch up on writing letters to my parents and an aunt whom I wrote on occasion. After that, I realized that once again, I had witnessed actual combat in a war zone firsthand. Normally, I saw it from the sidelines or after the fact when I talked to the men who experienced it. Every day, I gained a new perspective about why we were here and what we hoped to accomplish. I wasn't sure I had an answer, and worse, I wasn't sure the men running the war had one either.

The next morning at the headquarters building, I stopped by to thank them for letting me accompany the unit on a mission. While I was there, I overheard the S-2 talking about a defector who had been picked up in the Pleiku area and was being held there before being sent to Camp LBJ or the Long Binh Jail. I knew I had something else to add to my list.

I grabbed a seat on a flight back to Saigon and marked riding in a tank in combat off my to-do list as I added one more.

DATELINE: SAIGON, SOUTH VIET NAM

Like many people, probably more men than women, I grew up

watching war movies as feature films on Saturday mornings at the movies. We saw the Americans defeat the Germans, the Japanese, and anybody else that got in our way. This included various men from faraway planets, especially Mars. Many times, the battles were fought with tanks.

Real wars generally include battles between tanks, but the one here in South Viet Nam was an exception. The last real tank battle happened during the war in Korea, but that did not stop the United States from sending tank units to this one as well. I wasn't sure what they were here to do, so at the first opportunity, I found a tank unit that would let me tag along. Not only did they let me tag along, but they also made me the replacement for a crew member who was in the hospital.

Within an hour of moving out from the base camp, we ran over a mine, thus giving me my first taste of tank warfare. The tank was well prepared, and the mine did no damage, so we continued on. Later that day, we were the target of a nasty little piece of Russian or Chinese weaponry called a Rocket Propelled Grenade or RPG. It hit the side of the tank and since we had a crew that was prepared for such things, it did little damage. I can't say the same for the person who fired it since the commander of our tank peppered him with rounds from a .50 caliber machine gun to show him the error of his judgment.

One of the bad guys thought that his rifle or light machine gun could stop this fifty-nine-ton piece of Detroit engineering. All it did was make a series of pinging noises as he, too, was engaged with our heavier machine gun.

Going to war in a tank today is not like in the WWII and Korean movies. We did not face, or even see, an enemy tank. The two times we came under fire were minor inconveniences for us, but much more so for the other team.

I found out that a tank is like a rolling city for the crew. Before going on a mission, they pack it with everything they think they will need. That obviously includes ammo and spare parts, but for the crew I was with, it included cases of C-rations, a cooler filled with beer and soda, and rolls of concertina and razor wire to be used around the tank when they set up for the night. The tank crews were as close-knit as the plane crews of WWII that my dad talked about. Some named their tanks, made up bits and pieces of uniforms they wore in the field or when officers or senior NCOs without a sense of humor were around, and all wanted nothing more than to face an enemy tank in tank-to-tank combat.

It was an experience I will never forget and one I hope never to repeat. It took two days for my ears to stop ringing from the RPGs.

Chapter Seventeen

When I first arrived in Saigon and was trying to get my feet on the ground and determine just what I had gotten myself into, I asked a lot of questions to a lot of people. I spoke to as many different types of individuals as I could, and then I filtered the answers I got back to see if I could make sense of them. I talked to officers and enlisted men from all the services, civilians, government employees from the United States, South Viet Nam, other allied nations represented in the country. When I went out with Nguyen, the interpreter who worked in the office with us, I tried to talk to some of the locals to get their fix on the war. Did they think the South Vietnamese government would win the war? Did they care, or did they just want to be left alone? The answers were as varied as the people who gave them.

I remember one day, Nguyen took me to the local market in Saigon near the river. We drove, and once we got close, he parked and paid a South Vietnamese *Binh si,* or Private, to watch the Jeep. He added, as he told me later, that he threatened him with loss of life if anything happened to the jeep.

We walked among the stalls selling everything from fresh fish and produce to black market items like cigarettes, radios, cameras, watches, and even old US coins. "We will buy some *tom.* I had no idea what he was talking about until we came to a stall that had a mat made of rice straw on the ground in front of it. Beside the mat was a large tub filled with water. The mat was covered with hundreds of large, dried prawns. He pointed. "Tom. You call prawns." He made it sound like he was saying "pawns," but after seeing them,

I understood, although I was not interested in picking up a handful from the mat.

"More in water. All alive," he said as he stood by the tub. "She sells for a very long time." He then began a long conversation with the old woman. Women age differently in Viet Nam. She could have been in her mid-fifties or nineties. She squatted on the ground beside the tub. Her head was wrapped in a blue cloth, her teeth stained from a lifetime of chewing Betel nut, and the black pants she wore came to just above her ankles.

"You sure these are fresh?" I asked.

"No sweat. She sells for many years. My *ban oi*...uh...my mother's mother."

We were standing at a stall where Nguyen's grandmother was selling prawns. "She start with her Ba...mother when she six. Sell to Japanese soldiers, then to French."

It immediately registered that this old woman in front of us had gone through three wars and was still selling prawns. It was said as simply as one would say "bless you," to someone who sneezed back in the States. I filed that away on my board and planned to do a story on her soon.

We left, and I returned to the Mass BOQ, and Nguyen went to his house in Saigon to continue his life like his grandmother had done for more years than either of us had been alive.

That night, one of the first men I spoke to was a First Lieutenant about to make Captain, and an Army Advisor on his second tour. He volunteered for this one. When I asked why would a man volunteer to come back to a war zone where he stood a chance of never returning home?

"Lots of reasons," he said as he finished the bottle of beer I purchased for him at the bar at the Massachusetts BOQ. "First, I got no real family back in the world. I'm an only child, and both my parents are deceased. I don't own a home and I sold my car before I left, so I got no debts other than my bar bills over here. Pay is pretty good in a war zone. No taxes and combat pay, so I can save most of that." He held up his hand for the bartender to bring us another round. He looked at me for concurrence since I was paying, and I nodded in approval.

There was a Korean band playing on stage, and a few men had brought their girlfriends to the club, so there were three couples on the floor attempting to dance.

"The women over here are, for the most part, decent and available for a price. The way I got it figured is I'll spend six months in the field and six months as a REMF. Midway through the twelve months, I'll get an R&R someplace. Last time I went to Bangkok. May do it again, but I thought about Australia for this one. Probably get sick or wounded and spend a week or two in the hospital, so that breaks it up to four ninety-day blocks. I can do that sober and standing on my head." He took the beer the bartender handed him. "How about you? What are you doing here?"

I thought I had an answer, but the more I tried to explain my presence, the more difficult it got.

"You're like me. You're looking for something, but you don't know what it is, and you probably won't recognize it when you run across it." He sat his bottle on the bar. "Just keep your head and your ass down, and maybe we'll get to have a drink again," he said as he slipped from the bar stool and left.

A lot has happened since that night, and I'm a little closer to knowing why I'm here than I was then. I've seen most of the country, met almost all of the senior military leadership from both sides at one time or another. I received some awards for a few of the columns I wrote, and best of all, I may have met the love of my life.

After several months in country, Wess and I were at the club one night when every head in the room turned when she entered. It took some time, but I finally got to know her. I don't believe in love at first sight, but it was something close. After a while and several dates or as close to a date as we could manage, we both knew we were getting in over our heads.

Once, when I was chasing a story, I was wounded, and after spending several days in the hospital, she came and brought me to her home. From that day on, we have been inseparable. Last year, we went back to the States and visited both our homes to meet our parents. Although I had not made it official, I assumed that at some point, we would get married. All we had to do was survive a war and make it home.

She traveled as much throughout the country as I did, so our schedules seemed to never match. Finally, we got three days together in Saigon. She had her housekeeper, Mai, prepare dinner for us, and we were finishing when Mai came in and took the dishes away. I brought a bottle of wine from the PX, and we were deep inside it when Carmen suggested we go upstairs to her bedroom.

She had a villa that was provided to her by the US State Department, where she worked. It was an old two-story French villa. It had three rooms on the first floor and two on the second. She had a large bedroom with a sitting area facing west, so it was not uncommon for us to sit and watch the sun set.

"I have an idea," I said as I settled next to her on a large loveseat. "How would you like to go to Hawaii? We can catch one of the R&R flights. A week there would be a welcome respite for both of us."

It took three weeks for us to arrange a week off at the same time, but we boarded the flight along with men going to meet wives and girlfriends in Honolulu and a few who were leaving the flight there to catch another one that would take them home and away from South Viet Nam forever.

The military managed a hotel on the beach at Waikiki that was reserved for soldiers coming here on R&R. The facility had, or arranged for, anything the military and their families could want. It had a massive ocean front so there was no need to go looking for a beach. All one had to do was go outside, cross a picturesque area of native flora and fauna, and spread a towel. Tour busses left on a regular basis for all the tourist sights on the island. Luaus were planned for every night. Each one was complete with hula dancers and men who twirled flaming torches to the delight of the guests.

Across the street was another military facility. Between the two properties, I was certain that if they were sold to hotel developers, the national debt of the United States would disappear overnight.

Since both Carmen and I worked with, or for, the military, we were allowed to stay at the hotel. Like most of the men who came to meet wives and sweethearts, we spent the first day in the room only coming out long enough to have a meal and walk down to the beach, then it was back to the room. The second day, we ventured out to take advantage of some of the sights. Neither of us had been to Hawaii, unless you count a stop at the airport en route to South Viet Nam, so everything was new to us.

Carmen wanted to visit the Cultural Center, so we booked a trip for the afternoon. The morning was spent at a large shopping center where we made the obligatory purchase of souvenirs to send home. For reasons I still don't understand, I bought a large carved wooden knife and fork and sent them to my mother. Carmen was much more practical and sent her mother a necklace made from local seashells. We had lunch at a restaurant that served something that neither of us had managed to find in Saigon. We had a massive cheeseburger and an order of fries.

After the trip to the Cultural Center, we signed up for the evening luau. A whole pig was slowly being pulled apart as a main course. We tried poi and discovered it was something we could do without. When the dancers finished, we removed our shoes and walked along the beach hand-in-hand.

"I wish we didn't have to go back," Carmen stopped and dragged her barefoot through the dark sand and kicked it toward the surf.

"We don't. I don't know about you, but I can leave anytime I want to." I turned her to face me. "We can go back to the States and..."

"And what?"

"And...and I don't know. Whatever we want to do."

Before we could determine what we wanted to do, we were interrupted by a group of four very rowdy and very drunk young men. From their haircuts, it was obvious they were some brand of military, and since they did not have women with them, they were probably stationed on the island. We watched them stagger down the beach in the opposite direction from where we were going.

"Navy?"

"More like Marines," I said.

We continued to the next hotel with an outdoor bar. We walked through a double row of flaming tiki torches and selected a table. The waitress who came to us wore a brightly colored wrap that left one shoulder and arm bare. She had dark black hair that hung straight down her back almost to waist level, and a circle of flowers crowned her head.

"Do you have anything that doesn't come in a coconut or have an umbrella or a stick filled with pineapple?"

She laughed at my question. "Yes, but you'll probably get some strange stares from the others out here if I bring you something like that."

"Okay, bring us two of something you recommend."

A few minutes later, she returned with a tall glass with the umbrella and pineapple stuck in it for Carmen and an even taller glass for me. My drink was red and so sweet that I thought I might go into a sugar coma if I drank all of it.

A strolling group of musicians were playing and singing in what I assumed was native Hawaiian. They stopped by our table, and I tipped them for a song that they seemed to enjoy singing more than I enjoyed trying to figure out what they were singing about.

It was almost midnight when we made it back to our room.

The next morning, we had breakfast in the hotel's coffee shop and headed for the beach. I had spent some time in Saigon without my shirt, so I had a good tan from the waist up, but in a bathing suit, my legs looked like they had been painted a pale white. Carmen had a natural tan, so the sun was not too much for her. We took it in small doses as we moved from beneath our beach umbrella to the water and then back again.

I bought us two shaved ice cones from a beachside vendor mid-afternoon to cool us off. We were discussing our plans for the evening when we heard an argument coming from a short distance to our right.

A young man and a woman were seated on a blanket, much like us. Both were in bathing suits. Another man was standing beside the woman. Unlike the other people on the beach, he was dressed in shorts, a tee shirt, and tennis shoes. He was not there to enjoy the water.

Their conversation went from loud to yelling. Suddenly, the man seated on the towel stood up and, in one swift motion, swung his right fist and hit the other man on the side of his head, knocking him to the sand. By this time, they had the attention of everyone nearby.

Like a scene from a bad dream, the man who had been knocked down stood up, and when he did, he had a small pistol in his hand. It was pointed at the man who had hit him.

I heard several people yelling for someone to call the MPs, but it was too late. The man in the bathing suit, in a move that was so quick it was like a flash, pulled the weapon from the hand of the man holding it. He fired three times before the man had a chance to react to losing his weapon. By this time, the woman on the blanket was screaming hysterically.

Her companion dropped the pistol and took a seat on the blanket. Several men rushed to the wounded man. Two of them announced that they were medics and asked the crowd to give them room to work. In minutes, three uniformed Military Policemen came, and when the shooter saw them, he stood, placed his hands on his head, and was immediately placed in handcuffs. An ambulance crew arrived and, after checking vitals, placed the man on a stretcher and pulled a sheet over his head. It was obvious the woman in the triangle did not know which one of the men to go to.

It took two more days for the full story to come out. The couple on the blanket were married. The man with the gun was her boyfriend back in the world while her husband was at war. Not only was he her boyfriend, but he was also the father of the child she was carrying. I felt certain that the shooting would be declared self-defense since the shooter had taken the weapon away from the man holding it. Numerous witnesses came forward to give statements to that effect.

I wonder if anyone who saw it had any sympathy for the woman or the dead man.

DATELINE: SAIGON, SOUTH VIET NAM

Death is an occupational hazard in a war zone. It's something you must face, but never think it's going to happen to you. Each week, the Stars and Stripes, the official newspaper of the military published the casualty report. They break it down into categories. They have Killed in Action, Killed Not as a Result of Enemy Activity, and Missing in Action. That could be killed and the body not recovered yet or missing and taken captive. The one category they did not have was killed while on R&R.

I recently returned from a week's Rest and Recuperation or R&R

in Honolulu. I went with a lady whom I met over here and have grown quite fond of. More on that later, but we went together to take a week off from what we were seeing here in country. We had no idea it would follow us to Waikiki.

While on the beach, we witnessed the end results of a love triangle. A military man, I don't know which branch, met his wife in Honolulu. They were enjoying a day on the beach when another man approached them. A heated argument ensued, and the third man pulled a gun on the husband. Without hesitation, the husband took the weapon away from the third man and shot him three times, killing him instantly.

He was arrested as he should have been, but it was later revealed that the third man was also military but was stationed near the shooter's hometown and his wife. Do you see where this is going? Turns out the dead man and wife were having an affair, and she was pregnant by him. He came to Hawaii to confront the husband to do what….we'll never know.

The result is that the woman left Hawaii pregnant. Her husband was in jail but later released as the charge was deemed self-defense. The father of her child lay dead on the beach at Waikiki.

Some men refer to R&R not as Rest and Recreation but as Rape and Rampage. Maybe they're more right than they imagined.

Chapter Eighteen

At the Five O'clock Follies, the briefing officer mentioned that an operation had captured a North Vietnamese senior officer who had defected from the ARVN. Not only that he had been trained at the Infantry Officer's Candidate School at Fort Benning. He had been a plant from day one. Join the ARVN, learn English, attend OCS, and then defect. This was a man I had to see. I had heard about him when I was with the tank unit, but this was the first time I knew it was true and where he was.

Since arriving in country, I had heard rumors, of military personnel from all the services who had defected to the enemy and were fighting against the Americans. The two most popular ones were a "salt and pepper" team. One was a Caucasian with bushy red hair, and the other was a black man. Sometimes, they were described as former Marines, sometimes Army. There was never any verification that they actually existed, so they were like the infamous "three-step snakes" that were supposed to be so deadly that after being bitten, you could only take three steps before falling over dead.

If MACV was briefing on this person, it had enough credibility for me to follow up and see what I could find out. When the briefing was over, I and two other correspondents went to the briefing officer to get more information.

"I told you about all I know at this point," he said.

"Where is the man being held?" One of the other guys asked as he pulled out his notebook.

"Last I heard, he was up in Pleiku or the stockade in Long Binh. I imagine he'll be brought down here at some point, but they want to get as much hot intelligence from him as soon as possible."

"Did he defect, or was he captured?"

"Wounded and captured." He turned to walk away, then stopped. "Way I heard it, and I haven't verified it, was that one of the company commanders whose troops captured him knew him when he was an officer candidate at OCS in Fort Benning." With that little golden nugget of information, he left us to find our way to Pleiku. We couldn't leave the building fast enough.

Fortunately, we worked for different syndicates so even if one of us got to him first, it was a story that would get widespread distribution.

I left MACV headquarters by catching a ride in a jeep with an Air Force Captain who was going to Tan Son Nhut. The airfield was a warren of activity as planes, both fixed-wing and rotary, took off and landed in rapid succession. Someplace, there was a group of air traffic controllers who were responsible for the activity, and I did not envy them their jobs. Many of the pilots they spoke to were Vietnamese and did not speak the best English. They had interpreters in the control tower, but by the time something was translated, it could be too late. I tried not to think of that when I went to the terminal and looked for something heading north.

I didn't see either of the other two correspondents, so I assumed they had an arrangement with one of the services to fly them out of Saigon. I was just taking a chance.

As usual, the terminal was filled with men and women. The women acting as the girlfriends of the military personnel who were catching the Freedom Bird that would take them home, leaving South Viet Nam and the war behind them. For the women, it usually meant they were free to find another G.I.

I watched the line of men as they hustled out to the ramp leading up to the entrance of the large commercial airliner. It would be packed, every seat filled with men heading home or a few going to Hawaii to meet wives and girlfriends for a week of R&R. At the head of the line were the senior officers who loaded first. Their seats were just as uncomfortable as the lowest rank enlisted man on the plane, but they didn't have to stand in line on the hot tarmac as long as some of the others. For many, it would be the last time they had an officer pull rank on them.

There was a line in front of the counter where several Air Force enlisted men worked flights that were about to leave. When I got the counter, the Airman Second, gave me a long look. "You a civilian?" he asked.

Since my fatigue jacket didn't have any indication of rank and it clearly said CORRESPONDENT instead of a military service tape, I didn't know if he was screwing with me or not. Since I needed him to get me a flight, I played nice.

"That's right, but I have authorization to fly on military aircraft. I can show it to you if you need it." I wanted to add that he could stick it up his ass after he read it, but I didn't press my luck.

"No, that's okay. I just need to do a special form when we have a civilian on one of our missions." Now, he was playing nice. "Where do you want to go?"

He got me a seat on a C-47 Chinook headed north. We made a stop at a firebase, and after what seemed like an eternity in the air trying not to hear the overpowering noise from the twin rotors and the massive engine, we landed on the runway at the airfield at Long Binh.

The Air Force base at Pleiku was a mass of tents and buildings constructed on a red dirt clearing in the shadow of lush green-covered mountains in the distance. Each tent was built up off the ground on a wood platform. Walking from where the Chinook landed and dislodged its passengers, I was quickly overwhelmed by the smell of the tents. Each General Purpose or GP Large was constructed of oiled canvas stretched over wood poles with a metal rod at the end, which was fitted into holes in the canvas.

Each tent had a row of filled sandbags around the base. The bags were a great idea if the person shooting at the residents in the tents was aiming three feet off the ground, otherwise it was an exercise in futility. I saw nothing in the compound that would withstand a direct hit from artillery, mortar, or rocket fire.

The streets, and I'm being nice when I call them that, between the rows of tents and other buildings, were rutted from vehicles running on them. It was the dry season when I arrived, but I could imagine a sea of thick, stick-to-everything red mud during the monsoon seasons.

The entire setup was something the Air Force did not advertise to prospective recruits. The Air Force had a justly deserved reputation for having some of the best military bases in the world. The general opinion was that when the Air Force decided to establish a new base, the first thing they built was the golf course, followed by the officer's club, then housing for the personnel. The base at Pleiku would never make it to a recruiting brochure.

The place where we landed was beside a runway of sorts, so I followed it to the end, where I found a well-established flight operations office. Chalkboards indicated the time and destinations of upcoming missions. Several young airmen in OD tee shirts worked behind the counter, pointing out passengers and equipment that was destined for the next flight. I saw one who was either the senior man in charge or who had managed to find a way to screw off while the others did all the work. He was holding a small plastic bag with a straw sticking out of it. The bag was filled with a dark liquid. The Vietnamese had a thriving industry of producing a knock off of American soda brands. They would put the drink in a bag, stick a straw in it, and sell it to the military, who always took a chance when taking the first pull on the straw.

"Got a minute?" I asked as he slurped the last of the drink from the bag.

"Yeah. What'ch need?"

"Just some directions. What's the major command on the base?"

"Shit, man, we got so many different that think they're on the top of the totem pole that you got to be a little more specific." He tossed the empty bag into a box sitting in the corner. The box had rope handles on each side, indicating it had originally been packed with hand grenades.

"Okay, how about starting with the Provost Marshall?" In the military, law enforcement was the duty of the military police, and the senior command for them was the Provost Marshall.

"You're in luck. They're not far away. Since I know you came in on that Chinook out there, I know you're on foot. It's an easy walk unless you can catch a ride."

"I'll start on foot and see what happens."

He gave me the directions for the PM office, and I headed out. Two jeeps passed by me, and finally, a three-quarter-ton utility truck stopped and asked if I needed a ride.

The red dust kicked up by the previous two passing jeeps was still floating in the air and settling on me and everything in the area, so I was happy to get inside the truck. The driver was a black man who was puffing on a small cigar.

"Provost Marshall's office or as close to it as you can take me."

"No sweaty-da," he said, using the Vietnamese version of the American phrase. "You in trouble?"

"No," I laughed. "I'm just looking for some information." I noticed that he was wearing the stripes of a Staff Sergeant. "Information usually comes from the G-2 or PIO," he offered.

"I may have to talk to the intelligence or the public affairs officers at some point, but I think the PM is my first stop." I thought for a minute and then took a chance.

"I heard about an NVA officer who was captured who used to be one of us. You know anything about that?" Before he could answer, we were stopped at a road junction of sorts by an MP who was holding up traffic so a convoy of trucks could pass by.

"Hell, ever'body's heard about him. Said he was an officer for the GVN, then he hauled ass north." He turned to face me and I noticed that he had several day's growth of beard on his face. There was a skin condition that affected primarily black men that kept them from shaving. It was common enough that many of the senior black NCOs referred to it as something that only affected men in the rank of staff sergeant and below. It was a good excuse not to shave, but if the man was around a gas grenade tossed by one of the bad guys, he was hurting as he could not fit his gas mask.

"That's why I'm here. I'm a correspondent and I want to do a story on him. I figured he would be kept by the PM until they drained him of whatever good intelligence he has."

"I think you're right," he said as he pulled the floor-mounted gear shift into first gear when the MP signaled us across the intersection. "He'll probably wind up down in LBJ."

LBJ, in addition to being the initials of the president, was what everyone called the large stockade at the Long Binh compound. It was referred to as the Long Binh Jail or LBJ.

"I think you're right, so I want to get to him as soon as I can."

He pointed to a wood building across the street from where he stopped. "That's the PM over there. Good luck getting to see him. He's a prize, and they're not likely to want too many people to talk to him until they've rung him dry."

I thanked him and crossed the dusty street to the building with a sign with two crossed pistols on it, which was the insignia of the military police.

Inside the building, it was a combination of a mid-sized city's police station and a military unit. Men in uniform with an armband that indicated they were AP or Air Police moved freely about. Others in duty uniform were at desks doing what I assumed were clerical duties related to keeping the good order and discipline of the air base. I was approached by a Master Sergeant.

"Can I help you?"

"Yes, maybe you can." I explained who I was and what I wanted and he took his time responding.

"I'm not the one who can make that happen, and I'm not sure anyone here will let you see him."

"He's here?"

"I didn't say that. I said…" He stopped and looked around the room, finally settling on a door marked Office of the Provost Marshall. "Hang on. Let me talk to one of the officers. This is above my pay grade."

He left me standing in the middle of the room as he knocked three times on the frame of the door and waited to be invited in. When he heard a voice from inside the office, he opened the door and entered.

The building was one of the permanent ones constructed when the Americans moved in and took over the base. There were some made of wood, and a few trailers or mobile homes for senior officers and visiting VIPs dotted the area. I assumed that somewhere in this building, there was a secure area that was the jail or stockade. I was still looking around, trying to get a feel of what was going on, when he came back out.

"The colonel said give him a few minutes, and he'd come out and talk to you." He gave a slight nod and disappeared down a long hallway.

The few minutes turned out to be only a few seconds. The colonel came out about the same time the master sergeant left.

He extended his hand. "I'm Colonel Martin, the Provost Marshall. I understand you want to speak to our prisoner." He motioned for me to follow him back into his office.

We entered an office that would be the envy of many senior officers back in the world. It was paneled with wood that had once been part of ammo boxes. The wood had been scored with a torch to give it a knotty pine appearance, then coated with a stain to give it a high gloss sheen. Numerous photos, award and decoration certificates, and war souvenirs hung on the wall. He had a large North Vietnamese flag with a yellow fringe border, an AK-47, an SKS rifle,a Mountainyard crossbow, and a bamboo quiver filled with arrows scattered throughout the room. His desk was handmade and not the usual steel-grey government issue. I don't know how long he had been here, but it looked like he planned to stay.

"Take a seat and tell me more," he said as he motioned to a green couch like those I had seen in most of the offices at MACV.

"Like I said, I want to do a story on this man. He seems like he may be a one-of-a-kind. I think the public will find his story very interesting."

"I agree if it's done in the right way. He may be a hero to the NVA, but he's just another enemy officer who was captured in a firefight as far as we're concerned."

"I agree, but since the Air Force is not known for running operations on the ground, how did you happen to have him?

"We're just holding him for the 4th Division. Some of their men from the Third Brigade captured him, and our facility is much more secure than the one they have at their base camp. It's a temporary thing. He'll be moved to the facility at LBJ in a couple of days."

This was good news in a couple of ways. If I could talk to him here, I might be able to speak to the men who captured him since they were on the adjoining compound.

"I'd like to get his story first and then, if possible, talk to the men who captured him."

The colonel was quiet for a minute as he considered my request. "Sounds reasonable. Follow me."

I was taken to a small room, not unlike the ones found in most police stations where interviews were held. The room had a table, two chairs, and heavy bolts secured into the floor where a prisoner's handcuffs or leg irons could be fastened during their time in the room. The colonel told me to take a seat, and then he left me alone.

In less than two minutes, three APs escorted a short but well-built man into the room. He looked to be in his mid-twenties but I've found with the locals, it's difficult to guess their ages. He wore a pair of cut-off pants and an old shirt, neither of which had once been a part of a uniform. He smiled at me when they loosened on hand and then snapped the handcuff to a chain attached to one of the bolts on the floor.

"The colonel said you have ten minutes. We'll be outside the door in case you have a problem." One of APs said.

"You are not in a uniform. You are a civilian. Government? CIA?" He spoke with only a very slight accent.

"Wrong on all counts. I'm a correspondent. A reporter—"

"You do not have to explain yourself to me. I know what a correspondent is."

"Good. Let's cut to the chase. I'm here to do a story on who you are and why you did what you did. How's that?"

He laughed. "Do I get paid for my story?"

"No, but you will have the opportunity to tell the world the what's and why's. That should stroke your ego."

"I like you, so we can talk."

For the next ten minutes, he told me of his youth in Saigon, his decision to first join the GVN, learn English, and attend Infantry Officer's Candidate School at Fort Benning in Georgia, and his disillusion with the war and who was going to win.

"In 1964, I knew the Americans did not have a chance of defeating the will of the people to determine their own fate. Firepower can kill the bodies but not the will of the people. When you accept that fact, no more Americans will be killed, and the people of what you call North and South Viet Nam will live in peace. My decision was simply to hasten that day as much as I could."

"You lived as an American at Fort Benning. Did you ever think that you might be killing some of the men you met there?"

"You're wrong. You are in Viet Nam. Does that make you any less an American? I don't think so." He banged his hand on the table to get the AP's attention. "I have told you all that I want you to know. Tell your readers that to continue is to lose more American lives than they can imagine, and they will still not see any positive results."

The APs came in and took him away.

DATELINE: SAIGON, SOUTH VIET NAM

ARVN

OCS

NVA

I met a man this week who could have put all three of those initials on his military signature block at some time in his military career.

Born in Saigon, he was brought up to believe that military service was an honorable thing to do. He joined the Army of Viet Nam, or ARVN, when he graduated from a Catholic high school. At the school, he learned both French and English, and once he was in the army, he was selected to attend the US Army's Officer Candidate School, or OCS, at Fort Benning, GA. He graduated and was commissioned a Second Lieutenant in the ARVN. After a year of service, his opinion of the war and its eventual outcome began to change as did his loyalties. After two years of fighting the Viet Cong and North Vietnamese Army, he defected to the other side.

In our conversation, where he was chained to the floor in the interview room, he said he had to prove his decision to leave the ARVN by leading a patrol to ambush an American unit. The ultimate proof was to deliver the head of an American to his commanding officer. I did not ask if he did, but when he was captured, he had risen to the position of commanding a regiment of North Vietnamese Army regulars.

He was wounded and captured by a patrol commanded by a First Lieutenant who was also a graduate of the Fort Benning OCS program. They were not in the same class and not at Benning at the same time, but sometimes, payback takes its own way of doing things.

Dressed in cut-off pants and an old shirt and chained to the floor, he maintained his dignity and made several observations that gave me pause to think. The one that I remember most was his saying that American firepower can kill the bodies but not the will of the people.

What is the will of the people of South Viet Nam?

Chapter Nineteen

When you join any branch of the military, it's almost required that you learn a foreign language. Not one like French or German or even now Vietnamese, but the use of military acronyms and slang. The first day in country, when I reported to my new office and met my fellow workers, I was told I was the FNG and that my hootch was at the Mass BOQ. I had no idea what they were talking about. It was explained that I was the Fucking New Guy, and my room was at a hotel called the Massachusetts, and it was taken over by the military to serve as a Bachelor Officer's Quarters or BOQ.

Every day since then has been a learning experience. Each branch of the military has terms and acronyms that are unique to that service, but many are universal. The forests are the *boonies* as is the soft hat most of the men wear. Helicopters are *slicks, dust-offs,* or *medevacss.* The most common name for them is either dust off or medevac. Both are used interchangeably. I had to ask when I first heard the term. It relates to the cloud of dust they create when they land, and if it's to pick up wounded, it's for medical evacuation.

The C-130 aircraft outfitted with mini-guns are *spookies* or *Puff the Magic Dragon.* If your time in country is drawing to an end, you are *short* and awaiting your *dros* or Date Returned from Overseas. If you are just leaving the country or your *ETS,* Expired Time of Service, if your time in the military is over and you will be discharged when you arrive in the United States or *the world.*

If you have your orders to leave South Viet Nam for release or reassignment, you get a *FIGMO* or Fuck 'em, I Got My Orders attitude. What can they do to me now? Send me to Viet Nam?

The two I find to be most prevalent are slang. One is *Steam and Cream,* which is the name for the hundreds, if not thousands, of massage parlors just outside the gate of almost every military compound in the country. It's a place that has hot water where you can wash away the dirt and grime that you've accumulated since your last visit. It has a steam room where the pores of your skin expand to allow grease and grime to pop out, but most of all, it has a little room where an actual massage is offered. For a few more *piasters,* the local currency, you can have a *happy ending.* The total experience will cost the same as two or three dollars in *MPC,* or Military Payment Certificates, the multi-colored funny money used by the military to keep US currency off the black market.

The other universal term is *Round Eyes,* it's used for any woman in country who is not Asian. The term is normally used to refer to a dedicated group of young women who work for the Red Cross and are known as *Donut Dollies.* These ladies run the canteen services in the larger cities where the men can go and have a few minutes or hours of peace and quiet, watch a movie, have some snacks that don't come out of a can, write a letter home and a conversation with a woman who speaks the same language as they do.

For those men who spend their entire tour of duty kicking the brush as *grunts* or Infantrymen, the Donut Dollies come to them. It's not unusual to see a trailer set up with coffee, sodas, donuts, and real, American round-eyed women waiting for a unit coming back to a remote base camp. After an hour or two at the base camp, the women load up on a helicopter and head out.

Donut Dollies are all volunteers. Most are the same age as the men they are visiting, so they have the same tastes in music and current events and can discuss them with the grunts. If time and enemy activity permits, they may pull out a Monopoly game and challenge a couple of guys to a game. They try to make it as pleasant as possible.

My first meeting with a group of three Donut Dollies was when I caught a hop on a C-119 headed to a Province Headquarters in the Mekong Delta near the Cambodian border.

I did not mention why I was going to the same place as them on the ride there. The plane had hardly stopped rolling when a three-quarter-ton truck pulled up to the tailgate as soon as it was lowered. They were quickly hustled off the plane alone with several boxes, which I assumed contained their supplies of donuts, coffee, games, and whatever else they brought with them.

After the truck loaded, I grabbed my small bag and walked to the single building at the edge of the taxi strip that served as flight operations. I was not a part of their group and I did not want to impose on anything they were planning for the men, so I waited to see if I could catch a ride from someone heading toward the province headquarters.

"You that reporter?" I heard someone say.

"I guess that depends on who you ask," I said as I turned toward the voice.

It came from a staff sergeant who was working behind a counter that, like most of the construction in South Viet Nam, was made from 3.5 rocket boxes. The boxes held the rounds for the rocket launcher, commonly known as a bazooka. The old-style anti-tank weapon was being replaced by the Light Anti-tank Weapon or LAW. The LAW was a one-and-done. Each tube was loaded with a round that was sufficient to destroy or disable an armored vehicle or a bunker. The only problem was that if the tube was not destroyed, the VC would pick it up and make a booby trap out of it.

"Crew chief on the bird that brought you here called ahead and said he met you on another flight, and the two of you had a good conversation. Said you were one of the good guys." He reached into his pocket and pulled out a pack of C-ration cigarettes. Each box of Charlie Rats contained a packet with salt, pepper, a roll of toilet paper,a small pack of cigarettes, and a book of matches.

Like the rocket boxes, I soon learned that everything in the military has several uses. Eat C-rations for several days, and you won't need the toilet paper. Need to heat your C-rations? Soak the little roll in bug spray, and it'll burn long enough to heat a large can of rations.

"I wish I could remember, but I talk to a lot of people over here. I'm just happy he gave me his seal of approval."

"Need a ride to the head shed," he asked as he blew a cloud of smoke skyward.

"If it's not a problem."

"I got a couple of grunts hanging around waiting for the freedom bird to take them home so I can let one of them drive you." He walked to the far corner of the room where two men were sleeping, using their duffle bags as pillows. He kicked one of them on the foot, then quickly stepped back.

The man jerked awake, and I could tell from his body language and the way his arms flew out to his side that he was reaching for a weapon. The sergeant knew that would be his reaction, thus his quick movements when he kicked the man.

"Wake up. I need you to take this man to the head shed. You can use my Jeep. It's outside."

The ride to the headquarters took us down a typical unpaved road that was the way to travel in the Delta. Many areas were only accessible by water or air. The few roads had been carved into the earth so long ago that Chinese conquerors probably trod on them centuries before.

The landscape was rice paddies, canals, and, unlike most areas to the east and south of us, mountains. Across the nearby border in Cambodia, I could see the beginning of a mountain range the Americans called The Three Sisters.

When we got to the headquarters, the Donut Dollies were already handing out coffee, sodas, donuts, and, most importantly, smiles and a kind word to the men gathered around them. When I saw the joy they brought to the men, I decided that this was the reason I was here. At first, I wanted to talk to the men who were so close to the border yet could not cross it to chase the enemy, but coffee and donuts were more important.

I waited until the men in line had grabbed a donut and something to drink before I approached one of the women. After introducing myself, I asked the question I knew they had been asked every day since they arrived. Why were they here?

She introduced herself as Katherine Davis from Atlanta, Georgia, and told me to call her Kate.

"I've been asked that question so many times that every time it comes up,

I have a different answer," he pulled a wisp of blonde hair that had escaped from a ponytail tied with a piece of camouflage cloth. "My mother was a nurse in World War Two. She was stationed in England and I grew up on stories about the men she met and helped." She stopped as if recalling those conversations. "I think she still remembers the names of every man she worked with who didn't make it home."

I knew I was talking to a woman who had a story, but I also knew it might be too personal for her to relate it. "Why didn't you go into nursing? Has she made that much of an impact on you?"

"I thought about it, but I didn't think I was that dedicated. This was closer to what I want out of life."

"And what is that?"

She laughed. "I don't know what it is, but right now, I can tell you it's not a house in the suburbs with a white picket fence." She looked around. "Maybe it's a landing zone in a place that nobody ever heard of, and those who have can't wait to forget about it." I got the Donut Dolly smile. "How about you? What's your story?"

"Oh no, this is about you. I thought Donut Dollies disappeared at the end of the Korean War. I didn't even know the Red Cross still had them until I got here, and I think most people back home don't know about you either."

The other woman came up to us. "Kate, they said the chopper will be landing in about ten minutes. We need to wrap it up here." The woman extended her hand. "I'm Linda Statler," she pointed to the name tape on my jacket. "You're a correspondent?"

Kate answered for me. "He's doing a story for the folks back in the world to tell them we're here and what we're doing."

Linda grabbed Kate's hand and pulled her away. "Spell out names right when you do." With a wave she and Kate hopped in the back of the truck that was there to take them to another base to bring some joy to the lives of the men who needed it.

DATELINE: SAIGON, SOUTH VIET NAM

A war zone has its own language. It's made up of slang, acronyms, and local language with an American twist. In South Viet Nam you hear short, slicks, dust off, ets, dros, di di mau, short, figmo and more. The one that is as important to the men as any of the other terms, and most of them don't realize it, is Donut Dolly.

The incredible young women who volunteer as Red Cross workers bring a few minutes of normalcy to the lives of the men who are here. They can be found in most of the larger cities and bases running recreation centers and helping in hospitals, but the most important job they perform is in the field where the men are, and the war surrounds them.

They hop on a helicopter loaded with urns of coffee, boxes of donuts, coolers filled with cold sodas, and a box of board games. Many times, the helicopter has to avoid ground fire to drop them off, but that does not deter the ladies.

A smile, a kind word, and a promise to make sure a hastily written letter home gets mailed is as important to the men as is a resupply of food, water, and ammunition.

Unfortunately, since the ladies go to remote locations where death is all around them, that smile may be the last thing a young soldier remembers.

Chapter Twenty

Many of the leads the correspondents, newspaper and magazine reporters and others who were non-military got came from casual conversations in bars at the various clubs throughout the country. There were members of every military service the Unites States had, and the same thing was true for all the allied nations who supported our efforts in the war scattered throughout the country. Most of the ground troops and their support was stationed in South Viet Nam. There were some serious Air Force assets stationed at the large air bases in Saigon and at a couple of other bases where they launched air support mission that were confined to south of the border with North Viet Nam. The same went for the Navy. They have some aviation assets down in the Delta region that flew support for allied ground forces. We occasionally ran across Air Force and Navy officers at the clubs in Saigon.

Wess and I were at our usual hang-out in Saigon when we were not in the field. The officer's club at the Massachusetts BOQ was the favorite watering hole for most of the men assigned to the Saigon area.

We were talking about everything and nothing when a Navy commander pulled up beside me. "Did I hear you say you went to the University of Georgia?"

I turned to face him. "Go, you hairy dawgs," I said in response. The dog being the name of the football team.

"Hell yes," he said with a southern accent that made *hell* come out with three syllables. He extended his hand. "I'm Fred Holliday, class of '59. How 'bout you?"

I took his hand. "Sean Kelly. I'm a few years behind you, but I'll still buy you a drink." I motioned for the bartender. "And this is Wess."

"You don't have a service tape on your uniform. You some kind of spook? CIA or something?"

"No, nothing that exciting. I'm strictly a civilian." I used the time it took for another round of drinks to be brought to us to explain what Wess and I did, and why we didn't have a military service on our shirts.

"I took a few writing courses at UGA but found out I couldn't spell, so I went into accounting. I could count much better than I could spell. Got a degree in business and found out I couldn't get a job, so I joined the Navy, and now I'm a bean counter for the Navy."

I picked up my glass and touched it to his. "Here's to the good times in Athens." We toasted.

"What kind of stories do you write? Ever do anything on the Navy?"

I detected an opening, so I nodded. "I have, but I'm always looking for something the other guys are not interested in. I try to do the more personal pieces. Stuff that generally wouldn't make the evening television news."

He took his time to let that sink in. "Ever been on a carrier?"

Two more rounds and an agreement to meet him at TSN the following morning, and I left the club with an invitation to fly out to an aircraft carrier as the guest of a fellow UGA graduate.

We met the next morning, and a twin-engine Navy plane was sitting on the tarmac at the TSN airport. "That's called a COD-3. People think all we have on carriers are jets, but we have fixed wings and helicopters as well. Bet you didn't know that."

He was right. I had always just assumed that what we saw on the flight deck was all they had. I knew this was going to be an eye-opening experience for me.

We waited while the pilot and crew of the aircraft did their flight plan and other paperwork. We knew when they finished, they would motion for us to come to the plane. The crew did a walk-around behind the pilot after he did his ground inspection before getting inside to continue his pre-flight inside the aircraft.

There were several sailors who were standing beside their sea bags, waiting for the word to get aboard. The Navy is the most rank-conscious of all the services, so the enlisted men waited well away from the Commander, Wess, and me. Finally, we saw the crew chief from the COD-3 wave for us to come to the plane.

Wess had his camera gear in a large case along with a small bag with clothes and other personal items in it. Fred told us it might be a few days before we could get a flight back to Saigon, depending on the ship's mission, so we packed accordingly. He had been on R&R in Australia, so he had a week's worth of clothes and a lifetime worth of memories that he was taking back to the ship.

We loaded onto the plane, and the crew chief stood up and gave us the normal safety briefing. At least, I thought it was normal until they mentioned the tail hook part. I looked at Wess, and he had the same expression as mine. Tailhook? As in landing on the deck and being grabbed by a cable to keep us from running off the end of the ship and dropping into the South China Sea? That kind of tail hook?

It was too late to change my mind, so I was literally along for the ride.

The pilot knew what he was doing, and when the hook on the plane grabbed the arresting cable, we slammed forward, and the plane rolled to a stop.

The door opened, and the ramp was lowered so we could get out and on the deck. Fred said as soon as we stepped on the deck, we were to turn to the flag and offer a salute. He was a little fuzzy on the rules since we were not military, but said it would make the captain of the ship happy if he saw us do it. Outside on the deck, it looked like a roll of lifesavers. Men in shirts and helmets that looked like half of it was missing in a variety of colors were doing a multitude of jobs. It didn't take long to realize each color was specialized. I didn't know what they meant, but I knew I would soon find out.

Fred quickly pulled us to the side, and we watched as a swarm of colors prepared a jet for take-off. A crewman approached with three sets of ear protectors and handed one to each of us. The heavy protectors muffled most of the sound until the pilot revved his engine to full blast, and he and this aircraft were launched off the deck. As soon as that one was off the end of the carrier, another one was moved into position to follow it into the sky beyond the ship. Before it could be hooked up and prepared to launch, Fred told us to follow him.

He led us into the depths of the carrier. We made our way down passageways that were so narrow that if two people tried to pass, one had to turn sideways. Once, Wess had to place his camera case on the floor, or deck as we were told it was called, to allow the person to pass. He could not hold it and still give the man room. Finally, we were led into a large room that looked like a small movie theater.

"This is the ready room for one of the squadrons. I asked the ship's XO to meet us here. I want to let him know who you are and why you're here."

Wess placed his camera case on a chair and pulled one of the cameras from it. "Okay to take pictures?"

"You can now, but if you're here when they're getting a mission brief, no cameras are allowed."

The room had several rows of chairs that looked like they came from a nice movie house. Each had a heavy brown cloth-covered seat and back and wood arms with a flat surface. There was a large whiteboard at the head of the room with the squadron's number and name on it. Since it was a permanent part of the board, I assumed if there was more than one squadron on the ship, each had a similar room. Around the room, on the walls, were plaques indicating places the ship had been. According to them, it had been almost any place on the planet that had a port. I was looking at one from Subic Bay in the Philippines when another man entered the room.

"Gentlemen," he said in a voice that was more often used to call "attention" to a room full of sailors.

Fred turned at the sound. "Commander, this is Sean Kelly and Wess Price. They want to do a story on the crew."

He came to me first. "I'm Commander Roger Digby. I'm the Executive Officer. You'll meet the old man shortly. He's in his stateroom right now. Have a seat, and let's talk."

For the next thirty minutes, we told him in general terms what we wanted to do, who it was for, and what we had done in the past. He only took ten minutes to tell us what we could and could not do. When he finished, he looked at Fred. "Take them to one of the empty ward rooms. While they're onboard, they're our guests and your responsibility. If you need anything, let me know." He looked at us. "Gentlemen," he said again and left the room.

"What do you want to do first?" Fred asked after he showed us to the wardroom. It was one that had been occupied by one of the ship's officers who was no longer there. I did not ask what happened to him.

"I'd like to start at square one. Since this is an aircraft carrier, I'd like to see what goes into a typical mission from beginning to end."

"That would start with the operations briefing in the ready room. There should be another one in an hour or so. In the meantime, let me take you around the ship."

An aircraft is like a floating city of five thousand people. It has everything you would find in a city of that size. We were taken to places I never thought about that were floating around in the oceans. It had a fully functioning hospital with doctors, nurses, and all types of medical specialists. Over a hundred cooks and bakers worked around the clock to prepare and serve four meals each day. Meals were breakfast, lunch, dinner, and what they called mid-rats. A meal was served at midnight for the men who worked the midnight shift. I had been on more operations on the ground than I want to remember, and most of them required me to open a can of C-rations. No such thing here. We arrived midway between the breakfast and lunch meals, and as we walked through the kitchen area where the food was being prepared, I noticed that steaks, baked potatoes, and fresh baked rolls were on an upcoming menu.

Fred explained the ship was completely self-sustaining while at sea. It would be refueled and resupplied with ammunition, stores, and fresh food at regular intervals. We could not come up with a skill or a situation that they were not prepared to handle.

I'm not sure how many decks we walked through on the journey, but finally, Fred looked at his watch and said it was time for the mission brief, so he took us to an elevator that carried us to the right deck for the ready room.

The room was filled with rows of seats set in twos. One would be for the pilot, and next to him would be his co-pilot. The first two seats at the head of the room were empty. Fred pointed to them. "The old man or ship's captain will take one, and the XO will take the other."

Each seat was covered in a brown cloth or leather fabric and had a fold-down armrest that served as a table for the man to use when making notes or referring to their maps and charts. The seats were soon filled with men who looked like they would be just at home in corporate America, except for the way they were dressed and the shoulder holsters they wore. All were young, athletic-looking, clean-shaven, and they joked with each other as they took seats and pulled out notebooks and folders. We stood at the rear of the room and, except for a few glances, were generally ignored.

An officer stood by the door and called the room to attention when two officers entered. "Take your seats." A man wearing a set of silver eagles on his collar said as he moved to the front of the room. The "old man" and his XO were here, and the briefing would start.

A Lieutenant Commander pulled down a map that was rolled up over the whiteboard. He looked at Fred. "Commander Holliday, can I proceed with the briefing with our guests in the room?"

"Roger that. They are both cleared." He pointed to me. "This is Sean Kelly. He's a correspondent and wants to do a story on our operations and the man next to him is Wess Price, his photographer."

The briefing officer nodded in agreement and began his briefing of the upcoming operation.

"Here is the map of Package Six, our normal area of operations. The Air Force has had several Thud sorties in adjacent areas today, and we're just now getting damage reports." He took a long pointer with a red tip and tapped it against the map. "We think they have moved some SAM sites to this area closer to Hanoi. As usual, the people who plan these strikes don't know their ass from a hot rock, so we're still restricted to the ten-mile zone around the city." He tapped several more places and told the men to look at the maps they had in their folders. Each one was a known heavy weapons site on the ground. He asked for questions and answered a few, then dismissed the men to prepare for the mission.

I wanted to talk to some of them, but I knew this was not the time. I'd do that when they came back. In the meantime, Fred said he'd take us up to the flight deck to watch the crews prepare for the flight.

On the deck, all I saw was jet aircraft. I asked about that, and Fred said everything else was below deck. Another area I wanted to see.

The first thing I wanted to know was the various color coding of the men on the deck. "Each color represents a particular job. It's so noisy during flight operations that colors and hand and arm signals are the safest way to get things done." He pointed to a group of men in red, wheeling large bombs across the deck. "Red is the ordinance guys. They handle the bomb, and they are also the crash and salvage crew guys."

I saw one guy in green walking around the first plane in the row. "Green is maintenance personnel. They make sure everything is where it's supposed to be on the plane. On other planes, they load cargo, operate the ground support equipment, and make sure the catapult and arresting gear is operational and properly attached."

Each man went through a series of waves, circles, flaps, and other movements with his hands and arms as they went about their jobs.

We continued to watch, and Wess took photos of the activities until Fred took me by the arm and led me to the side. He pulled the covering from my right ear and yelled. "I want to take you to the bridge. Follow me."

High above the flight deck is the nerve center of the body. This is where the ship's commanding officer runs the city below him. To say it was a beehive of activity is to shortchange the men working there. Radio operators were in contact with units and individuals all over the ship and in other locations. Radar screens scanned the sea and the air. The weather was updated on another screen. After a few minutes, Commander Digby came to me. "Are you being well cared for?"

I assured him we were.

"We don't have much time for anything other than the care and feeding of the ship's mission for the most part. I'm sure Commander Holliday can fill you in on anything you want to know. We've got a mission about to go, so you'll see that, and you can do it from here if you want to."

How many times will I get the opportunity to see a combat mission of A-4 Skyhawks take off from an aircraft carrier? I jumped at the chance. Wess asked if he could get some shots from the deck and was told he could. We were ready for something I had wanted to do for a long time.

I watched the pilots come out,walk across the deck, and climb into their aircraft. Each one had the pilot's name, nickname, and call sign stenciled just under the canopy. After the pilot was assisted into his seat, it was time for the colored shirts to do their part. Everything was checked. When the pilot was given the signal, he fired up the engines and taxied to a position where the catapult attachment was secured to the front gear. Salutes were exchanged with one last man called the Shooter, who gave the signal for the steam-powered catapult to launch the plane forward at over one hundred miles an hour so it cleared the deck. If all went well, in less than five seconds, the plane was in the air headed for North Viet Nam and fate.

I watched several other launches and then Fred said they all look alike. Once you've seen one, you've seen all there is to see, so he suggested we try to find some of the crew who were not working, so I could talk to them.

The ship had a gym, so we went there. A large space was filled with treadmills, stair machines, weight racks, and other workout equipment, and most of it was in use. Several men were working up a serious sweat on the machines, and one man who looked like he spent every free hour here was lifting weights with arms as big as my thighs. When he stopped to wipe sweat from his face, I walked up to him.

"This your first day in a gym?"

He didn't know if he should laugh or not, so Commander Holliday came to his rescue. "These gentlemen are here to see what we do and how we do it. They want to talk to some of the crew, so if you want, you can talk to them."

"No problem, sir. He just kinda threw me a curve when he asked me that." He had a mid-west accent.

"How long have you been in the Navy," I asked as Wess took a photo of him.

"Bout three years now. I re-enlisted to get on a carrier. I figure if I'm gonna be at sea, I want to be as comfortable as I can."

"You comfortable here?"

"Oh, yes, sir. I was on a much smaller ship for two years, and this is like…I don't know… like being in a big city."

We continued to talk for a bit and then left the gym. As Holliday took us around the ship, I realized just how much it really was like a city. Need a post office? Barbershop? Clothing store? Candy bar? Pack of gum? Steak dinner? Plumber, electrician, radio station? It's all here someplace in the depths of the carrier.

"I want to take you to the operations center. You'll be able to monitor the radio traffic from the mission." We were taken to a room, and as soon as we entered, the voices of the pilots on the mission filled the air. The voices had to compete with static, which made it hard to filter them out for the first few minutes until I got used to it.

"We're ten out from target."

"That's the flight leader. His call sign is Sparky. Each pilot has a nickname as his call sign. They pick their own, but sometimes the others in the squadron do it for them."

"Roger, Sparky. I'm hot and ready for those little bastards today."

"Save some for me, Q Ball."

"I think they'll be enough for everybody. Just keep on a swivel."

"I just took a hit from the ground. They've moved some of the anti-aircraft guns."

"You okay, Smoker?"

"Roger, Sparky. Everything's still working, and I'm dropping down to ruin his day."

"Kick his ass, Smoker…"

Before he could finish, we heard the flight leader break in.

"Bear, you got a Mig on your ass. Break left, and I'll come under him."

Everyone in the room was holding their breath.

"Another one at three o'clock. I'll take care of him."

"Help me out, Sparky."

"Fuck me, Sparky. You put one up his ass. Nothing left of him or his plane."

"I'm taking heavy ground fire, and I got a problem."

"You okay, Smoker?"

"Not good, Sparky. I'm losing hydraulics."

"Head for the coast Smoker, I'll follow."

Holliday touched my arm. "If he can make it to the coast and has to bail out, we stand a good chance of recovery. They'll launch a mission now, just in case."

"Not good, Sparky. Ain't gonna make it. I'm punching out."

Without asking, I knew he was saying he was not going to make it to the open ocean and was ejecting over what was certainly hostile territory beneath him.

"We'll cover you, Smoker."

"God bless."

"Rescue has been launched already."

The other pilots offered encouragement to their downed shipmate.

"Once he's on the ground, he can communicate with the planes and us with his hand-held radio. All the pilots carry one. We should hear him shortly."

It seemed like an hour before we heard a voice that was soft, as if the speaker was whispering.

"I'm on the ground outside a village. I know they saw me coming down, so I'm heading east."

"Roger, Smoker. I'm making a gun run on the villagers. That should give them something to think about. Bear and Q Ball are circling your location."

"How long will they stay in the area now?" I asked.

"This is the tricky part. If there is a military unit around, they're already headed to the village. They've radioed back and they'll probably be Migs in the air by now, so the others in the mission will have their hands full, and there's the question of fuel."

We, like everyone else in the room, were glued to the radios for the remainder of the day. The downed pilot managed to keep moving and reported hearing Vietnamese voices once. Just prior to darkness, the remaining planes had to return to the carrier due to being low on fuel.

"Smoker, we're breaking off now. Hunker down, and we'll be back."

"Tango Yankee, Sparky," he said, using the code for "Thank you."

Smoker made several reports during the night and at first light, we were back in the operations center to monitor the action.

Holliday was already there. He pointed to a large coffee urn. "Grab a cup if there's any left. The team's been working all night."

He waited until Wess and I had a mug in our hands. "He reported once in the night, that he was still moving in a southeasterly direction and he was near a canal." Holliday pointed to a large map. "We think he's about here. That'll make him seven miles from the coast and right in the middle of some heavy anti-aircraft locations."

"Not good," Wess said.

"No shit. If we don't get to him soon, we may not be able to affect a rescue. We've got a helicopter as close to him as we can until we know his exact location. That's his best hope now."

Ten minutes after we arrived, we heard the static-filled voice of the man we now knew as Smoker.

"I hear dogs."

The operations officer had been monitoring his radio and talking to him during the night. He turned to Holliday when we entered. "He said he thought he broke his arm when he ejected. He's got some cuts and bruises from the jungle, but he's still moving, which is good."

The radio crackled again. "The bastards are almost on me. I can see them about twenty meters away….tell my parents I was captured alive…" His voice disappeared as he continued to hold the "talk" button on his radio. We heard the excited voices of the Vietnamese and the barking of dogs, and then everything went silent.

It was like a dark cloud descended on the room. I saw one young man cross himself and mouth a silent prayer. I think we all did.

We stayed on the carrier for two more days and then caught a flight back to Saigon that was taking a group of sailors who were going to catch R&R flights.

After the last broadcast we listened to, nothing else was heard from the downed pilot. He was the fifth pilot who went on a mission from that ship and did not return. Of the five missing pilots, three had been seen ejecting from their crippled aircraft. The other two evidently rode their planes into the ground.

I had heard stories of the hardships and torture the VC and NVA did to captured Americans. It was something I did not even want to think about. Somehow I knew I owed it to the people who read my columns to tell them what happened to Smoker.

DATELINE: SAIGON, SOUTH VIET NAM

Q. Ball

Sparky

Smokey

Call signs of some of the pilots I had the pleasure of meeting on board a US Navy aircraft carrier recently. I met them when I joined them in their ready room, where they got a briefing on their next mission. It was to fly over North Viet Nam, knock out some anti-aircraft radar and gun position, dodge or engage Russian Mig fighter planes, not get shot down and return to do it again the next day. For the men who did this, it was a calling not unlike that of a minister or a doctor. It was something they did because they were good at it. The inherent danger they faced every time they climbed into the cockpit was the cost of doing what they enjoyed.

Enjoyed? How can you enjoy screaming through the air at speeds you will never reach on the ground, dodge sites on the ground that are tracking you with radar in order to shoot you down, engage Russian Migs in a dog fight, just to bomb a bridge or a railroad yard? I can't explain it, and most of the men I met couldn't either.

I was there when the one thing they feared happened. One of the men was shot down. We monitored the radio as he fought off the Migs and the anti-aircraft fire until a Mig slipped up behind him and crippled his plane to the point he was forced to eject.

The other pilots had a single mission now. Protect their fellow pilot, suppress the ground fire, keep the enemy away until he could be rescued. No rescue meant he was destined to become a prisoner of war or POW. Perhaps that was feared more than being killed in action or a KIA.

He made it to the ground. We listened to him all night as he slipped through the countryside, pursued by local villagers and militia. At daybreak, he was seven miles from a possible rescue location. For him, that was the same distance the Earth was from Mars.

His last broadcast said he heard dogs, and he could hear voices less than one hundred meters away. His final words were to tell his parents he was captured alive.

Was he?

Only time will tell.

Chapter Twenty-One

Early in the conflict, both sides realized we were not fighting World War III or even Part Two of World War II. It was a new type of war that had its own rules, or lack thereof. One of the most unique of these rules became known as the Tet Offensive Cease Fire for the Viet Cong and North Vietnamese and the corresponding Christmas Cease Fire for the Americans. Tet was a time when families gathered to celebrate making another year without getting bombed, shot, napalmed, gassed, or otherwise killed or maimed by the Americans. The Americans did the same at Christmas time to celebrate the time-honored tradition of exchanging gifts, a too-big dinner, and a tree if one was lucky enough to find one.

The Red Cross and other civic and community organizations soothed their collective consciousness by shipping massive amounts of packages to Viet Nam to be distributed to the men and women who could not be home during the festivities. Even Bob Hope got in on the act. His annual Christmas Tour was a thing to behold. The man who had been entertaining troops since WWII knew how to pitch a party. He'd surround himself on stage with a bevy of young women, most of whom the men in the audience had never heard of, but it didn't matter. They were "round-eyes," and they all looked like the girl next door or the girl they wished lived next door. He had one or two recognizable headliners. He told a few jokes that never made it to the sterilized version of his shows that appeared after the holidays on television back in the world and always called a few men up on the stage to dance with one of the women. A few times, the man selected never made it home, and the last thing his family saw was him twisting his way across the stage with a blonde in go-go boots.

It was a week prior to my first Christmas in country, and everything was beginning to wind down in anticipation of the upcoming holiday. The Americans got a holiday first, and the treatment the Viet Cong and North Vietnamese got during Tet in February depended on how nice they played in December. On the 20th of December I got a small package from my mother back in Florida. She sent me a couple of cassettes of music I liked that I had mentioned once in a letter. She also sent me a bottle of sauce from a small barbecue stand that my family had been going to since I was a kid. I had asked for a bottle in the past and after a month of adding it to meals both in the field and in Saigon, I started doling it out almost by the drop, it was so good. She wrapped it in newspaper, put it in a sock, and then packed it in a small box of cotton, which she put in the larger box. I had to admire her ingenuity as it came in completely unscratched after having been tossed, thrown, dropped, probably run over a couple of times and then airlifted halfway around the world.

Wess and I were in the office alone. "You got plans for Christmas? I don't think there's going to be much we can do around here." He asked as he poured himself a cup of coffee from the pot we always kept brewing.

"I thought I might find a unit to visit. Do some hometown news releases for the guys. Christmas in Combat. That sort of thing. Why? You got something special going on?"

I knew Wess had been spending a lot of time recently with a woman who worked as an interpreter at a government office we sometimes had to visit. Her mother was Vietnamese, and her father was a French military officer who had been in the country in the early 1950s. I never asked, and I don't know if Wess or even the girl knew if he had been a Legionnaire and had been killed or captured at Dien Bien Phu.

"The Vietnamese don't celebrate like we do, but with most of the offices shutting down for the day or at least cutting back, I thought I might spend some time with Bae." He took a drink from the ultra-strong coffee we made and looked at me. "You really gonna spend Christmas with the grunts?"

On Christmas Eve morning, I went to the helipad at Tan Son Nhat and caught a bird headed for Da Lat. The city boasted being one of the highest elevations in the country and, on occasion, even had snow on the mountains in the vicinity. I thought since it was Christmas, I might as well get as close as I could to cold weather and snow. Da Lat was my choice.

We landed at a small airfield, and I hopped down from the Huey as the pilot cut the power and the blades slowly wound down. A Specialist stood nearby with a large red fire extinguisher mounted on a platform between two bicycle wheels. He was ready to put out any fire started by the helicopter as he casually held a hose in one hand and a lighted cigarette in the other. As I ducked down to get under the still slowly spinning blades, I remembered a sign I saw at the airfield in Can Tho. It said: ATTENTION ALL FLIGHT PERSONNEL. REMEMBER THE FIRST RULE OF FLIGHT IS NO SMOKING 24 HOURS PRIOR TO FLIGHT AND NO DRINKING WITHIN 50 FEET OF THE AIRCRAFT. HAVE A SAFE FLIGHT.

I had a small AWOL bag with my shaving gear and a change of clothes with me, so with that in hand, I made my way to the flight operations center housed in a small Quonset hut at the end of the taxi strip. It served as an operations center, waiting lounge, and passenger counter for anyone passing through, coming or going.

Once inside, I asked a soldier much too old to still be a Private First Class if there was any transportation headed to any of the field units in the area. He sat on a stool and was reading a well-worn men's magazine. On his right sleeve was a patch indicating he had been in combat. I recognized the patch as the 7th Infantry Division, a unit that had been in Korea during the fighting there in the early fifties but was not in Viet Nam. He also wore a Combat Infantryman's Badge and a Senior Parachute Badge. My guess was that someplace along the way, he had been on the wrong end of a court martial and had lost whatever rank he had acquired in the past fifteen years.

He pointed to a jeep and said, "Check with Sergeant Ball. He's headed out in a few minutes with a dispatch that came in on the chopper you were on."

Sergeant Ball hardly spoke as we drove the five miles to the small company-size

firebase where a unit was doing a "stand-down" in conjunction with the

Christmas truce. In a stand down, the men who were fortunate enough to be brought in from the field got hot showers, fresh uniforms, mail, hot chow, and a chance to rest and sleep in something other than a hole in the ground. Many used the time to go into local villages and catch up on their lack of sexual activities. Unfortunately, many came back with more than a pleasant memory of their time with the local "boom-boom" girls. The company medics were used to treating a variety of sexually transmitted diseases after a fellow soldier spent a night in the village.

I met the Company Commander, introduced myself, and told him why I was there and what I wanted to do. He had no objections and suggested my first interview should be with his First Sergeant, a veteran of both WWII and Korea. I did the interview and took a few pictures of him. "I'm having a formal retreat ceremony tonight. You might want to see it. Ain't no other unit in the field gonna have all their men in one formation."

I took him up on the offer, and I watched the men gather into a company formation for the retreat ceremony while the flag was hauled down from the flagpole. As the final notes from the recording of the bugle spilled from the loudspeaker, he dismissed the company and invited me to his hooch for a drink.

For the next few hours, we drank and talked with the other senior NCOs who drifted into his room for some Christmas cheer and to wish him a Merry Christmas. One of the topics of conversation was a man they called Chef Bill. He was the Mess Sergeant and was almost worshiped by the men for the way he cooked. He would be in charge of the Christmas meal and everyone was looking forward to it. By eleven, I was feeling no pain, and he directed me to a cot in a small room in the building that housed the medics, the supply room, and served as the armory. By the time I hit the bed, I couldn't have cared less if it held a locomotive repair shop. I was asleep before I turned over the first time.

The next morning was Christmas Day, and unless the man had to be up for guard duty, KP, or some other requirement, no one was required to be up and around. There was no morning formation, no reveille, and no other reason to get out of bed. I staggered, somewhat hungover, into the mess hall a little after nine, and was immediately taken back to my childhood as I was consumed with the smell of roasting turkeys, dressing, and the spicy memory of pumpkin pie, and fresh bread baking in ovens. I immediately checked my watch to see how long it would be before we would be served a home-style Christmas Dinner.

At noon, Chef Bill had a detail place tables on the outside of the mess hall. The room he used was big enough to cook but did not have enough room to feed everyone at the same time. He knew if he tried to do it in shifts, he'd have a riot on his hands by those trying to be first in line, knowing if they were in the second feeding, they might not get anything but leftovers. In the next sixty minutes, the company was in a line stretching around the tables and extending across the open area that served as the place for company formations.

Half the company had been fed when I got in line. I spoke to several of the men in front of me, explained who I was and why I was there and pulled out a notebook and wrote their information so I could do the hometown news releases once I got back to Saigon. I had been in line for a few minutes when I saw the First Sergeant making his way down the formation, speaking to each man, wishing them a Merry Christmas, and inquiring about home and anything else they wanted to talk about on this special day.

I wanted to wait until the mean was finished and then talk to Chef Bill and find out how he managed to work miracles with Army chow.

Even in the higher elevation of Da Lat, Christmas in Viet Nam was not like Christmas in any place in the United States. The weather may be warmer in Hawaii, colder in Alaska, or the same in Florida, but it was not home. It was ten thousand miles and a lifetime away. It was a place most of the young men in the chow line ahead of me had never heard of until they got a notice from their draft board that their number had been called and they were about to be sent away to war.

While the men moved up and down the feeding line, Chef Bill watched over them like a mother hen. This was his gift to the men in the unit and he wanted it to be perfect. In honor of the occasion, he wore his normal whites that cooks wore, but in addition, he wore a tall white chef's hat.

Some of the men in line wore their fatigue jackets, some had on the dark colored tee shirts issued to them. A few wore flak jackets and carried their rifles slung over their shoulders as they balanced the metal trays being filled with their Christmas dinner. There were about ten men in front of me in line between me and the stack of trays where the food line began. I was talking to a young man from Kentucky when the first shot rang out.

Men used to being shot at respond in different ways. Some hit the ground immediately, those with weapons unslung them and turned towards where they thought the shot came from. At least three men simply ducked down and continued down the line as if nothing had happened.

I heard someone yell, "Medic," and I knew that we had a problem. A small group of men gathered in a knot around the end of the serving line. Trays filled with food littered the ground where they had either dropped them when they heard the shot, or they had been discarded in order to assist a wounded comrade. As I got near, I could hear something that was not what I expected in a situation like this.

I saw a person on the ground and at least one medic bending over him. Others in a circle around him were pointing. A few had pulled cameras out of their pockets or from the spare ammo pouch, and many of them carried small cameras stuffed in the plastic bags from radio batteries. I heard someone call out, "Holy shit. You ain't gonna believe who's been wounded." After that, you could hear a peal of laughter move through the crowd. Since there was only one shot, it was assumed the shooter had done a "hit and get." He'd fire one shot and haul ass before anyone could determine where he was shooting from.

I realized what was causing the laughter and the need to take photos when I eased my way through the ever-increasing thong gathered around Chef Bill, who lay on the ground and swore at his fellow Soldiers while his whites turned red with the blood from his wound.

Chef Bill was overseeing the meal he had prepared for his men. He made sure they had a meal closely resembling one they remembered from home when a sniper fired one shot. Chef Bill was the unlucky one who was shot, and for the rest of his life, he will be able to tell the story of how he was standing in the chow line on Christmas Day in Viet Nam and was shot…in the right cheek of his ass.

DATELINE: SAIGON, SOUTH VIET NAM

Medal of Honor: Above and Beyond

Purple Heart: Below and Behind

If a person is not good with names, the military service is something they should consider as a life's work. Everyone wears a name tape or name tag, so you always know who you're talking to. Every uniform has an indication of rank, so you know if the person is Sergeant Smith or Captain Smith. If they are in a uniform other than fatigues or a duty uniform, they probably have a rack of ribbons. The ribbons are a living document of where they have been and what they did while they were there.

In Viet Nam, everyone gets several of the same medals. They are called "I was there" or "I was alive in '65." Do something other than what is expected of you, and you'll probably get an award or a "hero button" for that. There are numerous medals and awards for achievement: doing a better job than was expected of you. Next at the top of the ribbon rack you'll find those ribbons indicating the wearer received some recognition for a heroic act.

Mixed in with the "'atta boy" and the "I was there" is one that most people avoid. It's called the Zag Zig Badge or the VC Sharpshooter Badge. Its official designation is the Purple Heart. All you have to do to earn one is get wounded or killed. That's why it's not a popular decoration.

I have been on operations where several people earned the Purple Heart, some by getting wounded and some by making the ultimate sacrifice. Recently, I was in a place where I nor anyone else ever thought about earning the Purple Heart.

An outdoor chow line.

On Christmas Day.

I heard the shot ring out, and like many of the other men in the chow line, I immediately ducked and looked to see if I could find the shooter and to see if anyone had been hit. It only took seconds to know that someone had been hit. A crowd was gathered around a soldier who was on the ground, surrounded by the Christmas dinner prepared by the man they called Chef Bill. In the chow line they were holding metal trays filled with turkey, dressing, cranberry sauce, and anything else on the chow line.

Mixed with the calls for a medic was the beginning of a ripple of laughter. Several men had pulled small cameras from pockets and ammo pouches and were taking pictures of their comrade who lay on the ground in pain. Chef Bill, one of the most beloved men in the unit had been shot by a sniper.

On Christmas Day.

In the chow line.

In the right cheek of his ass.

Funny to everyone but him.

Chapter Twenty-Two

L ife in a war zone is a full-time job. There are no forty-hour weeks with Saturday and Sunday off. No overtime pay. No vacation. No accumulated sick days off. No calling in because you slept late and would be in later. For most of the military who were in South Viet Nam, the workday began as soon as their foot touched the ground as they were getting off the plane that brought them here. That day ended when their freedom bird's wheels broke the ground, and they were safely on their way back to the world.

If you were a soldier or a marine in the field, you sometimes went on operations that lasted for up to a month. During that time, you may be able to catch a few hours of sleep if you are lucky. Most of the time you took power naps of fifteen or twenty minutes. Just enough to recharge your batteries so you could push on. Once the operation was over, you'd come back to your base camp and get a few days off to rest and catch up. Even then, you may be called on to pull a variety of details from cleaning equipment to pulling guard duty. Then it was back humping out in Indian Territory, as anything beyond the security of your perimeter was called.

For a few lucky ones who were assigned to major headquarters, they sometimes got a half day off on Sunday. If you chose to attend a religious service, you traded that for your half day off. An afternoon off was usually spent in a nearby village, drinking, visiting a steam and cream, or with a lady of negotiable affection you met in a bar.

I was lucky. I made my own schedule, and I took a day off on occasion. Most of the time, it was not so much a day off, but one when I was in Saigon, and I could catch up on missed dispatches and columns. I usually wrote one or two in advance so if I was not in the office, Wess or one of the others who shared the office with us could send it to Nielsen News Network, my boss back in the United States.

Several times since meeting and…what…falling in love with Carmen, we had managed to get a day off at the same time. When we did, we tried to take full advantage of it. We'd have dinner the night before, spend the night at her house, and try to come up with something to do during the day. We went to the Saigon Zoo once and I was amazed to see the number and type of animals they had. Animals we take for granted in the United States were on display. I guess if you've never seen a goat or a lamb, the zoo is a place to see one.

I finished up at the office, wrote a second column, put it away in case Wess needed to send it out for me, and told Nguyen and Clayton Stanley that I would be gone for the next two days. Carmen had the same time off, so we planned to do something together. What that "something" was remained to be determined.

I got to her house around noon, and Mai already had lunch prepared for us. She made a trip to the local market each day that Carmen was home to pick up fresh fruit, vegetables, and sometimes fish. Carmen had forbidden her to purchase red meat at the market. It was not unusual to almost become friends with a large hunk of some kind of unknown meat if you went to the market each day. The meat hung in the same place, sometimes covered with flies until there was nothing left.

Fish were brought in every day, so they did not stay long. The prawns were especially good that Mai purchased and served to us on occasion.

After a light lunch, Carmen suggested that we have a drink on the terrace of her villa. She lived in a house that had, many years in the past, been a French dignitaries residence. The State Department leased several of them throughout the city for their employees. Other US government agencies did the same for their higher-ranking or more important employees. I never asked what Carmen did for State, but the fact that she had the villa spoke for itself.

"I would have liked to have seen the city before the war. It must have been beautiful." She said.

"I think you would have had to time it precisely between the end of World War Two and the beginning of the French's war with the Viet Minh."

"Most of the French action took place far north of here, but you're right. Timing is everything in life. Don't you agree?"

My getting a job as a journalist. Getting assigned to South Viet Nam. Meeting Carmen. Good timing or fate? Whatever it was, I couldn't have asked for more, I didn't say it aloud, but I certainly thought it.

"I do, but I think we have to nudge it a little bit on occasion."

Without speaking, she stood, took my hand, and led me inside to her bedroom. The timing was perfect.

It was almost nightfall when we finally left the bedroom, showered together, and dressed to go out to dinner.

We went to a French restaurant that she knew about through some of her friends at State. The meal was excellent and I was amazed, as I so often am with her, when she ordered in French. I knew she spoke Spanish, Vietnamese and now I added French. The lady was amazing.

"Carmen, are you taking an evening off?" A man asked as he and a very attractive Caucasian woman stopped at our table.

Carmen placed her napkin on the table. "Jack, this is my friend Sean. He's a correspondent." She turned to me. "Jack works where I do." That was enough explanation and introduction for either of us.

Jack extended his hand. "Glad to meet you, Sean. You freelance or work for a network?"

I stood to shake his hand. I remembered that my dad said a man never shakes hands while seated. "I work for a syndicate. I do a weekly column that has a fairly wide distribution."

"Impressive. Do say something nice about Carmen sometime." He and his un-introduced companion turned and left our table.

"I guess I'll have to rewrite my next column. I have to say something nice about you now." I scratched my head. "Let me see…what can I say? She's beautiful. Multi-lingual. Has an armed guard with a shotgun in front of her house and a maid that can fix a mean Gin and Tonic?"

"How about if we skip the Carmen expose and figure out what to do with the rest of the night."

"Do I get a vote? If so, I have a great idea."

"I can imagine what that is, and you may get your chance, but first let's do something we haven't done before."

"Like what?"

"I want to go to the cinema."

The cinema was what the Vietnamese called a movie. There were several cinemas or movie houses throughout the city and I had been to one once with Wess. We saw a western with John Wayne in it. His voice was overdubbed in Vietnamese. Believe me, you haven't lived until you've seen the Duke speaking Vietnamese.

"I saw a marquee advertising *Bonnie and Clyde* when I was coming through the city a couple of days ago. It's supposed to be in English with Vietnamese subtitles, so at least we can watch it without having to read the dialog."

Thirty minutes later, we were in the lobby of a cinema in downtown Saigon that, with few exceptions, looked like a lobby in any theater in the United States. They even had a popcorn machine.

We watched the movie, and when Bonnie and Clyde got their reward by being shot to shit by the good guys, the theater erupted with applause and cheers. I couldn't read the subtitles, but I think they may have indicated the couple was from Hanoi.

We left the theater and waited outside for a taxi. In Saigon there are numerous ways of getting from one place to another. Use your own transportation, catch a motor scooter or man-peddled pedicab, or take a real taxi. Most of the taxis were ancient French Citrons left over from when they were a status symbol for their owners.

I hailed a taxi, and it pulled to the curb. I knew Carmen's address and could pronounce it in Vietnamese, so after helping Carmen in, I climbed in, leaned over the seat, and told him where we wanted to go.

It was approaching the self-imposed curfew that most of the residents respected. Traffic was not a thick as it was when we arrived at the cinema and there were more motorcycles on the streets.

The big cities in South Viet Nam, and especially Saigon, are the most crime-free cities in the world. Anything from purse snatching to murder is blamed on the Viet Cong. There are no criminals in the country.

Five minutes into the ride, Carmen gave me a concerned look. "This is not the way to my house."

Before I could say anything, she spoke up. I couldn't keep up with what she was saying to the driver, but I got the drift. She was telling him he was not going in the right direction.

When he ignored her, I knew we were on the edge of being in deep shit. I reached behind my jacket and pulled out the snub-nose .38 revolver I kept in a holster in the small of my back. I placed it against the head of the driver. "*Dung lai. Dung lai. Ba ya.* Stop now."

Before he pulled to the curb, I saw two men on a motor scooter bearing down on my side of the car. There was no doubt who they were and what they wanted. The young men on motor scooters and motorcycles who did the robbing and killing in Saigon are called Cowboys, and we had two approaching from my side and two more on Carmen's side.

I had just enough time to take a hard swing at the driver's head with my pistol. It did the job, and I scrambled over the seat, opened his door, and shoved him out and onto the street.

"Get down. I'll try to get us out of here." I yelled to Carmen as I put the old car in gear and hoped it had sufficient power to get us away from the two sets of Cowboys.

When I turned back, the two on the passenger's side of the car had stopped, and one of the men was pointing a weapon at me. I still had my pistol in my hand, and for the first time since coming to this war zone, I fired it. The small revolver had a gentle kick, so the second round was on target. The double tap caught the Cowboy in the center of his chest, and he fell back toward his companion, who was holding the motorcycle steady. Before I could hit the gas to leave, I heard two similar shots fired from behind me.

I quickly looked to my left and saw a man fall. Two more shots caught the driver of the motorcycle, and he crumbled to the side, and the machine fell on him.

"Get us out of here," Carmen yelled from the back seat. She did not have to tell me twice.

Carmen climbed over the seat and sat beside me in the front passenger's seat. She was holding a small automatic pistol in her hand.

After getting directions from her to get us on the right street, I pulled up in front of her villa. As usual, the guard with the shotgun opened the gate and let us in.

We got out of the car, and I looked at Carmen. In the last ten minutes, we both had killed at least one man each, avoided a probable kidnapping and planned robbery, and were now safe behind the walls of an old French villa.

"What the hell just happened," I asked as we left the car and went inside.

"We did what we had to do. And now I must report it," she said as she went to the telephone she had in her main room.

By the time she had fully explained what had happened, a dark American sedan was admitted to the compound. Two men got out. One was dressed in a suit and tie, and the other looked like he was about to go on a safari. He wore a bush jacket and boots. He had a shoulder holster with a large caliber revolver in it. They ignored me and went straight to Carmen.

"Sean," she said, and I knew she wanted to be alone with whoever they were, so I went upstairs to her terrace and watched the tracers from a firefight off in the distance flicker through the night sky.

Ten minutes later, she joined me. We watched the guard open the gate and let the black car out. It was followed by the Citron.

"Is everything okay? Are you in any kind of trouble?"

"No. We're good. A report will be made, and our names will be left out."

I did not ask how they planned to cover the death of at least three men or why Carmen carried an automatic pistol.

"Hold me," she said, and we continued to watch the bullets fly from other weapons in the war zone.

DATELINE: SAIGON, SOUTH VIET NAM

Bonnie and Clyde

John Dillinger

Cowboys

Remember Friday or Saturday night dates. You and your girlfriend would stop by a hamburger joint, have a burger, some fries and maybe a soda or a malt. Then it's off to the movies. If you were lucky, you got to sit in the balcony and steal a kiss or two. If it was a double feature, you might even get a few more kisses. Popcorn, a Coke, a box of Junior Mints, and then a walk or a ride home. The next morning, you awoke with a pleasant memory of a night out with your special girl.

That's the way it's supposed to happen, but here in South Viet Nam, it was an entirely different experience.

I've written about my very special friend, Carmen, in the past. I don't quite know what to call her, so a special friend will have to do until I come up with something better.

My special friend and I managed to have two days off at the same time. Days off in a war zone are as rare as hen's teeth, as my grandmother would say. Nobody works by the clock. If the job, no matter what it is or where it takes you, must be done. You work until it's done. Ours were done, so we planned to make the most of our days off.

Saigon has a zoo which we visited. Along with the usual exotic animals, they had goats and sheep, but I guess if you've never seen one, a zoo is a good place to do it. A leisurely afternoon and then dinner. After that we decided to do what "normal" people do on a date. We went to a movie. Bonnie and Clyde shot their way across the screen while the dialog was superimposed in Vietnamese at the bottom of the screen.

After the movie, we caught a taxi to take us to Carmen's house. That's when we realized we were in a war zone and not back home. We soon realized the driver was not taking us to Carmen's. When we did, we also saw two motorcycles approaching the taxi, one from each side. The bad guys in Saigon are called Cowboys, they ride motorcycles are always considered Viet Cong, even though their intent was to rob us.

I quickly understood what was about to happen and jumped in the front seat, threw the driver out, and…drew a pistol I always carried. As soon as I did, I yelled for Carmen to duck down into the back floorboard of the old French Citron taxi.

In the next five minutes both mine and Carmen's world changed forever. We did things that I did not believe myself capable of, but in a war zone you do what you must do to make it to the freedom bird that will take you back to the world.

That night, the crime-free streets of Saigon got a little less crime-free. Those who planned to rob two innocent people coming home from a night out for dinner and a movie made a tragic mistake. It's one they will never make again.

Officially, no crime was committed. Four VC tried to infiltrate the city and were stopped by two Americans who were there to help the GVN win the war.

We made it back to Carmen's house.

The cowboys were not so lucky.

Chapter Twenty-Three

I was with a company of the 173rd Airborne Regiment. They made the only combat parachute jump so far in the war. For the men involved in the airborne assault, it was something that had not been done since the Korean War. They got a gold star in their parachute wings and the right to brag to anyone who would listen.

Airborne troops have had bragging rights since the first man jumped from a military aircraft prior to World War Two. Those who made combat jumps in the war never let anyone who didn't make a jump forget about it. They considered themselves a notch above "leg" troops, or those who were not airborne qualified.

I saw a sign in the office of a brigade commander who wore the parachute wings with the star and wreath on top, indicating he was a Jump Master, or Master Blaster, as they like to call themselves. He had a photo of a sign that stands proudly at the Airborne School at Fort Benning, GA. It says, "There are only two types of men. Those who are airborne qualified, and those who wish they were."

Bravo Company had been on a nine-day patrol when I arrived at their compound. They were a part of the larger brigade compound, but all the organic units had their own areas. My first night there, I spent a lot of time with First Sergeant Haley and Captain Miller of Bravo Company.

"It was a rough time," Miller said as he opened the top of a chilled can of beer. I watched it spew out as he covered the spray with his mouth in order not to let any of it be lost.

"Define rough," I said. That word could mean any number of things.

"We were up to our ass in bad guys at one time, and then when they slipped back into the woods, I had problems with one of my soldiers."

"It wasn't just a problem," Haley spoke up. "If it had been me, I would'a shot the son of a bitch on the spot."

Those were very interesting comments, so I wanted to know more.

"It was a Specialist that I had given an Article 15 to just before we left base camp."

There are three levels of military justice. An Article 15 in non-judicial and is administered by the unit commander. It usually results in a reduction in rank and a fine. After that, the other two levels can issue anything from a fine to the death penalty, so I knew the soldier had just screwed up and was going to get a fine and a bust in rank at the most.

"What did he do?"

"He is one of our village rats. Goes to the local ville every chance he gets and is almost always late for morning formation." Miller reached for another can. "He did it a couple of times, and a couple of weeks ago, he came dragging in just as I had the company formed for morning report."

"Late again?"

"Yes, and this time I told the First Sergeant to have his squad leader take him to the orderly room and hold him until I could get there."

"Did you do that?" I asked the First Sergeant.

He laughed. "Never got the chance. Little bastard stood up in front of the company, looked at the Captain, and said, 'Fuck you. I ain't going. How you like them apples?'"

"You're kidding."

"Wish I was, but he said it. Gave me no choice. I turned the formation over to my XO and went to the orderly room, read him his rights, and administrated Article 15."

"How did he take it?"

"Not well. He told some of the other men in the company he was going to take revenge. Even said he was going to kill me if he got the chance."

Outside the orderly room I heard the sound of a deuce-and-a-half truck pass by. The deuce was the workhorse of the military. It served for everything from a troop transport to a gun platform for convoys. We could smell the diesel smoke that belched from the pipe turned skyward by the cab of the truck.

"In the field, his platoon leader told him to take the point position, and he refused," the First Sergeant pulled out a pack of cigars and fired one up. "I hate these damn things. I wish they would get some decent one in the PX," he said as he blew smoke across the room.

"What happens when you refuse an order in the field?"

"The other troopers usually take care of it. When he refused the man who replaced him shook a tree full of red ants on him. Them little mothers will make you get naked and stop the war. Everyone except Specialist Tompkins thought it was funny, and he deserved it."

We talked about the operation and the war in general for about an hour. I went to the mess hall with them and met some of the other men in the company. Later that night I went to the Enlisted Men's Club that serviced the entire base and watched two of the biggest men in the room challenge each other to an arm-wrestling contest. It was a friendly one and the winner bought the loser a beer. The biggest loser was a man who was taking bets on his friend whose arm was finally slammed down on the table. Everything quieted down around ten and I went to the vacant bed that the First Sergeant provided for me in the hootch where the senior enlisted men slept.

We were jarred awake a little after three when there were four explosions in rapid succession. My first thought was a mortar attack, which would usually be followed by sappers cutting the wire surrounding the camp and slipping inside. The explosions came from our side of the camp, so if it was sappers, they would probably hit the opposite side.

The alert siren was spinning and men were heading for bunkers until they found out what was happening.

"Head over there," the First Sergeant said as he pointed. "That's the closest bunker. Keep your head and your ass down until we can figure out what's happening."

"Roger that, First Sergeant. I'm on the way." He didn't have to tell me twice.

Twenty minutes we heard the "ALL CLEAR" announcement over the camp PA system. I was still in the bunker when the First Sergeant came in. I could tell immediately that he had bad news from the look on his face.

"He did it. The bastard did it. I knew I should have shot him in the field."

"What? What did he do?"

"Wasn't no mortars. No VC or NVA. It was him. He tossed a grenade into Captain Miller' hootch and then tossed a couple more to cover it."

"He tossed…" I didn't get to finish.

"Killed Captain Miller. Fragged him. Never thought he had the balls to do something like that." He tossed his half-smoked cigar to the ground. "We'll find him if I have to burn down half the village. Miller was one of the good guys. Took care of the company, and the men respected him."

By the time we emerged from the bunker, a team of MPs and a Colonel were standing outside the building where Captain Miller lay with a camouflage poncho liner covering his body.

The Colonel came to us. "First Sergeant, you know who did this?"

"I have a good idea, sir, and I'm going to find him."

"And you, you're the reporter?" He looked at me.

"Not so much a reporter but a correspondent."

"Now is not the time to talk semantics. I don't care what you call yourself, if you put a word of this in print until we find out for certain what happened…" He stopped. "Well, it won't be good."

I left the next day after an Army Criminal Investigation Division or CID agent took a statement from me, since the First Sergeant and I had been the last ones to see Captain Miller alive.

The First Sergeant promised to let me know if they found Specialist Tompkins. Three weeks later, I got a message that Tompkins had been found in the village by some MPs checking the local whore houses. He put up a fight, and there was a shoot-out. He managed to wound one of the MPs before he was shot and killed.

Captain Miller was killed in bed in his quarters.

His murderer was killed in a Vietnamese whore house.

What a war.

DATELINE: SAIGON, SOUTH VIET NAM

Frag

Frag

Frag

The same word with three completely different meanings. Some commanders use a frag order to let their troops know what they are about to do or what is going on. It's a fragment or a mini version of a much more detailed order. It doesn't go into great detail. "We're going to this point on the map. We can expect light enemy activity along the way. At the objective, we will set up a perimeter and wait for further orders."

One of the things every soldier and marine carries with them when they go on an operation is a couple of fragmentation grenades. These frag grenades resemble pineapples and carry that as a secondary nickname. The steel body is designed to break into fragments when it explodes. These frags fly through the air at a tremendous speed for a killing radius of about five meters, but if you are within fifteen meters, they will put holes in you and your uniform.

The third and most deadly term is to frag someone. This is when a grenade or other explosive device is booby-trapped, usually beneath the target's bunk, and detonated in order to kill them. The reason is almost always personal and directed toward officers by those in their command.

This cowardly way of settling a dispute has gained some notoriety in this war zone. I'm sure it happened in previous wars, but I wasn't in previous wars. I'm in this one, and I witnessed the aftereffects of a fragging incident recently. The disgruntled junior enlisted man did not like the fact that he was not allowed to show up late for formations and follow the rules like the other men in the company. When told to take point while on patrol, he refused, which caused another man to have to take his place. The others in the platoon did not like this and showed their anger later when they were back in base camp.

To get back at the unit, he planted a grenade beneath the bunk of the company commander. He waited until late at night, and when his booby-trapped grenade exploded, he tossed several other grenades to make his murderous act look like an enemy attack. The captain was found in his hootch, dead from a grenade, and when a head count was done after the supposed attack, the man was missing.

Three weeks later he was found in a local house of ill repute when several MP's were inspecting them. When recognized, he opened fire on the MPs, wounding one of them. He was subsequently killed by the MPs.

Karma can sometimes take three weeks.

Chapter Twenty-Four

One afternoon at the MACV, five o'clock follies after the briefing officer gave us the normal bullshit about how the Americans were racking up a body count of enemy soldiers that could not be sustained much longer. It was always the same. American losses were small in relation to the number of enemy killed. The *Stars and Stripes* and *The Army Times*, the two official newspapers for the military, published a weekly total of those killed and or missing in action. Some weeks, the numbers were well over two hundred. I never found a publication that backed up the briefing officers' claim about the number of enemies dead.

After he finished his briefing, he introduced the MACV Provost Marshall and the G-2, Intelligence Officer. The PM was responsible for law and order in the country, and the G-2 kept track of any intelligence matters that had a direct effect on the military personnel. We had never had them introduced officially at the follies, although most of the men in the room had spoken to them at one time.

"Gentlemen, I want to introduce Colonel Ferguson, the Provost Marshall who has asked for a few minutes." He stepped back, and a man in his late forties or early fifties, somewhat paunchy, wearing a freshly starched pair of jungle fatigues and highly shined jungle boots stepped to the podium. Most of the men, including myself, in the room wore the same type of uniform, albeit ours were usually faded from too many washings, torn or patched from field wear, and our boots had white stains from the salt in our sweat that ran into them. For many, he lost a lot of credibility simply from the way he was dressed.

"Good afternoon, gentlemen. I want to talk to you about something that we think you may be able to assist us with." He pulled a pack of cigarettes from his upper left pocket, knocked one out, and fired it up. For the men in the field, that pocket was their survival pocket. Most kept a photo of wives, sweethearts, and sometimes a car or a pet, a Bible, or a lucky charm in it. The advisors kept a small plastic container about the size of a soap dish in theirs. The plastic box had everything they needed if they had to do an E&E or escape and evasion. It had a small saw, matches, a mirror, and small red pills called "hill climbers." Some said if you took two of them you had enough energy to run to Bangkok.

"I want to talk about war crimes." As soon as he said it, there was a noticeable shifting of the men in their seats.

"There is no doubt in my mind that some of you have witnessed actions and behaviors that can be classified as war crimes." He stopped to let his words sink in, the leaned forward on the podium. He let the cigarette dangle for a moment before taking it out. "We're the good guys here. If we participate in or allow war crimes to go unreported, we will lose that designation." The room grew quiet as we waited for him to tell us what we were supposed to do if we witnessed something that fell into the category.

Every hallway and most of the briefing rooms in the sprawling complex was covered with posters of some type. They warned of the dangers of talking, especially to the women in bars who may be enemy agents. Venereal disease was another popular topic. I guess if you couldn't talk to the women in the bars, anything else was off-limits as well. There was a bulletin board that had a regularly updated list of clubs and other establishments that were Off Limits, meaning they had the best-looking women, the best black market exchange rate for turning MPC into Piasters, and the best chance of you bringing something back to your unit that would cause you to rip out the plumbing in two days when you went to a urinal.

"I don't doubt that almost every man who has ever been in a leadership position has committed or witnessed a war crime. The problem is that he may not recognize it or may let it go as a cost of doing business in Viet Nam. We can't allow those actions to go unreported and if appropriate, punished."

He motioned to the other man seated in the front row. "I'll turn this over to Brigadier Drizinski, the S-2 who can expand on this."

The one-star general rose to his feet. He must have used the same laundry and shoeshine stand that the PM did.

"Let me give you some examples we've had that used the excuse they were looking for intelligence that clearly crossed the line." He pointed to a Sergeant at the back of the room who turned off the lights. As soon as it was dark, an image was shown of the blank white wall behind the General.

"This is an image of an accused Viet Cong. If you will notice, his fingers are missing. If they were shot off during a firefight, I'd be showing you an awards ceremony where the shooter would be getting a shooting medal."

Another slide was projected on the wall. "Here, you can clearly see an NVA officer secured to the trunk of a tree. His face shows that he has been severely abused. Did either of these two incidents provide usable intelligence information? It's hard to say, but if the enemy sees this kind of treatment, what do you think they will do to our men."

One of the more senior correspondents spoke up. "General, do you have a slide of an American soldier's head on a stake warning us to stay out of a village?"

"I know that has happened, but that does not give us the right to respond in like manner..."

Before he could finish, there was a chorus of *"bullshits, why nots,"* and other comments to indicate we did not agree with him.

"Let me remind you that each one of you is over here at the invitation of the US Government. If we determine that you have information about war crimes and do not report it, your credentials can be revoked." He stepped away from the podium and motioned for the PM to follow him out of the briefing.

The briefing officer tried to start talking again, but by that time, most of the men were standing and leaving the room.

I walked beside a network reporter. "Have you ever heard such a line of crap? Does he really expect us to report any infraction of the rule we see? I mean, if I see an execution, you can bet your ass I'm going to report it...right after I file a story about it."

I nodded my head in agreement.

After going back to my office and catching up on some overdue paperwork and turning in a pay voucher, I found a report about a unit that sounded like one I had on my board that was one I'd like to visit. I sat on the edge of the desk where Wess was sorting through some photos he had just printed. We had a full-service dark room in one of the vacant offices. Wess found a way to get some of the chemicals he needed on the black market, and once a week, he sent Nguyen out to buy them.

One time, Nguyen returned with the chemicals and a stack of lottery tickets. I was the first to see them since Wess took the chemicals and went into the dark room. "What are those?"

Nguyen explained that South Viet Nam had a weekly lottery. From that day on, everyone in the office gave Nguyen money to purchase tickets for us. Wess was the overall big winner, once having cashed in a ticket equal to fifty dollars in American currency.

"You taking the rest of the day off?" Wess asked when he looked up from sorting photos.

"Yes. I caught us with some columns, and I'm heading out tomorrow, so that's it for today." I looked at my watch. "It's almost happy hour at the Mass. Wanna go?"

One thing the military was punctual about was happy hour. If there was a club nearby and you could get away, that was where you went. Since my association with the military was limited to South Viet Nam, I didn't know how it worked in other places, but here, beer cost a quarter, mixed drinks were thirty-five cents, and there were several slot machines set up to take nickels, dimes, and quarters. Later on, most nights a band would play and the local women would show up.

We took a seat at a table and ordered drinks. "What did you learn at the follies today? We still winning the war?"

"Interesting topic today. War crimes. The PM and the G-2 briefed us and said it was our duty to report anything that could be considered a war crime."

"Did they say anything about giving you a badge to make it official?" Wess picked up his beer bottle and, after wiping the top with a napkin, took a drink.

"No, but he made it clear that if we saw something and didn't report it, we could lose our press pass."

"Interesting. Did he define what a war crime was? Seems to me that there's a lot of shades of grey in that."

"I guess we have to use our judgment." I had a gin and tonic in front of me. I took a drink. "I left the briefing with a network guy, and he said he'd report any crimes he saw…right after he filed his story."

Three majors came in and took a table close to us. They had a US Air Force tag on their uniforms. I knew there was a great officer's club on Ton Son Nhut Air Base, so I wondered why they were here and not there. That riddle was solved a few minutes later when three young Vietnamese women came in and walked straight to their table.

"You ever witness a war crime?" I asked Wess.

"Probably, and didn't realize it at the time. How about you?"

I was hesitant to answer because I had been on a Riverine boat once in the Delta when I saw something that probably was just what the PM and G-2 were talking about.

"You're taking too long to answer," Wess said as he emptied his bottle and raised his hand to signal for another one. "I'll take your hesitation as an affirmative." He leaned over and whispered, "Tell 'ol Uncle Wess all about it."

I was on a PBR, or Patrol Boat Riverine, with some Navy personnel once. The boat was commanded by an American Navy Ensign. It was his first assignment after graduating from the Naval Academy, and he was determined to make it a good one. He had a South Vietnamese Navy Trung Uy, or First Lieutenant, on the boat with him. The Trung Uy was about to get his own boat, and he was shadowing the Ensign to learn how to run it.

We were cruising a canal, checking water traffic to make sure the sampans and other small boats did not pose a threat. I was on the bow with both officers when Trung Uy Ho pointed to a sampan coming our way. The sampan was occupied by someone in the front and another person in the back. The one in the back was an old man, and he had his hand on the long shaft with a motor on the bottom that propelled the boat down the canal.

As it got closer, Ensign Callahan ordered his boat to move closer to the sampan and at the same time, Ho picked up a bullhorn and called out to the man in the sampan.

By this time, we could see that the occupant in the front was an old woman. She was dressed in black pants that came to just above her ankles, and her head was wrapped in a blue cloth.

Ho pointed to the bundle in the middle of the sampan. On the floor was a long bundle wrapped in white cloth and tied with rope.

I noticed that Ho was now holding the bullhorn in one hand and had a US model .30 caliber carbine in the other. The carbine held a magazine with thirty rounds.

He spoke to them in rapid fashion in Vietnamese. I could only catch a few words. I know he told them to stop, and he would shoot. After that, I was lost.

They complied, and our boat pulled alongside the smaller craft. The remainder of the conversation was in Vietnamese, which he told us about later.

"What is in the bundle?" Ho asked.

"Our son. He was killed, and we are taking him to our home village to bury him."

"What did they say?" Callahan asked.

"They say it is their son."

"Not weapon?" Ho yelled into the bullhorn.

"No. Please. Our son."

"He is dead?'

"Yes, and we are taking…"

Ho didn't wait for the old man to finish speaking before he opened fire with the carbine.

"If he is dead, this will not hurt him," he said as he emptied the magazine into the bundle, ripping it apart.

In addition to the bundle, he practically blew out the bottom of the old sampan. It quickly filled with the dirty water from the canal and started sinking. The two occupants were about to be in the middle of a canal in the Delta region of South Viet Nam without a boat. Not a good situation for them.

"We can go now," Ho said as he reached into a nearby compartment and pulled out a fresh magazine for the carbine.

"What about the people…"

"They are someone else's problem now. Another boat will assist them. If not…" He did not finish the sentence.

"Holy shit," Wess said as he drained half of the fresh bottle. "Was the bundle their son?"

"No idea. Ho said it was probably weapons, but since he, or it, or whatever it was, sunk to the bottom of the canal, we'll never know."

We continued to sit for a few more minutes. The three majors left with the three Vietnamese women.

By the time we left, we had not decided if shooting a bundle of unknown contents, blowing out the bottom of a sampan, and dumping two old Vietnamese in a canal was a war crime or not.

DATELINE: SAIGON, SOUTH VIET NAM

Crimes of passion.

Crimes of opportunity.

War Crimes.

Take a gun and shoot someone in any city in the United States, and you will go to jail. It's a crime.

Take a gun and shoot someone in South Viet Nam, and you may get a medal…if the circumstances are right.

Confusing? Welcome to the war.

I attended a briefing by the head law enforcement officer and the head intelligence officer for the largest military command in South Viet Nam recently. The topic was war crimes. What are they? Who does them? Who knows about them? How can they be stopped?

The biggest problem is defining the act. Kill an enemy in combat, and it's okay. Capture an enemy, and kill him later, you go to jail. On the surface, that sounds reasonable. Once the enemy can no longer hurt you, he ceases to be a threat, but he is still the enemy and may be of some use, especially if he has valuable intelligence information.

This is where it gets tricky. Where is the line between gathering information and torture? Our counterparts in the military of South Viet Nam at any level do not have the same standards as we do. If you spend any time with them, you either witness or hear stories of how they gather information, and sometimes it is not pretty. For the Americans who work closely with them in an advisory capacity, they must either stop it or turn a blind eye to it as if it never happened.

Even the Americans use some intense interrogation techniques. Example?

Capture a couple of VC or NVA military, blindfold them, and put them in a helicopter. Start the interrogation process on the one you think is of no real intelligence value. Save the other one for later. Have the interpreter begin to yell and shout, asking questions. "If you don't tell us what we want, we will toss you out of this helicopter." The other man is listening. The first man still refuses, so there is a struggle, and he is tossed out...but the helicopter is now only a few feet off the ground.

His companion hears the screams, and by the time his blindfold is removed, the helicopter is at altitude. He assumes his friend has been thrown out at the altitude he is at when his blindfold is removed. Now, he is more than happy to talk.

In an interrogation, the American pulls out a very sharp, wicked-looking knife. Holds it in front of the enemy soldier. Most enemy soldiers know the Americans are not supposed to torture prisoners. War crime, remember?

The American slowly takes a slice across HIS OWN thumb,

lets the blood drip, slings it across the face of the man, and his interpreter says, "If this crazy American will do that to himself, think what he will do to you." All the intelligence the enemy soldier has quickly followed.

War crimes?

Don't ask me. I never saw any of those things.

But I heard....

Chapter Twenty-Five

Sometimes, we get a hint of a big push or operation during one of the briefings we attend in Saigon. I had a few pieces of the puzzle, which I finally put together, and decided that an American unit was about to knock the bad guys off a mountaintop. They had been using that position to place their artillery where they had been shelling the Americans at the base of the mountain.

I had not been with an American infantry unit in several months, so I headed for TSN to catch a flight north. The helicopter took me to a base camp that was part of a division. As I always did, I caught a ride to the major unit's headquarters.

This was a brigade base camp and was in what I thought was a very vulnerable place. It was surrounded by mountains, and I could see the damage the artillery had done. Like most base camps, it was built as low to the ground as possible. Bunkers were half underground with entrances fortified with sandbags. The few wood buildings that were totally above ground had sandbags three or four deep around all four sides and on the roof. The tallest structures on the base were the radio antennas. The enemy gunners used them for aiming stakes and they were often targeted just prior to an attack.

I caught a ride in a supply truck that picked up some replacements that had arrived on the same helicopter that brought me here. All of us were headed for the brigade headquarters building. They were destined to be integrated into the combat units scattered around the area. I was there to meet someone who would let me tag along on their upcoming mission.

My first stop was the S-3 or Operations Officer. He may not be the one to give me permission, but at least he would either confirm or deny what I already knew. I entered the building and looked around. Several desks were placed against the walls. The metal desks would offer a little more protection for those inside if the side of the building took a direct hit.

A young man who looked much too young to be wearing the stripes of a Staff Sergeant saw me come in. Since I wasn't carrying a weapon, which was a requirement on the base, he immediately knew I was not military.

"Help you?"

"Uh, yes. I'm Sean Kelly. I'm a correspondent, and I'd like to speak to your S-3."

He sized me up before answering. "Thing is, Major Nadeau's not here. He got hit a couple of days ago. Took a medevac to Japan. We don't expect him back. Captain Rosenburg is the acting. He's over there." He pointed.

"Thanks." I went to the corner of the building where a Captain struck me as old as the Staff Sergeant was young.

"Captain Rosenburg? I'm Sean Kelly." I extended my hand and explained that I wanted to accompany a unit on an upcoming combat operation, leaving out the part about my knowing what that operation would be.

"You're in luck, although I'm not sure if it's good or bad luck. We're gearing up for one tomorrow." He stopped for a second. "You have some kind of paperwork that says who you are and that you can do this?"

I had made so many copies of the original authorization documents that I had a new set typed up. He was the first one to see the fresh copy. After looking them over, he refolded them and then handed them back to me. "I can hook you up with Captain Keech. His company is leading the operation." He pulled a bush hat from a nail driven into the wall, grabbed an M-16 that was leaning against his desk. "Let's go."

I followed him to a bunker that was dug into the side of a small rise in the compound. Like the others, it was surrounded by rows of sandbags. When we entered the dark bunker, I saw that it was being illuminated by a strand of low-wattage electric light bulbs. I could hear the hum of a nearby generator which would also be surrounded by sandbags.

"Keech, this is Sean. He's going to go out with your company tomorrow. Be nice to him and he'll make us look good to the civilians back in the world." He turned to walk away. "And try not to get him killed." With that, he left me standing with Captain Keech.

"You a reporter?"

"Not exactly. I send dispatches back to several outlets, but my main focus is a weekly column. I try to tell the things behind what's being reported. More personal than blood and guts war reporting."

"Sounds good. From what I read, everybody back home thinks all we do is rape, pillage, plunder, and murder women and children. If you can change that, it'll be a miracle." He pointed to a table. "Come over here, and I'll give you the *Readers Digest* version of what we're doing." Keech took the next ten minutes to explain that they expected to be out for no more than three days. The objective was to do the broom and dustpan work after the artillery was destroyed by air strikes. "We plan on being out three days. One day up to the objective, one day there, and another coming back to base." He looked at the small bag I carried every time I left Saigon. I had a change of socks and my shaving gear, along with a camera, several notebooks, pens, and pencils. "If you're going with us, you'll need something more than that AWOL bag."

The bag got its name somewhere along the line by being used by the military to pack enough in it to sustain themselves when they went Absent Without Leave or AWOL.

"Specialist Lincoln, go find a rucksack and bring it here," he said to a Specialist who was dozing in a chair. "Get off your ass. You've been sleeping and snoring all day long. Getting on my nerves."

I spent the remainder of the afternoon walking around the compound, getting a good feel for the unit. The compound was built three years ago, and I didn't find anyone who had been here long enough to remember who built it. Sometimes, the Engineers brought in the huge Rome tractors, bulldozers and scraped a place for a base to be built. They may have completed it, or the first unit moving in was left with that responsibility, but every unit gave it their own personal touch. Sometimes, it was for security, and other times for aesthetics. After my tour, I joined the men for a meal. I had a meal of

C-rations heated in large garbage cans filled with water kept hot with a submerged heating unit.

All the cans containing the main meat meal were dropped in the can, and as each man passed by, a cook dipped a strainer in the water, fished out a can, and dropped it into a waiting tray or mess kit. You got what you got.

I got a can of spaghetti which was one of the better meals. The man behind me, one of the FNGs who arrived on the same helicopter with me, got Ham and Eggs, Chopped, the second most disliked can. The other, and generally most hated, meal was Ham and Lima Beans, commonly referred to as Ham and Motherfuckers.

After dinner, the compound was secured for the evening. Patrols and LPs or Listening Posts were sent out. Radios were checked to make sure they had a link to those outside the wire. All lights above ground were eliminated, although there was some glow from the open doors of bunkers.

I heard music being played on cassette and radio combinations, and the variety of music was indicative of the men in the unit. Country and western, soul and rock dominated the selections.

Keech had an airlift scheduled for zero six hundred the next morning, so I crawled into the mosquito net-covered bunk I was directed to after writing a letter to my folks. I gave it to the clerk who was manning the radio in the company headquarters bunker to mail for me.

I was awakened at zero-five hundred by a Specialist shaking my bunk. "Wake up, sir. Captain said you were going with us. If you want some coffee or something to eat, you got to do it now." He was dressed in full battle rattle. He had his weapon in one hand, and the other was wrapped around a K-Bar knife that was taped to the strap on his web gear harness. He was standing back and punching the edge of my mattress with the barrel of his rifle. He knew that to touch a man who was sleeping in this country was akin to a death wish, as there was no telling what the man would do after being suddenly awakened. Like many men in country, I always tossed my wallet into the pillowcase if I was sleeping in a real bed. Also included in the toss was the small pistol I carried concealed in the small of my back.

"Okay," I said as I sat up and pulled the mosquito net aside so I could swing off the cot. "I'm good. Where is the coffee?"

"Some in the company bunker and some with chow in the mess hall if you've got the stomach for it. Mostly powdered eggs and pancakes. Pancakes ain't so bad, but I'll die and go to Hell before I'd eat any more powdered eggs."

I dressed, put my essentials in the rucksack that I had been provided, and went outside. I stopped by the water point long enough to scrape the damage the previous night's meal had done to my teeth and tongue. The small can of toothpowder I used was returned to my ruck. Shaving was out of the question, so a quick splash of cold water was all that I put on my face. Nobody used aftershave or deodorant before going on an operation, or while they were on it for fear the smell would be picked up by the enemy. That usually meant that when a unit, no matter the size, returned from the field, a green cloud of funk hung over it until they could all get cleaned up. I had added to that cloud many times.

Once, during a two-week stay with an advisory team, I did not bathe for the entire time. Toward the end of my time with them, I kept smelling a rank odor. I finally realized it was me, and every time I raised my arm, the downward movement forced air out from inside my shirt. If you stay out long enough the smell doesn't bother you as much. I hoped to never get used to it.

I had a mug of coffee in my hand when I heard the first outgoing artillery barrage. The hilltop would be targeted by 155-millimeter artillery pieces located at another, larger compound. The smaller 105 at our base did not have sufficient range to reach the top of the mountain, so they would fire on three possible landing zones for the operation. By prepping three possible LZ, an enemy observer would not know which of the three we were going to use.

We loaded on five Huey helicopters and had three more acting as gunships for the lift to the selected LZ. The gunships went ahead of us and fired on all three of the LZs and then concentrated their fire on the one where we landed. The LZ was about the size of a backyard in a neighborhood back home. The ships came in, dislodged their troops, and then left in a matter of a minute. Five minutes after the last round was fired from the gunships, I was crouched beside Captain Keech behind a fallen tree that was the victim of the artillery barrage. He had his platoon leaders with him as he gave them their orders.

"First Platoon will take the lead." He used his finger to mark the route as he briefed them. "We'll move along this ridgeline, keeping just inside the trees. We can expect some action the closer we get to the top. They're not going to lose their artillery base without a hell of a fight, but if our intel is right, it's lightly defended. No more than a platoon but most of them will be manning the guns. You'll be followed by Third Platoon with Second in reserve. I'll be with Third." He looked around. "Any questions?" There were none since all his Platoon Leaders were First Lieutenants and had been on numerous operations. They knew what was expected of them. "Okay, go back and brief your platoons. We move out in zero fifteen." He was giving them fifteen minutes to pass the information down to the lowest private, so everyone knew what was expected of them.

We could hear and feel the effects of the massive artillery strikes hitting the gun positions on the mountaintop to our front. They would keep firing off and on all day, giving the company the opportunity to move into position to assault the guns the following morning. The plan was to have destroyed everything and everybody prior to the Americans putting boots on the ground. I was reminded of the military adage that no plan survives first contact with the enemy.

The lead elements of the First Platoon moved through our position. Keech motioned for his headquarters element to drop in behind the rear security element of the platoon. As soon as we did, the point man from Third Platoon made contact with the captain and told him they were on the move as directed.

The area was heavily forested with trees and thick underbrush. Two men moved behind the point man and hacked their way with machetes. The rest of the company was spread out in a fifty-meter-wide formation. Each man was maintaining visual contact with his fellow soldiers on his right and left. Overhead, the sun had a difficult time breaking through the thick canopy of leaves from trees that had stood undisturbed for longer than any man beneath them had been alive. Occasionally we heard the scramble of an animal as they were disturbed from their homes by the invading army of men moving through.

The radio operator or RTO, who walked behind Keech and to the left of me, whispered, "I heard from a friend that there's tigers out here. Ain't never seen one and don't want to either." I had heard the same thing and didn't want to tell him I had actually seen one that the Marines killed a little further up north from us.

The first sound we heard was that of an AK-47. It was rapidly followed by several M-16s returning fire. The enemy knew we were in the area. The small arms fire was quickly accentuated by the muffled WHUMP of grenades. Keech grabbed the handset for his radio that his RTO was already holding out for him.

"Bronco one six, this is Bronco six. Status?"

"Six, this is one six, we're taking small arms and some grenade fire from three different locations to our twelve."

I had heard enough radio traffic to know that Six was always the unit commander, subordinate leaders would have a designation in front of their six, and twelve was the direction of travel since everyone used the clock method.

"Get a good recon and let me know what you're up against."

Before he could get an answer, we heard the unmistakable sound of a heavy machine gun. Since we didn't bring one with us and they were not something a normal patrol carried with them, I knew the First Platoon was up to their ass in alligators. The heavy machine gun was in a permanent position they would have to assault.

"Six, one six, we've got some serious shit in front of us. I'm going to try to flank it and take it out. It's got my lead platoon pinned down."

"Roger, one six. Third Platoon is moving up, and I'm calling for some air assets. Is it where they can see it?"

"Negative, but when they're on station, I can pop smoke and direct their fire."

Keech motioned for his RTO to lean down so he could change the frequency dial on the top of the radio, which the man carried on his back. When he leaned down, Keech pulled a small map from his cargo pocket. He had the frequency for all the support he would need written on it. He dialed in the frequency for division aviation. "Hot Shot, this is Branco Six, over."

When Hot Shot answered, Keech busied himself with giving them the coordinates for their location and making a request for gun cover. Once he got a confirmation and a time to target, he changed the frequency back to the one assigned to his company.

"Bronco One Six, this is Six, over."

"Six, go."

"You will have air assets in zero twenty. Can you hold out till them, or do I need to move Three Six up?"

"It's getting pretty intense. I've got three men down. One confirmed KIA and two WIAs. One will need a medevac."

"Roger. I'm moving through Three Six's location now. I'll be with you in zero-five." He looked at me. "You can come with me or stay with the Second Platoon in reserve. Your call."

"Lead the way." I fell in beside the RTO as Keech headed toward the action that had one of his platoon's pinned down.

We found the lead man from the First Platoon kneeling down behind a large tree. When he saw us, he motioned to his right front, indicating the direction the fire was coming from.

Keech signaled for me to keep low as we moved from tree to tree. We were only twenty meters from the first man when I felt the heat of a round as it passed by my ear on the right side. I didn't have time to second guess my decision to accompany Keech as I dropped to the ground and sought refuge behind a tree that had been the casualty of the earlier artillery strikes.

Keech was also lying prone in a small depression a few feet away. He was on the radio. The gunfire from both sides was growing more intense, and I only heard a few words that he said. I could tell that he had directed that a smoke grenade be tossed as close to the machine gun position as possible. Assuming the smoke could clear the overhead canopy of leaves and limbs, the incoming gunships would identify the color and take directions to the target.

In the earlier part of the war, men on the ground would indicate the color of smoke they were popping. If the enemy had a smoke of the same color, they would pop some as well, confusing the incoming gunships. The command from the pilots soon became, "You pop, I'll identify."

I heard the gunship. "I see green, over."

"Roger green. We're fifty meters to the south of the smoke. We're fairly secure, so work your magic and kill the bad guys."

"Roger on magic. Making first pass now."

I heard the roar of the M-60 machine guns as they fired from both sides of the chopper as it passed over our location. The helicopter took some ground fire, but it was not sufficient to stop the second pass. By that time, the action on the ground to our front had ceased, and all we heard was the very welcome *wop, wop,* sound of the chopper blades as it passed overhead again.

"I can stay on station for a while if you are moving out," the pilot radioed to Keech.

"Sounds like a plan. We'll move through the area and let you know the damage assessment and body count."

Winning or losing in South Viet Nam was not measured in ground gains, towns and villages liberated, or any other unit of measure used in previous wars. This one was measured in the number of dead bodies that littered the battlefield after a firefight.

Keech turned to me. "I can maybe get him to land and take you back to the rear if you're not interested in going on with us."

"No way," I said. "I'm in for the long count."

"Your funeral," Keech said as he motioned for his RTO to follow him.

I hope he was just using an old expression, and it was not a forewarning.

I pulled out my camera from the rucksack and took a picture of the now-destroyed machine gun location that had held up the company. Three men lay dead around the bent and twisted metal that had once been an instrument of death. I purposely avoided including the bodies in the photo.

We moved on for another hour. The helicopter stayed overhead and tracked our progress for most of it.

"Okay, Bronco Six, I've done all the damage I can do for you. I need to go back and rearm and refuel. If you get in over your head again, let us know. Out here."

The company had called for a medevac to take the wounded and the one KIA out while we were still near a good LZ, and we had the chopper overhead to cover the extraction.

It was now mid-afternoon when Keech called a halt. He had his Platoon Leader come to his location so he could brief them on what they were going to do for the remainder of the day.

"Put your platoons on fifty percent. Set out some LPs and let the men get a little chow and some rest. I want to get to the base of the mountain before nightfall. At first light, I want the second and third platoon on line for an assault up to the objective. First and weapons platoon will be in reserve." He pulled out his map and laid it on the ground. "We're here," he pointed, "And we're going to hold up in our RON or Remain Over Night position, here. Looks to be about two hundred meters to the top. I've got a pre-planned artillery barrage with 155s scheduled at zero four thirty. Daylight is at zero five hundred, so they will lift and shift at zero four fifty-five."

The other platoon leaders were taking notes and marking their maps.

"Any questions or concerns?" When there were none, he said, "Go back and take care of your men."

Under normal circumstances, they all would have stood, snapped out a smart salute, and left. Here, to salute meant there was a senior officer in the area, and you had just painted a very large bull's eye on him.

We made it to the RON location without further incident, and everyone hunkered down for the night. Foxholes were dug, patrols were sent out, LPs were established, and men dropped their rucks, started small fires, and heated cans of C-rations and canteen cups filled with hot water for coffee. All the fires were kept very small and disappeared long before dark.

A favorite method of heating rations was to open a Claymore mine, take a small, marble-sized chunk of C-4, the explosive in the Claymore, and light it.

It burned clean, was very hot, did not smoke, and heated anything quickly. The downside of that was if you forgot which Claymore you used and did it too often when you needed the mine to explode, it went off like a firecracker and not something designed to kill.

In lieu of C-4, some men soaked the small roll of toilet tissue that came in every C-ration box with bug spray. It would burn with enough heat and long enough to heat your meal. The toilet tissue was useless as a steady diet of Charlie Rats insured the last thing you needed in the field was toilet paper.

While Keech made his way to all the positions for the company, his RTO busied himself with digging a foxhole large enough for two. I did not think to bring an entrenching tool with me, so I was left to find a place on my own. I finally spotted a partial hole where a large tree had been blown down by artillery. Its roots were sticking up, and when they fell over, they pulled enough dirt with them to leave a small hole. Not exactly a tailor-made foxhole, but as darkness fell, I called it home for the night.

A ripple went through the line the next morning at zero-four hundred. The order was given to prepare to move out. The first artillery round crashed into the hilltop location exactly on time. Five minutes before we were to move out, Keech gave the order to "lock and load."

The smoke from the last round hung in the early morning mist as the lead element passed through the trees and overhead canopy of leaves and limbs that hid the morning sun.

Less than five minutes after the last man cleared the RON position, the enemy opened up. They were dug in between us and the objective, which was now less than the length of a football field away.

I heard the opening volley and the screams of the men who were hit. That sound was followed immediately by the lead element returning fire. To my amazement, nobody stopped moving forward. Their friends were in trouble and their only hope was the men coming up behind them.

Keech immediately grabbed his radio handset, which his RTO had already extended to him. "Sit rep. I need to know who's in contact."

"Six, this is Three Six, I'm taking heavy fire. At least four men down. Fire coming from our ten and two positions. My first is taking the ten; I'm going toward the two."

"Roger, Three Six. We're on your six and moving up. Let me know if we can flank either gun location."

"My First says they're in a fortified bunker. He's about to deploy a LAW. Stand by."

The third platoon leader indicated that his Platoon Sergeant was about to use a Light Anti-tank Weapon on the bunker. The law, a lightweight, self-contained replacement for the old bazooka, could be used on armored vehicles and fortified positions. It was a one-time use. Fire it, break the tube in half to keep it from being used to make another weapon by the VC, and throw it away.

I heard the heavy *Whump* as the round found its target. We waited to see if we heard the machine gun open up again. We got our answer. In less than a minute, we heard the unmistakable sound of a machine gun finding its targets.

"Son of a bitch," Keech said as he spoke into the handset. "I want mortars on that target. Put some steel on the bastards while I get second platoon to flank it." He looked at me. "You may regret not taking that chopper out of here."

I didn't have an answer. All I could do was stay close to him and hope for the best.

"Let's go."

He was in the middle of his reserve platoon and talking to his higher headquarters as we moved up. "I don't know what we're up against yet. May be just an outpost, but they're dug in, and they have at least one light machine gun. My third platoon is taking fire from two locations and we tried to take the bunker out with a LAW, and now I'm putting my mortars on it prior to a ground assault." He listened to the sound of mortars incoming over our heads. "I can use some gunships on station."

I heard the response that most of the air assets assigned to the unit had been diverted to another larger firefight to the east of the firebase.

"That may be a diversion since they have to figure we're heading up the mountain for their guns."

He ended the transmission and changed the frequency back to the one his company used. "Three six, we're on line with your trail element. What's your status?"

"Six, we took out the gun position on our two, and we're now moving forward."

"Don't get too far ahead of your First and the men with him. I don't want anybody caught in a crossfire."

"Roger, we're keeping eyeballs on the man to our flanks as we move."

Keech stopped and looked at me. "Okay, here's where it's gonna get sticky. The hilltop objective is about a hundred meters long. That means we have to assault on a line at least one fifty so we can flank them once we're on top. I gotta put everybody on line except for my weapons platoon, who will remain behind us to fire support until we reach the top. You've been lucky so far, but I'd feel a hell of a lot better if you stayed with the tubes until we secure the objective."

"I appreciate your concern, but you've taken good care of me so far, and it's too late to turn back, so I'll be with you all the way." I thought I saw him crack a very small smile.

"All right, let's do it."

Poets and songwriters talk about the "crest of the hill." In the military, there are two crests for each hill. There is the poetic crest at the very top, where they stand and write about the lovely sights below them, and there is the military crest. That crest is just below the actual top. It's a position where you cannot be seen silhouetted against the skyline and the NVA were using it to their advantage.

They were dug in ahead and above us as we moved through the trees. They knew we were there, so they did not have to wait for individual targets to present themselves. A burst of gunfire into the foliage below them was a sure bet to find a target.

Keech was busy on his radio, keeping up with the battle as we moved. Finally, we were stopped by the increasing amount of fire coming from at least three bunkers and an unknown number of individual enemy fighters between us and the objective.

He called two men forward to his position. "I want you to find the platoon leaders or their sergeants and tell them that I've got artillery planned to fire Danger Close in ten minutes. Tell them to pull back fifty meters immediately. As soon as the fire is lifted, I want every swinging dick up and moving full speed to the top. Tell them to acknowledge by radio. Now, move out."

I knew what Danger Close meant. "Are you sure?" I had to ask.

"Don't question my orders."

In ten minutes, we would be experiencing an artillery barrage between our lead element and the enemy which was less than fifty meters to our front. The artillery was planned to fall between the two locations. A deviation by less than a degree when the fires would put it in our pockets. I could only hope that the men plotting the fire had been math majors in school.

If you've ever heard artillery incoming or outgoing, you know the difference. There is a sound that you can't forget and a feeling that you hope you never feel again if you are on the incoming side. We heard the scream of the rounds passing overhead and the instantaneous explosion as they found their targets.

As I tried to no avail to get underground, I remembered my dad telling me about the German practice in the Battle of the Bulge of firing artillery at the American lines. They would set the timed fuses to explode at treetop level. This caused twice as much damage as men were wounded and killed by the metal from the shells and from splinters ripping through the air as trees were torn apart. I hoped we were far enough away so that if we got an airburst, we would not be picking splinters out of our bodies.

Keech had given the order for the barrage to last only seven minutes. At six and a half, he picked up the handset on his radio. "One Six, Two Six, and Three Six, move out in thirty seconds. Don't stop until we clear the area. Move out." He stood and led the way.

We were less than one hundred meters from where we were taking sufficient fire to keep us pinned down thirty minutes earlier. This time, there were no enemy soldiers firing at us. They had only shattered and twisted metal where weapons had been. The men I saw were unrecognizable except for the NVA uniforms they wore. Their own family would not be able to identify them. Limbs lay away from torsos. I saw one man's head still wearing his pith helmet but not the rest of his body. As I passed through this field of death, I silently chastised myself for not feeling more compassion for the enemy dead. That lasted long enough for me to realize it could have just as easily been one of them walking through our dead bodies.

The company was on line as we moved up to the top of the mountain. Keech was on the radio telling his platoon leaders to keep their men on line because we were certain to start taking fire from the man who had been manning the artillery pieces, assuming any were still alive.

At first, it was sporadic. One or two shots from an AK-47, then it began to intensify as more of the living defenders found targets when we cleared the tree line and got to the clearing that was their base.

The first man I saw hit was about twenty meters to my left. An immediate call went out for a medic. I turned my head back to look in front of me when several rounds dug into the ground in front of me. I saw a man standing beside a large artillery piece. He had his AK at his hip, and he was aiming at me.

This was not what I signed up for. I wanted to hold up my notebook and tell him I was just there to record the events for the folks back home. If he had not read my columns, my second choice was to pull my pistol and see if I could get lucky. Before those thoughts cleared my mind, I saw his body dance as several rounds from Keech found their target. He looked at me and gave me a "thumbs up."

Several other gun positions still had men who were able to fire at us. The guns had evidently been knocked out by the numerous artillery rounds that had fallen on them. There were craters all over the area where rounds fell into the mountain top. As more men got to the top, the enemy gunfire slowed and finally stopped as those men who survived the artillery either did not survive the infantry assault or decided life as a POW was preferable to no life at all.

After surveying the devastation at the three gun positions and determining they were out of action, he radioed back to headquarters that the objective was secure. His First Sergeant had been talking to the platoon sergeants, getting a KIA and WIA report.

"We've got three KIA and nine WIAs, three are walking wounded, but we need a medevac for the KIA and six of the others. We could use an ammo resupply, and some water wouldn't hurt either."

"Roger that, Top. I'm asking for an engineer demo team to come and destroy what's left of the guns and anything else that's up here." He referred to his senior sergeant as Top, which was a mark of respect for his being at the top of the enlisted command structure in the unit.

It took ten minutes for the first helicopter to land. It still had a red cross painted on it. Many of the medevac choppers had stopped using the international symbol for a non-combatant since the NVA did not respect it and fired on those choppers as quickly as they did the armed gunships. Three more helicopters were circling overhead. They were flying gun cover until the dead and wounded could be loaded, and then they would land if they were bringing in a resupply or the demo team. If not, they would continue to circle until we were clear of the mountaintop.

It took almost two hours for the demo team to arrive and rig the charges on what was left of the artillery pieces. When we heard the caution, "Fire in the hole," we knew it would be followed by a series of massive explosions. I was hunkered down in one of the artillery craters with Keech, his RTO and company medic, but I peeked over the edge with my camera so I could get photos.

The concussion from the explosive charges was enough to deafen me for several minutes. I knew I jerked when the charges went off, so I wouldn't know if my photos were blurred until I got back to Saigon and gave the film to Wess to process.

The original plan was for us to return the way we had come, but one of the truths of the war is that is you use the same trail coming back that you took going out, the chances of getting ambushed hovered around one hundred percent. With the enemy clearly upset because we destroyed their artillery position, there was a good chance that they would have several ambush locations between us and the firebase if we went back down the way we came. Going down the opposite side of the mountain was not a possibility since it would take us much too close to the border between South Viet Nam and Laos, one of the neighboring countries that was supposed to be off limits to American military. The NVA used the country as a part of the Ho Chi Minh Trail to move men and supplies to the south. I have heard rumors that we sometimes put small recon teams across the border to monitor their movement, but I can neither confirm nor deny that.

After the smoke cleared from the demolitions and the dead and wounded had been evacuated, Keech called in one last fire mission. "We hear heavy movement to our west. Request Puff the Magic Dragon."

That was the name given to the C-130 gunship equipped with the mini-guns. Seeing them in action, especially at night, was something you never forgot. The mini-guns spit out a stream of bullets at an unbelievable rate per minute. With tracers mixed in, the stream looked like a solid red line and sounded like half the bees in captivity were riding the line of fire. At night it was both beautiful and frightening at the same time.

It took Puff thirty minutes to get over us. Keech directed the initial gun run, and we sought protection in the craters that littered the mountain top. We watched and listened as the deafening *Buzzzzz* sound filled the jungle air. The pilot made three run. I could hear him speaking with Keech as he did so. I think he was enjoying the action as much as a kid with a new toy. "I can do one more if you think there are any targets left," the pilot said.

"No, I think you're good. If there's anybody left down there, let them think they won the lottery 'cause everyone else is chewed to bits. Tango Yankee," he finished with the initials for Thank You.

By the time the C-130 flew over us and did a wing dip, we saw our helicopter lift in the distance. We were being airlifted back to base. In the last few minutes prior to their landing, I saw several men go to some of the bodies and take belt buckles and other souvenirs. One of the men came up to Keech. "I found this on what must have been an officer," he said as he handed his company commander a Russian Tokarev automatic pistol.

The Tokarev was the highly prized side arm of high-ranking NVA officers. To find it and then present it to Keech was an indication of how his men felt about him. The man who found it could have kept it himself or sold it to a

REMF for several hundred dollars.

We loaded on the choppers and I watched as the devastation of the artillery position grew smaller as we gained altitude. I had been handed a headset by the crew chief when we lifted off. Keech tapped me on the knee and touched his headset, indicating he was about to say something to me.

"Take a good look at what it looks like today. In a week, it'll be back just like it was when we left out to destroy it. Unless we build a base on the ground, it'll go back to them, and we'll do this all over again in a couple of weeks."

DATELINE: SAIGON, SOUTH VIET NAM

DANGER: NO SWIMMING

DANGER: DO NOT ENTER

DANGER CLOSE

Most Americans are familiar with DANGER signs. We see them all the time in our daily lives. They warn us of places that may be unsafe. We understand and abide by them. If it tells us it's too dangerous to swim, we stay out of the water. If it's dangerous to enter, whether it's a building or a road, we avoid it.

What about Danger Close?

Unless you've worn a uniform, you probably have no idea what that means. I recently learned its meaning the hard way.

The United States hasn't occupied terror since the Spanish-American War. That's where we got the Philippines and a few other spoils of war. In both world wars, we were on the winning side, but once the shooting stopped, we packed up and went home. In World War Two, we almost singlehandedly rebuilt the devastation we caused in Europe and Japan, but once that was done, we left.

Besides the normal complaints about war in general, the biggest ones I hear are about incompetent leaders, the heat, and red ants. The enemy hardly ever makes the list. One universal complaint, especially from the marines and the army men in combat in areas north of Saigon, is that they fight sometimes for days for an objective, and after they capture it, they are ordered to leave, and the next day, the enemy moves back into position. We don't keep it.

In WWII, when the Japanese were kicked off an island, we moved in, liberated the civilians, handed candy to the kids, and built a runway. We occupied the island until the war was over, and then we gave it back. To the people who had been the enemy? Maybe, but the point is we left.

In South Viet Nam, we don't occupy territory. No matter what it costs to secure it. No matter the number of lives or equipment lost or destroyed. Not on our side or the enemy. Charge up the hill. Kick the bad guys off and do it again in a week or two when they go back to the same spot again.

What's that got to do with Danger Close? Glad you asked. Recently, I was with a unit that had to assault a mountaintop artillery position. On the way, we came under intense enemy fire. They were between us and the objective. The only way to dislodge them was to have friendly artillery fire so close to our position that we were in danger of being hit by our own artillery. We were so close the rounds kicked up dirt and debris that fell on us. Luckily, we did not suffer any casualties, but the bad guys were not so lucky.

The unit finished the assault up to the artillery position. It had been the target of numerous artillery barrages, and most of the guns were destroyed along with the men who were manning them. After a demolition unit came in and blew upwhat was left of the guns, we were airlifted out by helicopter.

As we departed, the company commander of the unit told me to take a good look at what it looked like now because it would be fully operational within a few weeks, and they would have to do it all over again.

A month later, I found out he was right.

Chapter Twenty-Six

The Massachusetts, or Mass BOQ, where I lived when I was in Saigon, was as close as one could get to the things we took for granted back home, wherever that may be. There was at least one correspondent from Korea in the building and two from Australia and New Zealand, so having never visited those countries, I was not sure what they had been used to. For me, the best thing about the Mass was a real bed, flush toilets, and a shower room.

I tried to make my room as comfortable as I could under the conditions. It came furnished, if that is a good description, with a bed, a bureau for clothes, a dresser, and a bedside table. Since arriving, I have added a small chest that was locally made. It has three drawers, and I keep my socks and underwear in one, miscellaneous junk in one, and the last one is still empty. I can only have so much clothing and other necessities, so I may never put anything in the third drawer.

Like most of the men, and probably the women as well, I bought a nice combination radio and cassette player. I have not gotten into the massive stereo components that so many have. My little cassette player provides all the music I need when I'm in my room. I can also record on it, so I do a voice tape to send to my parents several times a month. It's funny because I make my living using words, but when I pick up the little microphone that is attached to the player, I stumble through speaking.

Life in Saigon is as close to normal as those of us, military and civilians, can make it or the circumstances allow. There are three distinct levels of Americans and Allies in Saigon. The military runs everything. End of discussion. No questions asked, and if questions are asked, they may not be answered. The next level is the government employees from all the allies who are involved in the war. The US leads the pack on that one. At the bottom of the heap, you'll find me, Wess, and the other assorted civilians who are here for various reasons. There are a multitude of contractors over here making untold sums of money building, rebuilding, repairing, and providing services to the country.

For some that I have met, South Viet Nam is a second home. They have been here since the first shot was fired and probably don't intend on going home until the smoke clears from the last one, if then. They have Vietnamese wives and are raising a family. They make more money here than they ever could back in the United States, and it goes so much farther, that if they ever left and went home, the shock would probably trigger a heart attack.

My life in Saigon was in two parts. My job and Carmen. I had to spend a respectable amount of time in my office, or at my desk since I didn't really have an office. I was hired to ferret out the stories that didn't make the evening news. Mine were in print and not on television. I left the blood and gore reporting to the network guys. I wanted to get the stories, the feelings of the men who were here: who fought the battles, spilled the blood, missed their wives and girlfriends back home, and counted the days until they could board a Freedom Bird back to the world.

When I was with units in the field, all I could do was take notes, both written and visually, and put them together when I got back to my desk. My initial contract was for a weekly column, and for the most part, I made it. Sometimes if I was going to be in the brush when a column was due, I had a couple written that Wess or one of the other guys would put on the wire and send it to my syndicate so I didn't miss a deadline. On occasion I wrote something as it happened while I was with a unit. I'd send the copy back with someone heading for Saigon and make that week's commitment.

The other half of my life in Saigon was Carmen. When I was around her, I felt like a teenager about to ask the head cheerleader to the prom. She occupied my thoughts more than I ever thought she or anyone else would. There was never a day when I didn't think about her, and when I was in Saigon, and she was not out in the field, we were together as much as possible. She worked for the US State Department. I never asked what she did for them, but from the way they kept her traveling to all the military headquarters and the villa they provided for her. I knew she was not a clerk typist.

For several months, as my column began to gain a wider readership, I got a few letters from readers. I won't call them fan mail because some of them were quick to point out their distaste for the war and for my making it seem human. One thread that ran through many of them was from veterans who complimented me on how I handled the tragedy of war, but they all said I had missed one of the things they remembered, and for most of them, it was the only thing they talked about.

What about the funny things that happen in a war zone?

My mother always said there was a fine line between humor and horror. Either she was much smarter than I gave her credit for at the time (I have since learned just how smart she was), or she had listened to my dad and Uncle Jim tell their stories from World War Two so many times that she thought that was all that happened.

Funny? You want funny?

DATELINE: SAIGON, SOUTH VIET NAM

Recently, I was at the bar (where else) having dinner with a military police lieutenant when we saw a sergeant wearing a black and white MP armband enter and look around. The bar occupied the top floor of a building that was designated as a BOQ or Bachelor Officer's Quarters, meaning officers and senior civilians lived there. Their enlisted counterparts lived elsewhere, so an enlisted person on the floor was of great interest to all who saw him, especially since he was wearing an MP armband.

Back in the US a cop in a bar may have indicated a raid, here it indicated an emergency that only an officer could handle.

"Sir," he said softly as he came to our table. "I think we got a little problem."

The understatement of the night. The "little problem" we learned later was one of the junior officers assigned to the MP company in Saigon was visiting one of the local brothels. He had been drinking far beyond his capacity for consumption and decided to take a stroll across the roof of the building. Nobody knew why, but he climbed a ladder inside one of the rooms, and off he went. Five minutes later he crashed through the roof of the room occupied by one of the ladies and her guest at the moment. Unfortunately, her "guest" happened to be his company commander. Did I mention that all three of them were naked at the time?

Funny now, but probably not at the time.

I was on patrol with an advisor unit and a Regional Force Company when we came to a small canal. The fire was coming from the opposite side, so we had to cross it. No bridges, and it was too deep to wade, so the RF company commander had some of this Ben si's or privates cut several banana logs, lash them together for a raft so we could cross.

The first raft had a group of men who set up a line of fire to protect those of us who would follow. I was on the second banana log raft to cross. I had my bag containing my notebooks and camera on top of the logs, along with the weapons for the three other men crossing with me. Halfway across, the VC saw us and took us under fire. I remember as the rounds zipped through the water that it looked like some of the movies I had seen as a kid where the good guys are getting shot at, and then it struck me: Holy Guacamole, they're shooting at me, and I'm thinking about cowboy movies. The man who had gone over first returned fire, and we made it to the side where they were and took cover.

As soon as we did, the company commander yelled across that we should come back to his side of the canal. He must know something we didn't, so back on the banana logs and into the water, I went.

Zip! Zip! Zip! They were shooting at Cowboy Sean again.

After crossing under fire for the second time, we made it to the opposite side. We scrambled to the ground, and the team leader for the advisors asked the commander to explain. "We have boats now. We can cross," he said.

Some of his men had "confiscated" several sampans, and now he could cross, high and dry. I wanted to shoot the Vietnamese commander myself.

He looked like the painting of George Washington standing up in the boat while crossing the Delaware during the American Revolution. I wonder if any of George's men wanted to shoot him?

Almost every place in the country where there are more than ten men in a location, someone has taken a 55-gallon oil drum, cut it in half, put some legs on it, and made a grill. That same unit will have at least one man who is good at "scrounging" or acquiring things they want or need by any means necessary. Read...trade, re-locate, steal.

Recently, I was at a small compound near a Navy base, and the scrounger had gone to them and traded some weapons for a case of steaks. While in the meat locker, he "re-located" a large frozen hunk of meat that looked like a beef roast.

He came back, grilled the steaks, had a feast, and put the roast on the grill. It cooked. And cooked. And cooked. By nightfall he was standing by the grill with a flashlight that had a red lens cover, checking the roast that was now very well done. Every time he cut into it with his Kbar knife, it was still red on the inside.

When daylight came, and he was still checking it, one of the other men decided to cut it in half and eat the inside that was not cooked to the point of looking like a piece of coal. When he cut into it, they made a startling discovery.

The scrounger had stolen a very large, corned beef. He could have cooked it for days and never got it done all the way through.

He was relieved of his duties as the unit scrounger and left in disgrace.

There are signs all over the country. Some are serious, but most are ironic and funny if you understand them. They are grouped together as Murphy's Law.

Murphy Says:

Incoming artillery has the right of way.

Friendly fire, ain't.

If the enemy is in range, so are you.

No plan survives first contact with the enemy.

If it's stupid and it works, it ain't stupid.

You are not Superman. Marines and pilots take note of this.

And my all-time favorite:

Try to look unimportant. The enemy may be low on ammo, and they won't waste a bullet on you.

Sometimes, it's nice to have a laugh in the midst of the death and destruction all around you.

Chapter Twenty-Seven

I was sitting at my desk at my office in Saigon when I got the message from my boss at the Nielsen News Network back in Florida. We had a telex machine in the office that was used by most of us to send dispatches back to the States. Sometimes we got one from our agency or networks telling us to look for a specific topic for a story. This one was different.

It was from the head Nielsen of the Triple N, as we called it. The network had begun as a single newspaper in a small town in Florida. After expanding to several other cities and purchasing some smaller newspapers, it became a real player in the industry.

The telex informed me that the grandson of the founder had decided to sell the company. He was in the process of making a deal, and a part of it was that the new owners would have the option of keeping any and all current reporters. Since I was technically a reporter, my job and my future were in limbo. This information came as a complete shock to me as I had not even heard rumors of a sale.

Would I be leaving Saigon? Would I need to find a job? All those questions paled in comparison to the thought that was making me feel my heart beat in my chest. Carmen. Would I have to leave here and her? Could I? Better yet, would I? I knew men who had left the military and stayed behind after getting a job with a civilian contractor. Most of them had the hard skills that the contractors needed. I wasn't a mechanic, an engineer, a cook, a medic, or even an administrative support technician. What could I do if I stayed here?

I was staring at the far wall in the office when Wess looked over from his desk. "Man, you look like you just saw a ghost. You okay?" He asked as he stopped sorting through a stack of photos.

"Maybe I'm seeing my future…or lack thereof," I said as I held the telex.

Wess left his desk and came to mine. "Talk to me, brother. What's up?"

I handed him the message and waited for his comment when he read it. "You're kidding? You didn't know about this? Don't you have a contract or something?"

"I have one, but it runs from year to year. This one is only good for five more months. I suppose the new owners could either keep me or buy my contract out and let me go." It sounded scary when I said it. After graduating from the University of Georgia with a degree in journalism, it only took a few months to realize just how nearly worthless it was. Like all my classmates, I figured I'd get a job as a reporter, crack a hot news story, pick up a Pulitzer, and write my memoirs. The reality was that none of us would ever do that, and we'd be lucky if we actually got a job as a reporter.

I was one of the few who did, and now it might be fading like last night's sunset. I had to do something, but I wasn't sure what the first thing was. Did I go to the MACV headquarters and call the Triple N office and see if any decisions had been made and if so, what were they? Did I need to contact Carmen and tell her what was going on? Would she worry? Could she help? Maybe get me a government job if I needed it.

I decided to try to get a phone line back to the States and speak to someone at Triple N. "I need to have Nguyen take me to the MACV headquarters so I can get a phone call back to the States." The time and date difference was such that a call to or from Viet Nam to the States usually happened during the middle of the night in Viet Nam and the middle of the day in the States. I knew the offices for the network were manned twenty-four hours a day, so I called for Nguyen and headed for the door.

Thirty minutes later, I was walking down the familiar hallways that I had visited for the last few years. Each time in the past, I was looking for a story, this time I was the story.

I saw a major I knew and stopped him in the hallway. "I need to make a phone call back to the States. Who's got a good line I can use?"

"Good line? No such thing, but check out the Signal Office. They're your best bet."

I thanked him and continued down the hallway to a room that was wall-to-wall with radios and other signal equipment. I heard several one-sided conversations over telephones as the men in the room swore at the breakdown of communications between them and the units they were trying to talk to someplace outside of Saigon.

"Can I help you?" a lieutenant with crossed signal flags on his collar stopped me at the door.

"Yes," I pulled out my correspondence paperwork and showed it to him. "I really need to make a call back to my office in Florida. Do you have a good line I can use?"

"You're in luck. We're having good luck today. I can give you a line, and you can use that office over there if you need some privacy," he pointed. "Give me the number and I'll have one of my guys connect you."

I sat in the office and waited until he pointed at me and indicated that I should pick up the handset on the desk where I was seated.

"Hello...Nielsen News Network?"

"Yes, can I help you? You'll have to speak up. There's a lot of static on this line."

I quickly explained who I was and what I wanted because I knew the life expectancy of a good phone line from Saigon to Florida was not very long.

"Oh, Mister Kelly, I've really enjoyed your columns, and so have the others in the office."

I didn't want accolades from someone on the night shift responsible for answering the phone. I wanted to know about my future. Before I could ask, he continued. "I know you're like the rest of us and want to know what's happening with the sale. So far, all the reporters' jobs are safe. The new buyers are mainly interested in expanding their footprint in print media. They own a chain of radio and a few television stations right now. I don't think you have anything to worry about."

"That sounds great, but I'm ten thousand miles from the front office. No offense, but I'd like to hear that from someone who can sign a contract or a paycheck."

"I understand, and I'm making a memo to give to the personnel department as soon as they open tomorrow. I'll make sure they…"

His voice faded as the line filled with static, and I could no longer hear him…whoever he was since I did not get his name. I tried to get another line, but after an hour, the lieutenant said it was not going to happen, so I thanked him and returned to my office.

I sat and talked to Wess for almost two hours. We talked about the good and bad times we had shared during my time in country. Wess had been here a year longer than I, but we had shared a lifetime of experiences. "So, what are you going to do while you wait?" He asked.

"Carmen is in town so I'm going to see if she's free tonight and I she is, I'm going to take her to dinner and then I'm going to see if I can drink the bar empty of gin and tonics. After that I'll come to work tomorrow with a hangover that should qualify for an Olympic Gold Medal."

"At least you have a plan," he said.

I did as I said. Carmen and I had dinner, and for the first time since I met her, I got rip-roaring drunk. When she asked the reason, all I could tell her was that it was a good one and I'd tell her more later. I seem to remember her saying something like I hope it's not one of your parents passing away.

* * *

The next morning, there was a telex waiting for me when I almost crawled into the office. My hair hurt. My toenails hurt. My mouth tasted like the entire Russian army marched through it wearing muddy boots. My first thought was to get to the coffee pot and drain it.

Wess noticed my condition and came to me. "Mornin' sunshine. How's the head?"

"Give me ten aspirin, and don't slam the lid on the bottle when you do," I said as I poured my first cup of coffee.

"Here, this will make you feel better," Wess said as he handed me the paper he tore from the telex machine. Nothing that came in on our machine was secret, so when someone heard the bell on it ring, indicating an incoming message, they watched as it was printed and then took it to the recipient. Whatever the message, the first person knew about it before the person who was to receive it.

I took the page from his hand and had to focus twice before I could read it.

Sean, the potential new owners are delighted that you are a member of the Nielsen News Network organization. If the sale goes through as we expect it will, you will probably be called upon to expand your reporting to include radio broadcasts. Stay safe.

It was signed by the current owner of the Nielsen Network. I read it again and then rushed to the bathroom, where the previous night's gin and tonics were given up.

About the Author

Paul Sinor is a retired US Army Lieutenant Colonel.During his career, he had two combat tours during the Viet Nam War, and other diverse assignments, from company commander to being on the staff of the Secretary of Defense. His last military assignment was the Army Liaison to the Television and Film Industry in Los Angeles.In that capacity, he was the script consultant and on-site technical advisor for a multitude of feature films, including *Transformers* 1-3, *I Am Legend, The Messenger, Taking Chance, GI Joe*, and numerous episodic television series.

As a novelist, he currently has over twenty books in print from traditional publishers. This includes two mystery series. Eight of his screenplays have been made into feature films, with one: *Minutes to Midnight* resulting in him being awarded a People's Choice TELLY Award as a producer. His ninth feature film is currently in post-production. He holds a BA in Criminology and an MFA in Creative Writing and is a member of MWA and ITW. He has been a presenter at numerous writer's conferences and is active in all forms of social media, with websites devoted to his books and movies. Paul has taught screenwriting at the University of West Florida and the University of Washington.

AUTHOR WEBSITE (live link):

<u>https://paulsinorbooks.net/</u>

SOCIAL MEDIA HANDLES (live links):
<u>https://www.facebook.com/paulsinorauthor/</u>

Also by Paul Sinor

SEAN KELLY, WAR CORRESPONDENT
War Stories and Fairytales

JOHNNY MOROCCO SERIES:
Wrath of the Dixie Mafia
Fair Game
Picture This
Blackmail and White Lightnin'
Double Trouble

MAX MAXWELL SERIES:
Dancing in the Dark
Sentimental Journey
That Old Black Magic
We'll Meet Again
Racing With the Moon
Long Ago and Far Away
Blues in the Night

STANDALONES:
Where There's Smoke
Operation Thunder Strike
Demon Riders